# Razor Point

## By

## Eric Johnson

Published by Eric Johnson

Copyright © 2015 Eric Johnson.

ISBN-13: 978-1515306030
ISBN-10: 1515306038

To Christopher and Caitlin
Special Thanks To:
Stella Samuel
Ian Hugh McAllister

For readers who are challenged by Dyslexia a version of Razor Point is published using OpenDyslexic typeface. It is available in print through Amazon. OpenDyslexic is a typeface designed to make reading easier for some symptoms of dyslexia. Letters have heavy weighted bottoms to indicate direction. You are able to quickly figure out which part of the letter is down which aids in recognizing the correct letter, and sometimes helps to keep your brain from rotating them around. Consistently weighted bottoms can also help reinforce the line of text. The unique shapes of each letter can help prevent confusion through flipping and swapping.

# Books By Eric Johnson

### Book One
## Summer School Zombocalypse

## Coming Soon

### Book Three
## The Monster
## A Child Knows Best

Eric Johnson

## CHAPTER ONE
## HOW TO DISSECT A FROG

The third bell rang, and Tom ran for his classroom past lockers and posters of smiling kids eager to learn. Mr. Dickerson, the science teacher, stood in the doorway waving students in, "Come on people, this is my time too. You can't be late in the real world!"

Tom's shoes squeaked as he stopped at the door. "Sorry, Mr. Dickerson, I had complications."

"Complications, right. Just wait for today's assignment."

Tom entered the room, muffled laughter rolled to the front of the class. "What are they doing here, Mr. Dickerson?"

Past the Bunsen burner tables at the back of the classroom, Jackson, Chi, and Hernandez ducked down, hiding their laughter.

"Coach transferred them in," Mr. Dickerson said. "We've got a busy class today. Go and sit, Tom."

Seeking a friendly face, pressure built behind his eyes. "Will someone trade for a seat up front?"

"Come on, Tom." Mr. Dickerson motioned him in. "There's a seat at the back. Don't hold up the class."

Jackson held his arms out welcoming Tom. "Yeah, Tommy, we saved you a seat. Today's a great day for learning."

Mr. Dickerson adjusted his glasses. "Cut the crap, Jackson, or I'll have Coach give you extra laps."

"Anyone?" Tom asked desperately, his voice cracking. Eyes around the room averted. Three eggs too many, his breakfast twisted in his gut. "Anyone?"

Chi crossed his arms and pouted sympathetically. "What's the matter, Tommy? We saved you a whole row."

"Please, Tom," Mr. Dickerson said, waving his pen. "Let's get this class started. Sit."

Tom gripped the edge of the chair and pulled into his seat.

Gum stuck to his fingers.

Jackson whispered while keeping his eyes on Mr. Dickerson. "We heard you're having a beach field trip on Monday."

"Thought we would come," Hernandez added, poking Tom in the back between his shoulders. "Wouldn't want you to miss us."

Chi drummed his pencil on the desk. "Think of the photo ops. We wouldn't want to lose out on any beach fun for the world."

Mr. Dickerson emerged from the store room door at the back of the classroom, and stood at the front of the class. He pulled a large gray cover off a cart revealing a dozen frogs floating in jars. "We will be dissecting frogs today. Partner up, take a dissection tray from the shelves, and get your frog from the cart at the front."

Jackson ran his pencil across the back of Tom's neck. Current surged across Tom's face, his skin pulling tight as he batted Jackson's hand away, turning to face him. "Damn it, Jackson, cut it out!"

"Damn it, Jackson. Don't do that, Jackson. Boohoo," Jackson mocked.

Hernandez pointed a finger pistol at Tom and made a *tock* sound by moving his tongue against his palate. "Quiet, or you'll get in trouble."

Chi leaned over the table whispered in a sultry voice, "Bonnie needs a partner. He's so lonely."

Abruptly, he raised his hand. "Mr. Dickerson, I can't sit here." The world was a slow motion movie. Each second was like a minute, waiting for Mr. Dickerson to set him free.

"Tom, please don't interrupt," Mr. Dickerson instructed, as the class got their equipment. "You are required to cut open the frog and identify its basic organs and systems. Remember this for the test; the easiest way to tell the difference between male and female frogs isn't examining between the legs, but looking at the feet. Now come get your frog."

Bonnie approached Tom eagerly, shifting on his feet, stuttering for the right word. "Partner?"

"I don't need a partner," Tom scowled and pushed past him.

Hernandez laughed. "Hey, Tom, show us your feet."

"What pranks are you doing for us today?" Chi asked.

Jackson opened his frog jar and his nostrils flared at the stink of formaldehyde. "*Always defer to the materials provided by your instructor,*" he read aloud from the handout on his desk. "If you're not comfortable, Tom, we won't laugh at you. . . too much."

Hernandez tapped Tom on the shoulder, and Chi held his frog next to Tom's face. "Surprisingly few people have the stomach to use a knife on something already dead."

"Say ribbit," Jackson instructed as he took a picture with his phone and pushed send. "Frog face."

Tom shot up out of his chair.

Hernandez shoved him back down into his seat. "No telling, Tommy. We don't like tattle tales."

"He's turning green," Chi said, and drummed the work bench. "What's green and jumps?"

Jackson flicked Tom's ear again. "Don't slouch, Tommy. Sit up straight. Safety first when working with formaldehyde."

"Cut it out. Why can't you leave me alone?"

"Tell us why you didn't do what I asked?" Jackson said.

"Is there a problem back there?" Mr. Dickerson asked.

"No, sir," Hernandez replied, and flicked Tom's ear again when Mr. Dickerson turned.

"Stop! I did what you told me."

"Then where are my pictures?" Jackson demanded.

"I sent them."

"Send them again, or I'll kick your ass again."

"Just leave me alone."

"Déjeme en paz," Hernandez mocked. "You gonna cry like a little niña?"

Chi and Jackson laughed.

"What happens when two frogs collide?" Jackson asked with a smirk.

Tom's scalpel sank through the frog's skin, and the skin peeled back easily. "I can't send them. Don't you understand? I know what you'll do."

"Tom Tom. Tommy. Tom Tom," Jackson said with a mock sigh. "What did I teach you about the word can't?"

"Stop it," Tom hissed.

"Boys. Seriously," said Mr. Dickerson. "I need your attention up here."

"Sorry." Chi smiled. "Tom's having trouble with his frog."

Jackson read the assignment instructions slowly as he took the frog from the jar. "Pull frog from the jar. Place belly-up in the tray, and. . . launch!" The frog flew in an arc and landed perfectly on Tom's shoulder.

Chi and Jackson high-fived. "He scores!"

The formaldehyde-soaked frog teetered and fell from his shoulder, exploding on impact, and spilling guts across the floor. "This stops here and now!"

Chi and Hernandez erupted in laughter. "It doesn't say that in the instructions."

"What ya going to do about it, Frog Boy?" Jackson asked.

Tom's face turned bright red. Holding the scalpel in one hand, he threw his frog at Jackson. Frog guts spewed across Jackson's chest. Chi and Hernandez moved in to stop Tom, but Tom held them back with the knife. "What about STOP don't you understand?"

At the same time Jackson jumped back, his chair hit the floor. "Mr. Dickerson! Tom's gone crazy!"

"Stinson, put the knife down!" Mr. Dickerson ordered and moved across the room, keeping a chair between him and Tom. "Take it easy, Stinson. What's going on here?"

Tom swiped at Mr. Dickerson and pointed the scalpel at Jackson. His hand shook. "He threw the frog on me!"

"Then put the knife down and we can talk it through."

"No," Tom said. "They poked me with a pencil, and threw the

frog on me. I'm sick of it! I told the principal before, they won't leave me alone."

"You're the one holding a knife, Tom," Mr. Dickerson said. "Jackson, get out of here."

Jackson blurted out, "Tom smashed the frog against my chest! He's trying to send me pictures of his ass and got mad when I didn't want to see them, Mr. Dickerson."

"Out, Jackson. Chi, Hernandez, tell me what happened."

"No!" Tom's voice dispersed in the silent vacuum of the science class. "They are friends. You can't let them tell you."

Jackson wryly said, "He's always had troubles, since he moved here."

"Mr. Dickerson, don't you understand what they are doing? This is what they do."

"Tom," Mr. Dickerson said, stepping around the chair. "What are they trying to do?"

"We just want to be Tom's friends, and he goes crazy on us," Jackson said.

The scalpel blade flashed in the fluorescent light. "Every day they harass me. They threaten me and make me do pranks for them, so they won't get in trouble."

"Nobody's making you do anything," Mr. Dickerson said. "They are good students, and so are you."

"You don't know what they do!"

The school security guard entered the room, deploying a can of pepper spray from his belt, aiming it at Tom.

"Don't spray that in here," Mr. Dickerson demanded. "Get the kids out first."

"Procedures are to use it in a hostage situation," the guard said.

The faint sound of sirens hung in the air, and Tom rocked back and forth on his feet.

"We're not going there, are we, Tom? Nobody's a hostage here, right?" Mr. Dickerson asked.

"Mr. Dickerson," Hernandez said. "Jackson's right. We just got the frog out of the jar, and asked Tom for help. That's when he was like, don't talk to me. Then he went crazy."

Confused, Tom's eyes darted left and right. Most of the class had gone from the room, and he pointed the knife at Hernandez. "Don't believe him. He'll say whatever he thinks you want."

"Come on, put the knife down, Tom." Mr. Dickerson tried to make eye contact. "Help me out."

"Why won't anyone listen? Why won't you believe me? Didn't anyone see!"

"I'm listening right now, put the scalpel down. You don't want to do this."

Jackson stood behind Mr. Dickerson and mouthed, *Do it.*

Mr. Dickerson cupped his hands together. "Tom, I'm not the bad guy here. I'm your friend, right?"

"I can't let their bullying go on," Tom said.

"Come on, talk to me."

Tom screamed and lunged at Jackson, swinging the blade, aiming for his throat. Mr. Dickerson and the security guard tackled him. They isolated his knife-wielding hand, and he let the scalpel fall without a fight. His tennis shoes squeaked as they dragged him down to the office.

The detention room door closed, locking Tom in. The pink walls and ambient relaxation music ate at him. He dropped his face into his hands, feeling defeated again. *No one listened to his side, all they heard were excuses. He had the knife. He threatened Jackson. He was the one at fault, and they got away as they always do, time and time again. Never again. They had to pay for their crimes. He had to end it somehow.* The clock ticked, and he stared at his shoes.

The principal opened the detention room door, *what hell was coming now,* then his dad stepped into view. Tom tensed. Light from the main office outlined him, and he examined Tom for a moment. "Are you okay?" he asked sternly. "Let's go."

The chair squeaked across the floor as Tom stood. "Are you

mad at me?"

"I'm not mad, I'm disappointed. We talked about staying out of trouble, and it was your choice. For Chrissakes, a knife!"

The solitude of the halls between classes comforted him, and he ran his fingers along the lockers. "You're pissed."

"Damn right I am. I don't get it. What were you thinking?"

The school doors creaked and the push bar clacked. The car doors shut, seat belts clicked, and hope crossed Tom's face. "Can I be home schooled?"

"By me? I have work. If you won't tell me what's going on, I can't help you. You need to figure out your problem, and get past it."

"I can't go back there."

"You are lucky officer Ramirez is on my bowling team, and the principal was willing to work with us. Taking hostages is serious business."

"I'm not getting suspended?"

"No, or arrested. Is suspension what you want?"

"They started it. I had no alternative. You told me to always finish what I start, remember?"

"Not with a knife. What if you had stabbed one of those boys?"

The engine started. Tom stared out of the window as his dad lectured him. The twelve blocks home felt like miles. Gravel had spilled over from the drought resistant lawn onto the driveway and crunched under the tires.

"I don't like arguing all the way home from school," his dad said, as he got out and checked the mailbox. "Come on in."

Slowly, Tom followed his dad up the driveway.

The house keys jingled as the teeth sawed into the lock. His dad pushed and the door creaked open into the dark hallway. His dad turned abruptly and breathed deeply. "You're too old to send to your room, but go to your room. It's clear I've failed as a parent. I need time to think about what I'm going to say. No Internet, no TV. Understand?"

Down the hall, Tom entered his room. "Dad! What the hell! Where'd all my stuff go!"

"I can't have you acting up any more. We're supposed to have an open communication policy. Which means letting me know what's going on, so I can help you."

"You searched my room and took my stuff! When did you have time?"

"I didn't find anything, if you are wondering. Where do you hide it?"

"Hide what?"

"Don't lie to me, you know very well what I mean."

"You think I'm on drugs? You had to have done this before you knew about school. What the hell!"

"Then what is it? Why can't you talk to me? You've been acting strange for weeks; withdrawn, staying in your room, hardly eating."

Tom kicked his legs up onto the desk, grimacing at the ceiling. He couldn't look his dad in the face. "Can't you trust me?"

"Not if you won't talk to me. Part of trust is having an agreement of expectations. We can try that again later."

The door closed. Tom kicked off his shoes and turned to his computer. The keyboard and mouse were gone. "Dad!" He hammered his desk at the same time his phone vibrated. It was Curry.

Text:

*What happened?*

*Dude, lost it on Jackson with a knife.*

*?Ded?*

*No. Put a frog on me.*

*FRG? Whut U going to do?*

*On death row, FIIK.*

*Skip-n-skate.*

*Can't dad will kill me. Where r u?*

*Skating. Duh. What are you going to do?*

*On lock down until Monday*
*Dude.*

A knock on Tom's door made him jump. "Tom, can I come in?" his dad asked.

He texted quickly.
*GTG DAD*
*WTF IS DAD?*
*My D A D*
*L8R.*

Tom hid his phone. "What!"

The door swung open, his dad held a stack of papers. "I had your teachers email me today's assignments, here."

"Homework?"

"You're lucky only to be sent home for the day. Tell me what's going on, please."

Tom crossed his arms across his chest. "Nothing."

His dad leaned against the door jamb and scowled. "Mrs. Stevenson told me next time she would press charges and have you arrested. Do you want that?"

"No."

"You're not leaving the house unless I'm with you until Monday. You are grounded. Give me your phone too."

"Dad, no way."

"Give it, or I'll just call and have it turned off."

Tom slumped in his chair and held out his phone. "Here."

"Don't do anything stupid like climbing out your window."

"Now you think I'm going to run away? Dad!"

The door shut, echoing poor quality. Tom flipped through the pages; math, science, the whole gamut. *No phone? It had to end. School wasn't going to do anything, and if he spoke up they'd retaliate.* He threw the papers onto his desk and they spread out. *How much homework had they given him? Torture.*

"Dad," Tom called. "School work requires me to be online. I need my computer!"

"Homework only," his dad said from the hall. "Don't let me catch you doing anything else."

A moment later he entered and handed Tom the mouse and key board. "Need me to plug it back in?"

"I don't need your help. Just close the door."

Dad's footsteps faded down the hall. Tom locked his door and opened a chat window.

*Curry u there?*

*Wut?*

*I'm gonna end it. Need help.*

*WTF end it?*

*No not like that*

*:)*

*Get me your body camera.*

*Why?*

*Evidence. Tell Brew I need him too.*

*Wut u doing?*

*Gonna scare them. I need to video it.*

*U R nutz, they will beat you down.*

*Nobody who can do anything will help. Now it's up to me. Bring the camera for the field trip. Don't Skip-n-skate*

*Not going. I'll leave it outside your window.*

*Friends help out.*

*Not your way. I have my life ahead of me.*

*Don't be chicken Curry. I need back up.*

*Don't call me chicken!*

*Get me the camera!*

## CHAPTER TWO
## MONDAY

The three-story school loomed over the rows of houses, ominous and green. Tom scanned the parking lot; Curry and Brew weren't there. The clicked seat belt open and he held on to the strap. "Let me out on the corner."

"Want me to walk you in?" his dad asked.

"I can do this."

Students pushed past him, funny looks and freak club stares followed him up the steps. *What were they supposed to do? The whole school knew. He wouldn't know how to act either.*

The CCTV camera at the entrance pointed down on him. As was his ritual, he flipped it off. Through the door of the security check station, Tom could see the guard sitting in his chair. He was a tired looking man who's eye were glassed over. His job, mind numbing. He didn't look up as Tom approached. "Put your keys and pack in the tray. Down the dark tube of the x-ray they go, hooray! Protest and you go to the principal, not no way. Argue with me, get suspended for a day."

"You're not funny." Tom tried not to smile.

The guard's hand went to his mouth. "Oh. It's you. If I were you, I wouldn't be back here for a couple of months. Not that I, you know."

"Talk to my dad, he won't home school me."

"That's some harsh business. Step forward."

The metal detector beeped and Tom's shoulders fell. "Crap."

"Go on." The guard waved him through. "You've been through enough. I'm glad I didn't pepper spray you. You'd gone over the deep end and didn't need any more grievance."

"Thanks for not following the rules," Tom said. If someone was caught talking to the guard, he would be labeled Narc or some other unimaginably stupid name. Another way of committing social suicide. Who cares though, he was already dead. "You got kids?"

Surprised by the question the guard relaxed and smiled. "No one ever asks me nothing. I have three. Thanks for asking."

"That's cool," Tom said.

"Give a little kindness, get a little kindness. Have a good day, Tom, and don't stab no one."

"Very funny," Tom said, frowning.

He continued down the hall and up the stairs, then entered the office and leaned over the counter. "My dad says I should tell you I'm back."

The receptionist tipped her tortoiseshell glasses at Tom. "Oh, Tom," she uttered in surprise. Her crafty bead necklace tinkled as she popped up and skittered around the counter, quickly knocking on the Principal's office door. "Let me get the principal, I know she's expecting you. Please take a seat."

"I'll stand," Tom said, and stared at the fliers on the bulletin board.

Out in the hall, the noise of arrival boomed. *What the hell am I doing here?* Acid gnawed at the pit of his stomach.

"Tom." The principal tapped him on the shoulder. "Come into my office."

The principal, a stout, happy woman with a clean desk, motioned him to sit. He had been in her office too many times over the past few years not to feel contempt. "I know time is short," she said. "I'll get right down to it. You know what I'm going to ask."

He held his eyes closed, reciting to himself: *Keep it short, get out as fast as possible, and avoid any conversation traps.* Breathing deeply, he said, "Let's cut the crap. I hate school."

She folded her fingers together and tumbled her thumbs in a slow circle. "We don't think of you as a troublemaker Tom, you just don't try to fit in with any of the other students. You were so innocent when you moved here from Illinois. What happened?"

"You know what happened."

"I do. We appreciate individuality as long as it is expressed within the rules. But at times you go out of your way to agitate people."

"Individuality? Why should I fit in? When they don't try either? They herd me, they hit me, and it's all my fault. You're a joke."

"I'm not being funny, Tom. A little respect goes a long way."

"Are we done?" Tom rose and walked out the door. It closed behind him as he stepped out of the office into the hall.

The floors of the school were prison-like, complete with color-coded lines for the lost. Students jammed down the hall, bumping into him, rushing to class. Moving against the current, they parted around him. Someone yelled, "Don't stab me Tom-katana!"

They had nicknames for him, mostly stupid ones: *Tomnado, Dorothy, and now Tom-katana.* This was how it started: a scent that caught in the air and shifted conversations, subconsciously altering the entire school routine. Spooks of concern stretched faces and tickled drones into laughing nervously. It was the pattern: isolate, belittle, eliminate. These were the tell-tale signs; something predatory was coming.

Tom spoke into the blur of faceless kids. "Yea, I don't care about you either."

A pug-faced cheerleader approached. "What does it feel like?"

"What does what feel like?" he replied, confused. Dread washed over him; it was too late. A hand locked onto the back of his neck and slammed him face-first into a sticker-covered locker. His head hit the metal with a loud crack. Little sparks of light danced across his vision as he staggered back and stared into space down the hall.

"That's for Jackson, asshole," the voice said.

Tom held his nose and blood pooled in his palm. "Well, I didn't expect a warm welcome."

"Go kill yourself and die like you should." The voice faded into the crowd. Whoever pushed him was gone. One kid shook his head and shrugged as he passed. Another outlined a circle in the air like a face and mouthed the word *nasty*. Then a hand was on his shoulder. Tom winced, expecting more pain. Instead, a hand holding a tissue came into view, and the warm voice of a teacher asked, "You okay?"

"Yeah." He tilted his head back and pinched his nose. "I didn't do anything, either. Some cheerleader came up and told me to die."

"Would you like to see the nurse?"

"I'll be alright."

"Here's a couple more tissues, you need them. If I can ask, why don't you let them know who you are? Give them something positive?"

"I can't do that, they deserve nothing. The last thing I'll ever do is give them something to use. It's why they get on me."

"Even if it means being bullied?"

"I'm only bullied if I let them."

"You look bullied to me. You should talk with the principal. Tell her who they are."

Tom wiped the blood from his face. "Maybe you're right. I'll show them who I am. That'll work, sure."

Down the hall, Mr. Dickerson stood at his door waving students in. Tom stuffed the tissues into his pocket. He didn't want him to know. It would only interfere with his plan.

Mr. Dickerson nodded and held out a welcoming arm. "The principal told me you were back. Come in. Come in."

*Circus time and I'm the big top attraction,* Tom thought. Long-faced stares and nervous hellos greeted him. Chairs squeaked. Students scooted aside as Tom pushed down the aisle.

The teacher shut the door.

"Don't bother sitting, Tom, we are leaving immediately."

"Don't stab me!" Jackson yelled from the back of the class and burst into laughter.

"Jackson, behave," Mr. Dickerson said. "Remember, it takes two to tango. Okay everyone. Get your packs and coats. Let's head out."

Tom stood out of the way, back and behind Mr. Dickerson's desk, keeping his distance as Jackson, Chi and Hernandez danced their way out of the classroom, mocking him.

"See you on the bus, Stabby Stinson," they said, laughing.

Outside, the bus doors hissed open and students crowded on board. Brew and Curry were nowhere to be seen. He checked his phone, then sent a text:

*Curry where are you?*
*SK8 told you*
*I needed you and Brew's help*
*A wise man said, don't get your ass kicked unnecessarily*
*F U*

Pain burst at his shoulder, sending him staggering back. Hernandez, Chi and Jackson surrounded him and shoved him against the bus.

"I liked your little knife pulling stunt," Jackson said.

"Just leave me alone."

"Yeah, very creative," Chi said. "We should stuff you under the bus."

Jackson smacked Tom in the arm. "Ready for your assignment?"

"Take this." Hernandez thrust a paper bag into Tom's chest. "They're making us little tykes hot cocoa after we clean the beachy weachy. Make sure you put it in our drinks."

Chi flicked Tom's ear. "That way we are innocent."

Inside the wrinkled bag sat a blue capped bottle of Schnapps.

Jackson pushed his finger into Tom's face, flattening his nose. "Do it, or face the consequences, Sloppy D. No one can help you; don't make a sound."

"Get on the bus, you're sitting with us." Hernandez grabbed Tom's belt loop. "You need behavior coaching."

The bus stopped in the beach parking lot and the doors hissed opened. Mr. Dickerson spoke over the PA. "Heads up, people.

Clean-up partner assignments are listed here. Get with your partner and take a bag, we'll meet at the trailhead. Once we are on the beach, note the types of trash you find on the assignment sheet."

Hernandez escorted Tom off the bus, holding him by the back of his neck. "There's the Ecology Center. Make sure you finish first and get there before the teachers do. If you tell anyone or act weird I will beat you, understand?"

Tom nodded.

"Your girlfriend Bonnie needs a partner." Chi pushed Tom. "Go clean, Little Green Earthling."

Mr. Dickerson approached Tom. "I'm glad you were able to resolve your problem so quickly and be friends with Jackson."

Tom gave Mr. Dickerson a blank stare. "Yeah, right. No one will help me, not even you."

"What was that, Stinson?"

"Never mind."

Tom tapped Bonnie's shoulder. "Hey, over here. Lets go!"

*

The cry of a gull cut through the crash of a wave as water washed over the sand towards Tom. He shuffled above the wave line, keeping his feet dry, dragging his trash bag behind him. Tom motioned Bonnie over. "Hurry up. There's a patch of trash we can clean up."

"Tom, wait. We can't go past the rocks, remember? We should stay closer to the class."

Tom spun around and thumbed over his shoulder. "Come on, Bonnie, don't be a wuss. Why would we subject ourselves to their torture? Don't do this to me. The class is right there. Besides, we stay true to our class project if we pick up the most trash. It's Save the Beach Day, remember?"

Bonnie hucked a sand dollar at Tom. It whizzed past his head as he ducked, just missing him. "Don't call me Bonnie. What's your problem? You need all the friends you can get."

Tom laughed. "It's not my fault your parents named you Bonafair. Blame them."

"What's wrong with you?"

"Just hurry up."

A pile of cigarette butts was nestled in an artful circle of driftwood and shells. Bonnie pulled his fleecy tight and moaned as he bent over, picking them up. "This sucks. I'm cold, and cold sucks even more than picking up people's trash. Why'd we choose January?"

Tom picked up a rope-tangled plastic bag. "Seasons don't matter, we're saving the planet."

A dog ran up the beach, splashing through the wash, and stopped for a quick sniff. Tom patted its head before it continued on its path.

Bonnie dodged the dog and blew into his hands to warm them, then cupped his ears against the wind. "It's like being in a sand blaster, a freezing one. A class ski trip would have been way better."

Tom furrowed his brow. "Skiing isn't saving the planet, Bonnie. That's why we didn't vote for a ski trip. Pick up the trash and fill our bags, then we can jet. No big deal. There's hot chocolate waiting for us at the Ecology Center after we reach our quota. Besides, we're supposed to care as part of the assignment."

Bonnie frowned. "You don't care at all. It's obvious you think this is all a joke. Your problem is you don't care about the things everyone else does. Didn't anyone teach you to be part of the crowd, and care along with everyone else?"

"Part of the crowd?" Tom dug his foot into the sand. "How dumb are you? We both get our asses kicked by those dicks, but the difference between us is you want to be like them. You are a traitor to everyone bullied. So, how do I care? I love cats and do community fulfillment services on the weekends for my church. I can live with me, can you? Or Maybe I should do something to embarrass you, like make you wince and cross your legs like you have to pee. Is that what I should do? Fit in like you?"

"Tom, you are flawed. They aren't so bad, once you know them. You don't try hard enough, that's why you are stuck with those losers, Brew and Curry."

"Hernandez, Chi and Jackson? You are a tool for their amusement, Bonnie. Don't tell me 'Don't stress the haters' when they don't care one bit about anybody but themselves."

"Tom, if you show them who you really are, you would become more human, it's hard to hurt a friend."

"Hurt a friend, right. Bullies are really nice people, they're just under a lot of pressure. I'll remember that the next time when I'm pushed onto the ground, kicked in the stomach, locked in the bathroom, or wearing a frog from science class."

"Please try," Bonnie said with too much emotion for Tom to bear. "Have feelings for people."

A gust of ocean wind whipped sand into Tom's mouth. He spat. "The problem is bigger than just at our school. The amount of trash here shows how people care about other people. You are disposable, crumpled up and easily discarded when they use you up. And the joke is, no one will do anything to change, not until it's in everybody's faces like sitting in a burning house. The whole 'Save the Planet' ecology crap is just window dressing to keep the masses occupied as we plunge down the interstellar highway toward extinction. So while you worry if those dumb asses like you, toss another plastic water bottle into a recycling bin and wash your hands of any responsibility."

"Wow," Bonnie said. "You should become an activist. I do my part, so stop whining. Recycle, reduce, reuse."

*How unbelievably ignorant. Didn't he get it. . .? No, but then not many people do.*

"No Bonnie," Tom interrupted. "What we need to do is refuse, stop buying the crap, but that's too much of an inconvenience. So who cares, right? People will eat and shit and drink and fuck their way into extinction and all the while they will say is it's not so bad, because bad becomes good when it gets worse."

Bonnie kicked a clump of seaweed and ran ahead. "Whatever, dude, I have hope."

Tom picked up a rock and eyeballed Bonnie.

*They may both be social outcasts, but the difference is Bonnie wants in.*

He drew his arm back, the perfect shot begging him. He held the rock for a second but decided against it. If he faced Bonnie, he'd be in front of the school for everyone to see, with the jocks at his back to witness his demonstration of sociability. That's what people like Bonnie understood. He'd go from social climber to ass kicker in a swirl of punches and a 3-day-suspension. Bonnie would do it, too, if he he had enough balls.

Bonnie ran back, holding out a wallet. "Check this out! It's crusty and stuck together." He pried it open, brushing away the sand. "What type of money is this? This dude's face is serious."

Tom took the money from Bonnie. "It's Japanese. I'll alert Washington, and let them know of the change of plans. We're leaving for Vegas."

Bonnie grabbed it back. "You don't even care I found money in a wallet washed up on the beach. What are the odds that would happen? I could be rich."

Tom shrugged. "Keep trying."

Bonnie flipped him off. "Don't be a dick."

Tom laughed and walked away. They weren't friends even though they were on the same side of the punching bag.

"Maybe a Tsunami will wash you all away," he shouted out over the crash of the waves.

*No one would ever get all the trash. Damn the field trip. Damn it all to hell. It was all in the name of free labor and a lesson in futility. He'd finish first, but not the way they wanted.*

"Doesn't it make you feel good, Bonnie?"

"Dude!" Bonnie ran up pointing to the rocks in the surf, their argument forgotten. "A dead seal!"

Bobbing in the breakers out among a jetty of rocks, a black dot swayed with the waves. Tom dropped his trash bag and waded out into the surf. "Sick, change of plans, Bonnie. Let's check it out."

A dead seal was just what he needed.

The wash receded. Timing his movement across the rocks, he worked his way out between the taller waves. The rocks were slippery and covered in barnacles. A high wave soaked him and Bonnie laughed from the beach. The cold water bit into his bones as his shoe soaked it up like a sponge. "Damn it."

Bonnie stayed back above the water line, recording the rescue. "Whatever it is, it's too far out there. You'll totally get blasted by a wave."

"You'd like that, wouldn't you, Bonbon? Give you something to tool your way into having friends who don't really like you. Come on, camera man, don't be a wimp. The water won't hurt you."

Reluctantly, Bonnie followed him with his phone held out. "What if a shark didn't finish its lunch? What if a shark is waiting?"

A wave pushed the black lump closer. Reaching down, he grabbed it. "Get your phone over here. We can document this for Mr. Dickerson. Show him we are learning."

"That's nasty." Bonnie angled his phone. "Wait till I can get closer. What if it has a disease? You could end up in the hospital in an isolation ward with your dick falling off and pus oozing from your eyes."

"Dude, it's a wetsuit, not a seal. Plan change again, the suit is atypical sea trash from Japan, just like the rest of the crap we are picking up today. The remains arrived last month from Fukushima."

"If you had picked up a hunk of dead seal, I would have definitely told Mr. Dickerson. He'd quarantine you for being stupid."

Tom stuck his hand through a hole in the wet suit. "All part of the scientific beach cleaning process, Bonnie. Just ask our teacher, he'll tell you what's what."

"Whoa." Bonnie held onto the suit leg. "Is that a shark tooth stuck in it? It's huge."

Tom's eyes grew as he pulled the tooth free. "A keen discovery, Bonbon. The day may not be lost yet. Not shark, it's more like a fang."

"What kind of creature with fangs lives in the ocean?" Bonnie asked. "It's gotta suck, losing a suit. Then have some fish think it's food. Whoever lost this suit lost big. Now it's just a fish's chew toy."

"There's more." Tom dropped the suit, jumped down into the water from the rocks and waded out. "We're getting lucky today."

"Don't be dumb," Bonnie said. "Now you're gonna cry like a baby because you're wet. I don't think I can take your poor life decisions."

"The life coach at school is buzzing around your head. I say who's dumber, the dummy who makes the choice or the dummy who follows?" A wave lapped over Tom. "Damn, my nads!" he yelped. Putting aside his discomfort, he waded further out into the surf and pulled on a strap that floated up from between the rocks.

"Dude. Air tanks. It's mighty sea trash and something made holes in the tanks.

"Those tanks are punctured," Bonnie said. "You should get out of the water."

Tom jumped a breaking wave, bits of plastic debris clouding the water around him. "I don't think the suit was lost. I think it was some kind of monster. Mu ha ha!"

"Wet feet suck." Bonnie hopped back across the rocks onto the beach and slung his trash bag over his shoulder. "I'm gonna freeze. We better go back and show the teacher what we found."

Tom put the fang in his pocket and pushed his way on shore against the receding waves. "You just want hot chocolate. I know what you're about. Hey, a diver's bag over there!"

Tom and Bonnie raced, pushing each other aside as they ran. Tom was first, despite his wet clothes.

Bonnie grabbed for the bag. "Open it."

Tom twisted and reached in, pulling out a shell. "Abalone. You ever eat it?"

Bonnie's eyes darted up and down the beach and he grimaced. "We gotta tell the teacher: the tanks, the tooth and suit. This isn't cool, where's the diver?"

Tom fished his hand around in the bag. "What's spooking you? It's not like we found a body. There's something else in here. Too round for a shell."

Bonnie pressed in close. "What is it?"

"A hunk of sandstone." Tom held it up. "There's something in it."

"Sandstone? In the water? Give it!"

Tom twisted again, pulling the rock away. "Don't you have any manners? Grab for it again and you go in the water."

Hernandez, Chi and Jackson appeared only feet away.

"We told you, finish first or you'd get a beating," Jackson said. "You lovers failed."

"Oh shit," Bonnie yelped, and backed away, still taking video.

Tom turned the body camera on.

Chi punched into his hand and laughed. "It's beat down time."

"Back me up, Bonnie." Tom backpedaled, fighting for courage to face them.

"Scared?" Chi laughed. "Your pants are wet. Did you go a little wee wee?"

"Back me up, Bonnie. Back me up," Jackson mocked, then spoke grimly. "Run away Bonnie or you'll get a beat down, too."

He was alone, Bonnie wouldn't help him. He'd been a dick and hadn't cut him any slack. *Pain is only temporary*, he told himself, then flipped Jackson off. "Go ahead, beat me down. You'll pay for it."

Jackson's chest puffed up. "On the beach, no one can hear you scream."

"I have proof, there's no way you'll lie your way out of it. Hit me and you are finished."

Jackson kicked sand at Tom and ripped the camera from his shirt. "Nice try, camera boy. Beg for mercy, weakling."

Tom couldn't hesitate or he would lose his nerve. He swung his fist in a wide arc. "Not this time."

Jackson ducked. "Too slow."

Hernandez pushed Tom from the side. "Where's our bag? Give it."

Tom pulled the schnapps out of his coat and waved it in the air. "Is this what you want?"

"Give it!" Chi grabbed for the bottle.

Tom threw the schnapps far out into the surf. The bottle bobbed for a second before a wave crashed over it, pulling it under, disappearing into the unknown realm of Davy Jones' locker. "There's your drink."

"You are so dead!" Chi shouted and waded into the surf after it.

"It's lottery day," Hernandez cracked his knuckles and moved in. "You won a double beating!"

"It's gone!" Chi yelled from the water. "Beat the fag!"

Hernandez swung, missing. Tom jumped back and raised his fists in a defensive stance. "It's my turn to beat you!"

"Ha!" Jackson snorted. "Like you did when we beat you in the hall, and the bathroom? Like when we put the frog on you? Like when we tossed you naked into the girls locker room?"

Bonnie yelped. Hernandez and Jackson froze mid-grab. Then the three ran.

Tom cocked his head, perplexed, his heart pounding in his throat. "Fuckers, come back!" Just one punch, that's all he wanted, give one of them a black eye so he could claim a little victory. Chi was gone, too. *GOD DAMN IT!*

His phone vibrated and he reached for it, but it was the rock he found in the divers bag. He turned the rock over in his hand and flakes of sand crunched under the pressure of his fingertips. Gray aluminum appeared.

"What the hell?" he said as his eyes widened and he eagerly broke away more of the sand, uncovering a metallic oval with the layered image of a circle surrounding a square. It was warm despite the cold.

*Someone's got to see this.*

Bonnie, Hernandez, Chi and Jackson were almost to the class when they stopped and waved their arms in the air, pointing towards him. The class crowded around them. They all started jumping up and down, waving their arms in the air.

*What the hell are they doing?*

He took a few steps closer. *Really, what were they doing?* He flipped them off. Dark figures emerged from the surf behind the class. *Let them get eaten by seals, that would be justice.* He laughed, but they were too big to be seals. His lips curled in confusion.

Crumpled feathers blew past his feet on the wind, and the air burned with the smell of sewage and rotten fish. He closed his eyes. Fear flooded him. His class. They weren't waving a friendly, "Hey dude, what's up, bro?" or a playing new type of joke. Hernandez, Chi and Jackson weren't smart enough to pull off such a feat with the whole class. They were warning him.

A shadow loomed over his.

## CHAPTER THREE
## NO BULLETS?

Five hundred feet of sand gave way to the planks of a wooden walkway winding through the dunes and opening onto the asphalt parking lot. The school bus, unattended, sat still in the glare of the bright winter afternoon. Beyond it was the ecology center and the freeway. Tom blurred past the chaperones who huddled together outside the ecology center. Their faces rosy from the bite of cold sea wind, stared at him.

"Hey! Stop!" one chaperone called after him. "Watch out, car!"

A hybrid car entering the parking lot, gliding silently in front of him. The metal of the hood crinkled from the weight of his body hitting. He wasn't sure if he rolled or bounced off.

The driver leaned on his horn.

Tom skidded to a stop as his elbows and knees scraped across the pavement like pencil erasers. Pain shot through his body. Scrambling to his feet, he lunged for the door handle and pulled on the half open window. The glass snapped, shattering into little beads and peppering the ground.

"Get me out of here!" Tom demanded. "Let me in! Now!"

The woman in the passenger seat fought. She hit at him, cutting her arm on the broken glass of the window and reaching for the OnStar.

Panicking, the driver threw the car into reverse and floored it. The wheels spun on the sandy pavement. Unaccustomed with driving backwards, he lost control. The car crashed into a lane separating pole, the bumper crumpled and the airbags deployed. The driver sat stunned, holding his nose. Blood had burst across the bag and window, leaving streaks like splattered finger paint.

Tom blinked quickly. He had to run. The freeway. He could get a ride, but his feet were frozen in place.

A ranger charged out from the toll booth and grabbed for him, snagging him by his hoodie. The drawstring pulled tight, choking him. He spun around, slipped on the gravel and fell on his knees, cracking them on the pavement again.

"Stay down!" the ranger ordered.

Tom sprung up and the ranger grappled him into a pain compliance hold. She pulled at his arms, bending him at his elbow and then kicked the back of his knees. He fell again, and she landed on top of him.

He fought free under her weight, jamming his thumb into her eye. "M-m-monsters!" he strained. "Let me go!"

A second ranger grabbed him by the foot, pulled him straight and folded him at the knee. "Don't resist, or I will use severe force." He took out his taser.

Tom didn't understand what was happening and continued struggling.

"Clear on the count of three!" the second ranger shouted.

The ranger who had pinned him rolled away, leaving Tom flat on his face. The second ranger jammed the taser hard into his back. "Stay down!"

Pain shot across Tom's body as his tongue stuck out into the sand, and his eyes rolled up into his head; he felt like he had been hit by another car. Still he tried to get away, twisting for leverage, but his body wouldn't work.

The ranger shocked him again. "Stay down!"

His muscles knotted from the burst of electricity coursing through him. Sand crusted his face and burned in his eyes. "Let me go!" The words flew out of his mouth with a spray of sand. "We're all going to die!"

The first ranger dropped down onto Tom and pushed her knee between his shoulder blades, bending his arms back around him. "Stay still. Put your hands behind your back!"

The chaperones arrived and gathered around, their faces surprised and cautious. "No, don't. He's one of ours. He's a kid. Stop!"

The man whose car he hit ran up holding his nose between his fingers. "You goddamn punk! Why the hell did you do that?"

The second ranger turned towards the chaperones. "He tried to carjack those people. Who is he? What's his name?"

The woman from the car ran over, holding a baby. "Why the hell did you attack us? You ruined my car. How could you? What were you thinking, kid?"

"Back off," the second ranger said. "Everyone calm down. We have the situation under control." He faced the woman and the screeching baby. "Do you need an ambulance for your baby ma'am?"

She checked quickly, pulling back the fold of the swaddle as if it were an afterthought to her car. "Oh my God! Oh my God! I do! What if it's a sub-cranial hematoma or if his neck is broken? Call an ambulance!"

Shaking his fists at Tom, the driver lunged forward, kicking him. "Arrest him!"

The chaperones pulled the man back, holding him by the arms. "I'll make sure you go to jail for a very long time. You endangered my family."

Tom struggled even harder to break free of the first ranger's grip. "Oh, God. . . Monsters. . . Run. You don't understand!"

The ranger drove her knee into the back of his neck, pushing his face deep into the sand. She pulled a zip tie from her fanny pack. "I understand perfectly; you assaulted them. You are under arrest. You have the right to…"

A chaperone stepped up and got down on her knees beside Tom. Her eyes pleaded with him as she brushed sand from his face. "Stop struggling, Tom." she said softly. "Calm down. Relax, and it will be easy. They won't restrain you if you promise to calm down."

Standing, the ranger focused her attention on the chaperone. She unsnapped her holster and put her hand on her gun. "Step back, now! Do not get involved!"

The chaperone held her hands up. "Just wait. You may think

you are in control, but I'm a parent, and I am concerned you are using excessive force. There have been too many cases where law enforcement gets carried away, and a kid dies needlessly."

The ranger switched from her gun to the pepper spray and squirted her with a stream. "You are being placed under arrest for obstructing an officer. Get down on your knees."

The chaperone dropped her hot chocolate and screamed, covering her eyes with her hands. Her eye makeup streaked down her face and ran between her fingers.

Grabbing her by the wrist, the ranger pulled her arm, swung her around, and pushed her face into the ground alongside Tom's, zip-tying her like a hog in one swift movement. The other chaperones protested.

"Do you want the same?" the second ranger asked. "I have no problem hauling all of you in."

"No." They fell into their soccer mom line, dejected and obedient.

The ranger tapped his badge. "Then I suggest you get uninvolved quickly, before you get on my radar."

Cries for help captured the rangers' attention. Responding to the call, they let Tom go and jumped into action as the class funneled into the parking lot at a dead run. Searching for safety, they all headed for the bus. Chi, Jackson, and Hernandez were in the lead and pried the doors open, but it was too late.

Monsters appeared from rips in the light across the parking lot, stepping out from the darkness beyond.

Their red scaly carapaces glowed, fingers like rods of bone coral struck with deadly accuracy as they slashed the students, taking them down.

The air reeked like a tipped-over port-a-potty at a Tuesday fish market. The rangers fell back, and the chaperones ran to save their children.

Tom pushed at the ground and worked his legs. *Please, please, legs, just get up and run,* he begged. Fear puke ran from his

32

mouth as he pulled himself into a ball on the sandy lot, unable to look away.

More creatures sprang over the top of the dunes; horrors, but graceful in their bounds. Shimmering black nets fanned out from their hands, scooping up students and chaperones, and tossing them into the air. Their screams rotated with their spinning bodies as they were caught and taken away into the black.

Tom screamed hysterically, "What are they?"

A million thoughts trampled through his mind, but one stood out. *Not this way! My life will not end like this, not without a fight.* Forcing himself up, he grabbed the ranger's gun and stepped forward firing wildly, but the gun clicked uselessly in his hand. He turned it over, not knowing what was wrong. Then it hit him like a thousand daggers of dread piercing his eyes, *no bullets!*

"Run!" the ranger said, breaking free of her fear. Sprinted into the toll booth and slammed the door, sealing herself in.

Pulsing across the parking lot in and out of darkness, a creature stepped out of a split seam in reality, towering before Tom. There was nowhere to go.

A dazed and confused chaperone ran screaming past Tom, putting herself between him and the monster. It grabbed her, shook her violently and threw her away; her broken body landed and skidding to a stop like a lost lunch bag on the wind. The monster reared up on its spiny tail with a deafening roar, and the smell of sewage and rotten fish spilled out of its gaping mouth, burning Tom's eyes.

Whatever was left in his stomach drained down his chest as he tucked his chin in and shielded himself with his arms in a pitiful attempt in defense. Euphoria washed over him, and his breathing slowed. He knew he was dead, and there was nothing he could do. Gazing into the monster's eyes, he thought they were kinda cool in a way. Was this acceptance? It raised its claw to slash him, and he held its gaze. He wouldn't shy away. He would face death with defiance. With a roar it slashed, but stopped short from eviscerating him as the sound of gunshots pierced his ears. Tiny pockets appeared on its carapace and spurted vile blood.

The monster turned its head and Tom followed its gaze. The second ranger stood half shielded by the toll booth. Wisps of smoke streaked away from his up-turned gun barrel. Futility was on his face as he reloaded. A gush of slime ran down the monster's chest, dripping onto Tom, burning his skin where it touched.

The ranger forced out a yell. "Run!"

Stars filled Tom's eyes, and the taste of blood filled his mouth. He felt weightless for a moment, *it was such a nice day*, then everything went black.

## CHAPTER FOUR
## THERE ARE NO MONSTERS

In the darkness, Tom followed a faint but steady beeping with his mind and woke to the scent of flowers. Pain pierced through his eyes to the back of his neck as he screamed and struggled. "I can't see. We gotta get out of here!"

Gentle hands pressed on his shoulders, holding him down. "Tom. It's okay, you're safe."

His thoughts were confused as he tried putting it all together. "I'm dead!" he said, pulling at the bandages wrapped around his head. "Tornado? Dad? The monsters? Where am I?"

"Stay still, you are in the hospital."

"Don't try to move," a soft voice said. "You'll rip your stitches."

The whir of a motor sounded, and something squeezed his left arm. He pulled his arm away as a flash of the monster squeezing the chaperone until her eyes popped out filled his mind.

"Hold still and breathe normally."

He held back the urge to run, and breathed deeply. Every muscle in his body screamed. "Hold still? My whole body hurts. I don't understand?"

The band loosened its grip on his arm. "Are you a runner?" she asked. "111 over 68. That's real good considering how agitated you are."

"How bad am I?"

His dad held his hand. "I'm here, Tom."

"It smells like a funeral home in here." He shook off his dad's hand and felt his face.

"Don't worry about opening your eyes, and try not to touch your face. You have a lot of stitches."

"Here, drink." Tom felt a straw touch his mouth. "The doctors say you're all right."

It was cold and tasteless, pinching his throat as he swallowed.

"Why was I on Mars? Something went wrong. Lizardmen were trying to kill me. Emmett said he would come get me, make it right."

His dad sniffled and his voice choked. "You're okay, Tom-"

The nurse cut in. "You'll be a little disoriented. You have been unconscious for a while. It's typical for patients to remember traveling, being on a jet or a cruise."

"Who's Emmett?"

"We don't have an Emmett on this floor, you probably heard another nurse saying you'd be alright and help was here. Even if you are unconscious, you tend to pick up on the things around you."

"Monsters," Tom croaked. "There were monsters."

"No, Tom, there are no monsters. You're safe here with me. Don't you remember what happened?"

The IV line pulled tight as he lifted his arm. "My face is killing me."

"There was an earthquake off the coast. You were caught in a tsunami. It's a miracle you survived."

"Tsunami? Bonnie found the money. I was joking. Then we found a wetsuit."

"You've been out for over a week. Your mind may have played some tricks on you from all the drugs they've given you."

He pushed himself up, and his dad adjusted the bed. He ran his fingers along the bandages. "It's my fault, I wished for it to happen."

"Tom, you can't wish for a tsunami, that's nonsense."

"They're all dead, aren't they?"

"We can talk later. Right now, I'm more worried about you."

"Are they? Don't lie. Tell me! We agreed to be honest with each other after mom disappeared."

"I'm sorry, Tom, you're right. I can't help but protect you, and sometimes it means holding back the truth from you. You were the only one they found."

36

"Only one? That can't be right. There wasn't a tsunami. Monsters came over the dunes and threw my class into the air. Didn't anyone? Don't you believe me?"

"I do believe you, Tom. I believe you have had a hard time. Here, take another drink and try to calm down."

His dad pulled the cup away and they sat in silence. *Why didn't his dad believe him? He needed evidence and not an emotional explanation. That's how they argued. A game of prove it with fact or take a seat. He wasn't getting any answers from his dad, so he changed the subject.* "How many stitches do I have?"

"Thirty-eight. The cut on your face is a little more than four inches long. It runs down your forehead across your eye, and about an inch into your cheek. The doctor said we can talk about options when the stitches come out."

"I'm not going to be ugly, am I?" Tom asked. *How was he going to get any girls if he was ugly? He'd be stuck with his stalker, Stacey. Maybe it would be a cool scar. Like a war hero's.* He shook his head, trying clear his mind. He had to deal with the facts and be patient.

"The truth? It's a big jagged cut, and it will be a big scar."

Tom tugged the bandages. "Is it cool?"

His dad stopped his hand. "Don't, Tom, leave it alone. I understand you are curious, but I can't tell the future. It might be a cool scar, but it doesn't matter. What does is you are my son, and that will never change. So don't worry about how it. We will take care of it, no matter what it looks like. Besides, you were very lucky your eye didn't get cut, and I'm just happy you didn't lose your sight. That's more important than having a cool scar."

# CHAPTER FIVE
## MUM'S THE WORD

There was a commotion outside. A nurse stood in the doorway holding her arms out, blocking the hall. "Excuse me. You have some friends here. Is it okay, Mr. Stinson?"

"Visitors? Who?" Tom's dad waved his hand no. "He's not up for it. It better not be more reporters or parents."

The nurse turned in the door and spoke. "There's no visitors right now. You'll have to leave."

A familiar voice called from the hall. "You can't keep us out of there. Tom, you in there?"

"You can't come in here," the nurse said.

Tom lifted bandages, the light from the hall hurt his eyes, and he squinted; he was just able to make out who it was. "Dudes. Brew. Curry!" He tried not to smile, but it was hard not to. No matter how much they sucked.

Curry was a matter of fact thrower, he prided himself on pointing out the obvious. He wore his favorite shirt, printed across in bright green letters was the word, 'Moist'.

Brew was a golly gee yuckers dude who fell off a farm truck when he was a baby. He should be on the football team and wore his skateboard helmet on sideways. He was always joking and fell over at unexpected times.

Curry led the charge. "Holy guacamole. It's the mummy. The rumors of your incarceration are true. No wonder you don't reply to your texts, you're all wrapped up."

"The bandages tell me you did a face grind, dude." Brew pushed the curtains back, letting the sun spill in. "The light of truth be upon thee. Show us your face, Frankenstein's mummy."

Curry kicked the bed. "Yea, like your face, it's way messed up. You'll do about anything to get out of school. Huh, bro?"

"Shouldn't you guys be in school?" Tom's dad asked. "I thought they only closed it for a week."

"Nah, Mr. Stinson." Curry put his hands in his pockets and stepped back. "We're on extended grieving time. They know how sad we are at the loss of our fellow classmates. Rest their souls."

Brew bumped into a cart and squeezed past Curry. "Our parents said we could skip school and visit. It's true."

"Tom needs rest, so make it fast and keep your voices down."

Tom lifted his bandages higher. "I'm all right, just a little messed up."

Curry grimaced and turned his head. "Dude. Ugly."

"What's with all the flowers?" Brew asked as he fiddled with the drawers in the room and found one open. "They from your girlfriend, Stalker Stacey?"

"Hey, stay out of there," Tom's dad said. "That's hospital property."

Tom tried to sit up. "I don't even like her. If you knew half of the crap she did, you would have gotten a restraining order too."

His dad put a hand on his shoulder, holding him down. "Take it easy, Tom, don't get up just because they are here."

Curry punched Brew in the arm. "Bro, don't start on her."

"Settle down, boys. If you are going to play around, you'll have to leave."

"Shucks, we're just joking around, Mr. Stinson," Curry said.

"We're way glad you are alive," Brew grabbed Tom's foot and gave it a wiggle. "When do you spring from this joint?"

"Hit the skate park." Curry balanced on one foot and tucked his arms behind his back. "Grind it out and live like no others. They're almost done building the new pool. That's where I will be discovered and sponsored all the way to the Banzai Open in Hawaii."

Brew shook the heart monitor Tom was hooked to; it beeped wildly, and he tapped it with his thumb. "This thing is broken. You were hella lucky, dude. What was it like being smashed by a ginormous wave?"

Tom started to speak, but his dad shook his head no. He

hesitated. Why didn't his dad want him to tell?

"Whats up? Too awful to talk about?" Curry asked. "Octopus got your tongue?"

Tom let go of the bandages, and they fell back over his eyes. "I don't really remember. I just closed my eyes and held on."

Curry laughed, picked up a get well card and tossed it down on the table. "Don't remember? Man you sure are popular now, even that douche Coach wrote you a card. You know there's no way I would forget. You were like riding the big wave and lived."

The nurse appeared in the door. "You boys have to leave. There are other patients here, and you can't respect the noise levels."

"Who, us?" Curry asked.

The nurse eyed Curry. "Aren't you, Dr. Martinez's son? You should know better."

"Nah, not me. I'm an orphan," Curry said, and frowned at the nurse. "Your face, do you have an antacid?"

"Go now," she ordered. "Or I'll call security."

Curry zipped up his hoodie. "Dang, dude, we're just hanging with our contemporary. Talk about a hint. Guess we gotta bail now."

Brew flipped off Tom. "Yeah like, later skater."

"Don't fall on your head again," Tom said after them.

"Oh, and just so you know," Curry said. "I forgive you for losing my camera."

Brew smiled. "Safety third."

The nurse drew the curtains shut and dimmed the lights in the room. Brew and Curry stood in the door making faces. "Go on. Don't make me call security." She chased them out.

Tom grabbed his dad's arm. "Why didn't you want me to tell them?"

"Tom, there were no monsters. If you told them what you think you saw, how would they react? And if I know those boys like I think I do, they would tell everyone. I know how it was when I was in high school."

Tom let the bandages fall. "I'm so tired, Dad."

"It's okay, rest for now. I have to check into work anyway. I'll be back a little later."

## CHAPTER SIX
## ORTEGA

Tom felt a hand on his foot, and jumped. A man spoke. "Sorry, I didn't mean to startle you. You have your own room. How very lucky. Most people can't afford one."

Tom pulled up his bandage. "What? Who are you? My dad was just here."

A balding heavy set man wearing a dark gray suit stood next to his bed. He held a clipboard and flipped through the pages. Sweat dotted his forehead. "I'm the hospital counselor. My name is Doctor Ortega. I hope I didn't catch you at a bad time. How are you doing today, Tom?"

"You know my name?"

Ortega drew a finger across the clip board where his name was printed, and tapped it.

"Okay I guess. Are you here to talk to me about my class?"

He pulled up a chair. "Only if you want to."

"I don't know."

He glanced at the door, then removed a device from his pocket. It was no bigger than a smart phone. Two wires extended from it, each ending in monitoring electrode pads, which he quickly pulled adhesive paper off and reached to attach them to Tom.

Tom blocked Ortega's hands.

"What's that for?"

"This? Nothing really. It's a pulsing electromagnetic waveform manipulator."

"It's not even wireless, what's it do?"

"Helps you relax."

"I don't think so, where's the nurse?"

"The trouble with you kids. Nothing impresses you. This is bleeding edge technology, and. . ."

"Blah blah blah, it's harmless. Spare me the lecture."

Ortega reached forward, then pulled back and tapped the

monitoring pads together. "So may I? I'm interested in listening."

"Whatever."

"You may feel relaxed and a bit drowsy. But you don't want to use it, that's okay. But if you do, I'm here.

"Sure," Tom said.

"Let me begin. You had quite an experience. You have been the big story in the news. Lucky for you, we've been keeping the reporters out of here. They're quite persistent, but hospital policy it to protect the patients. The chart says you are making a nice recovery."

"Yeah, that's what everyone says. Will I have a scar?"

"I can't answer that. My job is to find out how you are doing up here." He tapped his head and smiled, and turned on the device. "The nurses told me you have been talking in your sleep, having wild dreams about all sorts of things. Mars. Lizardmen. Strange rocks that you found on the beach. Tell me about all of it."

"They're just dreams."

"I'm sure, but you have been through a traumatic experience, and sometimes it helps when people talk about their experiences, even if it doesn't seem like it would. Now close your eyes, you may see moving patterns of dark purple and greenish yellow. Don't be alarmed."

Tom let his bandages fall over his eyes. Ortega's voice sank back into a whisper, and he breathed deeply.

"Tom," Ortega continued. "If you feel uncomfortable or feel distressed while we talk, you can stop at any time, and you never have to tell anyone we spoke. Would that be okay?"

"Yeah." Tom yawned.

Doctor Ortega shut the door and drew the curtain. "Great, Tom. Tell me about your dreams."

*

An orderly cleared Tom's lunch tray as his dad entered the room. He sipped from a large cup of coffee and pulled a chair over. "Hey, how you feeling? I brought you a book."

"Thanks, Dad," Tom put a magazine down. "I feel like crap. My face itches like hell, and reading out of one eye sucks."

"It'll get better."

"It was cool Brew and Curry came."

"It's good having friends who care about you, isn't it?"

"Care about me?"

"Yes, care about you. They are the only ones who have come other than me, but I don't count."

Tom had never considered it before, his face scrunched up under his bandages. *Maybe they were glad too.* "That's stupid. Those guys are jerks."

"Sounds like you care too," his dad laughed. "But I still don't get why you hang out with them. They are loud and obnoxious, and they don't give a damn about anything."

"They are my friends," Tom declared. "You said, have friends who have common interests."

"Yea, but I also said have friends who like study groups and are academically focused."

Tom lifted his bandage and scowled at his dad. "We just hang out, you know. Skate, mess around, all the things we should be doing. School stuff is for school, and if anyone deserves to get out and live, it's me. I got a second chance, the nurse said so."

"You did, and I am glad. So, is working harder in school on your list now?"

"No, once I'm better I'm going sky diving. There's a place at the airport, isn't there?"

"You're not jumping out of a plane."

"It would be a great way to celebrate my second chance on life."

"Where are you getting this idea?"

"The magazine I was reading. Check it out."

"You didn't touch your lunch, aren't you hungry?"

"Hospital food sucks. It probably kills more people than injury or disease. Can you bring me something real?"

"Anything you like, a nice salad? An apple?"

Tom's mouth watered at the thought of real food. "Something with flavor that hasn't been cooked into paste. Like a cheeseburger or pizza."

"How about something with lots of fiber. It'll clean you out after all the nasty hospital food and drugs. A big cup of oatmeal?"

"Dad, how old am I? I want real food, not the high fiber, low fat junk you like."

His dad patted the bed and got up. "Okay, a whole grain veggie burger, it's settled."

"Dad, I want meat, grease, and fat. Anything but the junk here. I'm 17, remember? My body isn't falling apart like yours."

"Don't remind me," his teeth gritted. "Jello pudding, and cottage cheese coming up. The cafeteria downstairs has a great selection of old folk food. I'll be back soon if I don't fall and break a hip."

"Dad. Wait," Tom said seriously. "After you left, a doctor came and talked to me. He asked me about what happened. I told him, but he didn't seem right. He had a lot of questions, like he knew more than he was asking me. He was weird."

"What doctor? Weird how?"

"I don't know? Like really nervous, he didn't stay very long either. He told me to keep quiet about everything we talked about. It was to protect me."

His dad's voice increased in volume. "Did you get his name? I want to know who he was."

"Doctor Ortiz I think, but what does it matter? No one believes me anyway."

"He asked about your dreams? Why didn't the hospital tell me about it."

"Dad, it's no big deal, remember your migraines."

His dad's eyes flared. He breathed loudly through his nose. "I'll be right back. No one does anything without my permission."

45

Tom closed his eyes and put his fingers in his ears, *are all parents are determined to kill their kids by embarrassing them to death?*

His dad stormed back in the room several minutes later. "If I don't advocate for you, nothing gets done. They just stick to their check list, and that's not good enough. What did he ask you? Tell me every detail."

"Take it easy, Dad. It's not a big deal."

"It is; I don't like surprises. The more educated you are on a subject, the better you are able to protect yourself."

"Okay, but calm down. The doctor said it was my mind making things up. People who experience trauma disassociate to protect themselves. It's the mind's way of keeping the horrible thoughts out. He said I have survivor's guilt, and my mind made up all the things I think happened to repress those feelings. What does that mean?"

His dad's jaw worked back and forth for a moment. "It means you have had a rough time, and it's going to take a while before you get better."

"But I don't feel anything. I don't feel guilty, and there's all these cards. Why are they here? I don't know half these people," Tom crumpled a card and threw it on the floor. "They are from parents asking if I spoke to their kids. The only time the jocks ever talked to me was when they stuffed me into a locker or flicked my ear because they overheard me say a band they liked sucked. The cards from the people who I do recognize must be a joke. They never cared before. So why should I care about them now?"

"It's tough for everyone. . ." His dad picked up a card and mulled over it. "I understand why the parents want to talk. You're the last link with their children. They want anything they can hold onto for comfort. It's alright to care about these people, even if they have done you wrong. It's how we work through our problems, we forgive."

"It's not enough to make a decision one way or the other, I don't think I should."

"Tom, it's more complicated than a simple decision. You ask yourself, are they worth it? What good would you be for them, and they for you? And if either side is no, then it's not worth your efforts. Everyone has a place in the world, and you are one of the lucky ones. You are smart, you think about things, and you plan. Those are powerful skills to have on your side."

"Then, I know what happened. I found a giant tooth and a metallic oval. I had Curry's body camera. Both you and the doctor told me not to tell anyone about the monsters who took my class. Not everyone died, they were taken. They were pulled into the darkness. Bonnie saw, the whole class saw, and the rangers and the teachers and the chaperones, I need the truth."

"Tom, you have been heavily sedated for over a week now. Only in the past couple of days have they started to back off on the dosage. Who knows what tricks the drugs have played on your mind. I'm sorry, but what you think happened, didn't. An earthquake off the coast sent a wall of water washing over the beach, twenty feet high. You're lucky to have survived." He searched the floor as if he had lost something, and coughed. "I don't know what I would do if I had lost you, but I don't have to think about it anymore and that makes me lucky, too."

"Dad, I'm all right. I know what happened. I have proof. It's in my hoodie."

"Tom," His dad leaned forward and straightened his blanket. "You were found 500 feet from the visitors center in a hedge of beach brush, your clothes were shredded. You were barely alive. They didn't find a single other person."

"But the tooth? The metallic oval? It was my proof."

"Whatever think you had is gone. Forget about it. The doctors say you will be well enough to come home in a couple of days. Hang in there."

"Even my phone?"

"Everything you had with you at the beach is gone."

"Sir? Mr. Stinson?" An older woman said from the doorway. She wasn't dressed like hospital staff; she wore a gray business suit and held a brief case. "Can we talk in private?"

His dad patted the bed again. "Now we get some answers about who talked to you."

## CHAPTER SEVEN
## MEATY GOOD AND GREASY

Around the corner on Tom's block, half a dozen news truck lined the street, reporters in their semi-precious catalog clothes milling about waiting for something to happen. His neighbors were out on the street picking up trash from the gutters, they had stacked the bags against the news trucks.

Tom shifted in his seat and rolled up the window. "What's all this about? Why are they here?"

Seeing Tom, the reporters moved out into the street and blocked his driveway, crowding around the car. They shouted questions at him. His dad revved the engine and honked the horn, pushing the news crews aside to get into the driveway. "Damn vultures." He shook his fist. "They scurry like rats, just like rats. They've been here ever since they found out you were the sole survivor."

"What do they want?"

"You."

"That's crazy."

His dad hit the garage opener and pulled in quickly, he jumped out of the car. The door sprung back, slamming shut. "Apparently, you're a hot news item."

The reporters came up the driveway, toting camera's and microphones, with hopeful looks in story hungry eyes. "I don't want to deal with them now," Tom said.

"I'll take care of them, stay here." He grabbed a baseball bat from the workbench, and charged out waving it at the reporters. "Go on, git. My boy's been through enough. This is private property, leave us alone."

They backed off, but not fast enough. His dad singled out a reporter and went after him, clapping the bat in his hand.

"Wait," the reporter gulped. "We just want to talk to Tom. What ya say, Mr. Stinson?"

He swung the bat in the air and flipped the reporters off. "Sensationalize this."

The reporters retreated to the street and his dad returned, ducking under the closing garage door. Tom got out of the car. The smell of WD-40 and dryer lint permeated the air, making him dizzy. He held onto the door for balance. "Have they been here the whole time?"

His dad tossed the bat onto the table and hurried over. "Here, Tom, let me help. Hold my arm, and I'll get you in the door."

Tom staggered. "Dad, I didn't think you had it in you to scare off those reporters."

He smiled and held his arm. "You liked that, did ya? Well the whole experience is new to me too."

Tom let go of his dad and braced himself against the wall. The hall seemed longer, somehow different, indescribable, unsettling him. A sudden wave of nausea washed over Tom; he braced himself against the wall holding back the urge to heave. He half smiled at his dad. "It's good to be home."

His dad pulled a towel down from over the bathroom door and spread it out at Tom's feet. "Do it here if you need to."

Tom stared at the walls and the ceiling, trying keep his equilibrium. "I'm just gonna be in my room resting."

"Good idea, rest. Okay." He turned into the kitchen and spoke over his shoulder as he went. "If you need anything, just give a holler."

Orienting himself, his eyes cleared. The state of his room sank in, it was a disaster. "Dad, what did you do in here?"

His dad appeared at the end of the hallway from the kitchen and came running. "Are you okay, Tom?"

"No, what did you do in here? Why is my room messed up?"

"I cleaned it." He pulled at his ear. "I thought I would make it nice for when you came home. I took all the teddy bears and cards from your hospital room. See how I arranged them, looks nice. . ."

"It's not. This is my space. We agreed, remember?"

50

"I couldn't help it. You don't understand what it's to be a parent. I climbed the walls while you were in the hospital. I had to do something to keep from going crazy."

"You totally invaded my space. We had an agreement. I don't mess with your stuff when I'm worried."

"I'm the dad remember. It's my job to worry you know. Ever since your mom. . ." He choked up. "It's been me and only me. You can't fault me. In a few days everything will be back to normal. You'll be back at school tomorrow."

Carried by his anger Tom stepped into the hall and paced back and forth. "How can everything go back to normal? It's not. Everyone in my science class is dead. I'm told they were washed away into the ocean. They didn't even find the bodies. Not one. And I don't even remember it happening that way."

"Tom, calm down." His dad held up a pill bottle. "The doctor gave me these pills for you. Take one. You'll feel better."

"Pills? You've always said drugs are bad. I don't need pills. I need you to listen." Tom hit the wall with his fist and almost fell over from the force. "Leave me alone!" His bedroom door crunched shut.

His dad's feet pounded the floor down the hall. He stood at the door. "Don't hit the wall."

"What?"

"Can I come in?"

The door knob twisted and Tom rolled his eyes. "Don't you ever give up? This is the part of the argument where you leave me alone. Remember?"

"We can't let this slide. You're hurting. What happened is awful and tragic. And I know you're having trouble dealing with it. I would too, but. . ."

"Leave me alone!" The muscles on his face tightened, pulling at the stitches.

"Tom?" His voice sounded like he was pressing his forehead against the door. "I'm trying anything I can do or say to make it all better for you, but I can't. I'm learning how to help you. You have to live with surviving for the rest of your life, and you have to start dealing with it. We need to start somewhere."

Tom opened the door.

His dad reached into his coat pocket. "Here, take one of these. The doctor said it will help your mood. Please. And when you calm down you can tell me how you feel."

Tom spoke quietly not move his face. "Get out. I don't want to talk about it."

"I can't." He pushed past Tom and brought up a news video on the computer. "That's the foundation where the visitors center was, and the parking lot is buried in sand."

"You used my computer too? This sucks. What else did you do? Did the psychologist tell you to do this?"

"No, he didn't. I thought it might help you learn your dreams are just dreams and help you cope by knowing what really happened."

Tom scratched at his stitches as the video played. He dabbed the seeping blood. "That's not even where we were. It's not right. There's no visitors center, not even the foundation."

"Diamond beach, right? It's on KVTU 2 News. The whole building was washed out to sea, and the lot was covered in sand."

"It's not the right place," Tom wiped the blood on his sleeve and opened the window blinds. The reporters were alerted and came up the lawn taking pictures. "I'm trapped, everyone's eyes are on me and I can't believe it. It's not what happened. They're covering up the truth. Lying like they always do."

"How? How are they lying? Why would the news people lie? What would they gain? Reporters just don't make up stories."

Tom twisted the blinds, closing them tight. "I don't know. They are. I just know. It's like the 'don't text and drive' stories where a man hits cows on the road, and his last name is Cowit. What are the odds the drivers name would be Cowit. They make those stories up to promote their agendas, sell advertising space"

"That's ridiculous, you're confused. Lay down, and get some rest, like you said. I'll get you a new bandage and you rest for a few hours. Take a nap, you need it."

Tom sat. Cellophane wrapped flowers and teddy bears crunched and squeaked under his weight on his bed. He wanted to run.

"At least push that stuff on the floor."

"Just leave me alone."

"We're not done talking, Tom. After you rest, we'll straighten out our problems."

The door closed softly. *Sleep? Fake video!* Flowers and teddy bears fell to the floor as he got up and hit play. *His class was dead, and no one would listen. Why didn't anyone know? It wasn't a hallucination like the hospital shrink had said.* He stared at the pills. *It's not my imagination. If they knew what was in my head, I could explain it. I need evidence.* Tom threw the pill bottle at his trash can. He he missed and it bounced off the wall onto the floor. *Screw the pills.* His fingers clattered on the keyboard searching for more images. *Frog monsters, sea monsters, sea creatures, nothing is like it.*

Out of the whole Internet, someone must know about what he saw. Sea monsters with legs and girls in bikinis came up. Then Jelly fish, crabs, lobsters. *These are stupid*, he hit his keyboard. *People are dumb. A crab isn't a monster unless you get it from someone.*

The doorbell rang and a moment later his dad stood at his door holding a pizza and new bandages. "Triple meat combo, just like you like."

"I'm still mad."

He set the pizza on Tom's desk. "You've been in here for hours. Aren't you hungry?"

His stomach rumbled. The antiseptic smell of the fresh gauze was drowned out by the rising aroma from the box. "You want some?"

"No, not me. I can't eat that junk, too many carbs. I'm more of a salad guy these days. Let me clear the stuff off your bed. I have a midnight conference call with Beijing, so I'm going to bed. I'll see you in the morning."

"Dad, it's only seven."

"Andare a letto presto in modo da poter dormire in ritardo. That's my motto." He smiled and folded up all the stuff on Tom's bed in the blanket and slung it over his shoulder.

"Ya ritardo. We're not even Italian. How come you say it like that?"

"Go to bed early, so you can sleep in late. I live by it."

"It's still stupid."

The door closed, a chest of fortune sat on the edge of his desk. He flipped the lid open; the sound of cardboard scraping on cardboard was comforting. Pizza. Hot, still steaming. Meat, good and greasy too. He dove in. Cheese stretched. Crust crunched. Chewy. Hot. Hot. Um. Mm. Ah.

Tom typed with one hand, sauce fell on the keyboard, and crumbs clogged the mouse wheel as he scrolled down the page. *This is the lamest search engine ever. Found giant fang on the beach.*

Nothing.

He bounced his leg and rubbed the back of his neck, he wasn't getting anywhere. He felt something with his foot and kicked it. It rattled as it hit the wall and bounced back, resting at his feet. The pills; he picked the bottle up, maybe they would help him get his head straight like his dad said. The lid popped open, and two pills rattled out. He downed them with the last of his coke.

A picture came up, Mermaids. His vision blurred. It was hard to keep his eyes open, he strained to focus. *Mermaids are stupid. They were ugly, not pretty little cartoon crap. Cryptozoology? I'm not crazy like these freaks.* He felt drowsy and picked up the bottle. *Whoa? You little bastards don't mess around. Dudes are ugly, what about mermen.*

An image appeared on the screen, and his heart jumped; his eyes widened. He wasn't crazy after all, maybe delusional, but definitely not crazy. He let out a big sigh of relief as his head hit the keyboard, and he passed out.

## CHAPTER EIGHT
## I'M CRAZY, AND I HAVE TO GO TO SCHOOL?

Dreaming, he had to be dreaming. Flying through the air was both exhilarating and terrifying. A tingling sensation rippled across his body. Tensed muscles and force of will kept him aloft, navigating through power lines and past birds as a sandy plain spread out below. This is what it is to be free. A lizardman stood atop a hill, he spoke, "Tom, I'm coming to get you!" The lizardman's voice broke his concentration and he fell. "Emmett!" He woke with a scream and a thud, his shirt was soaking with sweat. The smell of coffee hovered around him, and he wiped the crust from his eyes. "Crap, what happened?"

The blue glow of the power light from his computer illuminated his dad's face in a devilish way as he knelt at his side, startled he jumped. "Tom, are you okay?" he said, and brushed Tom's hair to the side. "You fell asleep at your desk."

The haze of the pills hung around his head like a rubber doughnut. "I feel awful. I was dreaming of the beach. . . Dad, I know what I saw."

His dad's hands slid under his arms and propped him up. "Tom, you had a bad dream, that's all. I suspect you are going to have a few more before you get a grip on your emotions."

He scratched his head. "What time is it?"

"It's early, just after 4:30."

Tom kicked his desk, and the computer flickered on. "I found pictures of what I saw, mermen. They had spears and nets and claws, and they jumped high in the air."

His dad shook the pill bottle. "Sounds like it's from a video game or one of your comics. You took the pills the doctor gave you. Drugs do funny things to your mind. Let's get you into bed."

Tom braced himself on his dad's shoulder. "You told me to take them. Aren't you going to look?"

"Cut the nonsense, Tom. What do you want me to say?"

"I need you to believe me. Please. Then you will understand what I am talking about."

His dad grunted as he helped him onto his bed. "You're not a little kid anymore. I hope this is the last time I ever have to pick you up."

"Please."

"I'm not making any promises. The Internet is full of fantasy, and most of it is made up by people who like to tell stories so they can sell their ideas and products. It's a tool the manufacturers use through music and imagery to influence people to blindly follow them and their products. It's called product identity. They put people at unease and make them feel they are lacking something in their lives. Things they can't live without, and they have just the things you need."

"Dad, you are a nut job. Nobody would do that. Those are just commercials, banner ads. Nothing more."

"And you want me to believe in mermen?"

"Dad? The dreams I had at the hospital were so real."

"Nice art work."

"This isn't a joke."

He took a long moment. "And what should I see? What you want me to, or something else."

"Those are the closest things I could find. I know it's just drawings, but it was real."

"Even though you don't want to talk to anyone, I think you need to, before what you are feeling gets out of hand. I went ahead and made an appointment for you for this afternoon at the hospital. So I want you to go to school today. The rest of your school has been back for a couple of days now, and I think it will be good for you to get back to the school routine."

Tom held his hands out, pleading him to reconsider. What was his dad thinking. "Today? You can't do that. I can't."

"It'll be good for you. It's never good to be alone when you are hurting," he said again in a stern voice.

"So I'm just supposed to go right back to school? And I don't need to talk to a shrink. I already did at the hospital. We're supposed to take it slow and easy, that's what you said right. Talk it through, it's a learning experience for both of us."

"Tom, you need to move on, and heal your wounds."

"It's not like I am becoming a freak who stays in the basement. I only came home from the hospital yesterday."

"I want you to get better."

"Dad? I thought you trusted me. We work things out together remember?"

His dad pulled a blanket over him. "There's nothing to be afraid about. It's only an appointment where you talk to a doctor. You've been through a traumatic experience."

"I already talked to the doctor. I told you I'm fine."

"About that, I had a meeting with the hospital manager. It wasn't a doctor you talked to. It was a reporter impersonating a doctor."

"A reporter? Like the ones outside our house?"

"They're not sure who it was. They are going to check the security footage, and report it to the police. And if I find any story about what you told the reporter, there will be hell to pay. The hospital has promised full cooperation."

"What if they want to lock me up. I have proof right here on my computer."

"Cryptozoology? This isn't late night radio. This isn't the movies. They don't lock you up for being crazy. They just dope you up on anti-psychotics and let you wander the streets rummaging through trash cans. Try to go back to sleep, you need the rest. When you wake up I need to change your bandage; you are going to school."

Tom threw his pillow on the floor and sat up. "Sleep? How can I sleep. I'm crazy, and I have to go to school. What would you do if you were in my shoes. Don't you get how I feel? My school is a joke, and I hate going there."

Eric Johnson

"Suit yourself. I'd choose to sleep. Today is a big day."

## CHAPTER NINE
## NOW IS THE TIME

The mail slot cover slammed a dozen times on Tom's front door. His dad called from the kitchen. "That's for you. Guess who?"

He hurried to the front door. "Cut it out already, I'm coming."

"Tom!" Brew yelled through the mail slot. "Open up, loser!"

Brews cologne seeped through the door. "I said, knock it off, Dick."

Brew and Curry stood on the door step.

"Don't call me Dick." Brew flipped him off.

"It never gets old," Curry laughed.

Tom reached into his pocket and pulled out the finger. "It's not my fault your parents named you Richard Brewster."

"Shouldn't you guys be on your way to school?" Tom's dad stood behind him.

"Dude," Curry said. "I mean, Mr. Stinson. We can't go to school, they'll think something is wrong with our family life."

"Can't you be serious?" Tom's dad asked.

"It's like only seven," Tom said.

"What's with the hounds?" Curry asked.

"They heard you were coming." Tom stepped back from the door as the reporters came closer. "It's a perfect photo op for you, Curry. Go skate for them."

"Don't mind if I do. My amazing feat will only take a moment."

Brew speared his skate board at Tom. "I think you're getting uglier. You ready?"

Curry pushed Brew. "Yeah, let's go."

Tom gave Brew the finger. "What is your malfunction, Richard?"

Brew flipped Tom off back and thumbed over his shoulder at the news crews. "Don't these clowns have homes?"

"Grab your stuff," Curry said. "Don't be lame."

Tom grabbed his skateboard and backpack. "Dad, let me take the car to school."

His dad appeared behind him with a steaming cup of coffee in his hand, his face crinkled. "You go right to school. No detours. Right?"

"Mr. Stinson, our parents said it was okay to take the day off to hang out with Tom, to help him get better."

"He's going to school."

Brew pushed Curry out of the way. "Just kidding, Mr. Stinson. We're going, just here to keep Tom
company."

Tom's dad took a deep breath. "You should worry about your future a bit more."

Tom jingled the keys, grabbed his skate, and chirped the car. The reporters massed at the end of the driveway. "Right to school, thanks, Dad."

"Don't forget your appointment."

"I'll be back on time."

Brew ran to the car and tagged it. "Shotgun."

"Man, it's my turn." Curry raced around the car and pushed Brew out of the way.

"I'm too big to fit in back you know," Brew said. "I'll hang my legs over your seat so you can rub my feet."

"That will never happen." Curry pushed Brew again. "The fact here is your discordant tune makes you a front seat persona non grata."

"You mean get in the back, because I fit? You want me to do that for you?" Brew asked.

"Don't languish over your foibles. Prepare to be mesmerized!" Curry flipped the reporters off. "Pavlovian response, dude!"

A few reporters raised their cameras.

"Is that sign language for unicorn?" Brew asked.

"Narwhal east of the Mississippi. You know, local dialects,"

Curry said. "I'm fluent in many languages for saying fuck you."

"The ever learned student," Tom said.

"Get in back, or I'll sit on you," Brew said.

"It ain't over yet," Curry said.

"Get in the car, losers." The reporters shuffled about in the rear view mirror. *Puppies at the kennel*. The doors thumped closed, Tom pushed start. "Safety third, kids. Buckle up."

Curry choked and fanned his skate board. "Turn on the air. Turn it on. Hurry! Roll down the windows, something died back here."

"Asshole!" Brew held his nose and rolled down the window. "I'm going to beat you down."

"Curry!" Tom leaned his head out his window. "You're riding on the hood. Get out."

"Aw come on, it ain't bad. No more than what the farm boy is used too."

Tom honked the car horn and backed out of the driveway quickly. The reporters jumped out of the way. He hit the gas hard, and the tires squealed. Smiling he said, "It's been a total prison for the last two weeks. It's good to get out."

Brew said in a robotic voice, "Consideration for the safety of others is very kind. Not running over the campers was good."

"I hope they don't follow us," Curry said. "I got asked a thousand questions just walking up to your doorstep."

The tires screeched as Tom pulled the car around the corner. "They're hungry for any story they can sink their teeth into," he said. "Especially when they don't have to make it up."

"You mean news agencies fabricate news to fill in the advertising space they sold?" Curry asked. "Shocking."

"Precisely, my good man, precisely," Tom replied.

"Dude, the school is the other way," Brew said.

"I know." Tom turned down the radio. "We're going to the beach."

"The beach? It's January, totally freezing, are you nuts?" Curry asked.

"Sixty degrees ain't freezing," Tom countered.

"It is for my hot blood," Curry said. "Remember my heritage."

"What about your Dad?" Brew asked. "Isn't he going to be pissed with you just getting out of the hospital?"

"That's my man. Fight the power," Curry said.

"I have a few hours left of being a free man," Tom said. "Then who knows what's going to happen when I confess at the shrink."

"They're not going to lock you up," Brew said.

"Yeah, they will. It's what they do," Curry said. "I should know, if anyone ever did. They'll keep you calm, set you at ease, make you think they are your friend. Then bang, you open your mouth, and stuff you never thought you would say comes out. Next thing you know you are in a straight jacket doped up for a 72 hour evaluation."

"That's what I'm afraid of," Tom said.

"They don't do that, it's not like the 80's when they bagged and tagged teens on the anti-drug safari," Brew said.

"Trust me, they do. I have personal experience," Curry said. "And why are we talking about feelings? You guys are creeping me out like mini-clowns dancing on a birthday cake."

"That's what they said at school," Brew said. "Talk about your feelings to help you get over the loss. Remember?"

"Dude, I was skating," Curry motioned for Brew to roll up the window. "People were way too sad for me to be around. I couldn't bring myself to go. Think of the impact on my skating it would of had. I can't afford the hit to my concentration."

"No one will ever sponsor you," Brew said. "You are too much of a criminal."

"That's my angle. Like the Phoenix, I will rise from the ashes of a life of crime and become a role model to the youth of the underworld."

Tom laughed. "He's right, Brew, we shouldn't ever try to break his concentration. When he gets sponsored we can travel with him."

"That's right, be my sidekicks."

"I'm not a sidekick," Brew said. "Bad things happen to sidekicks. We're expected to do stupid stuff and get killed."

Curry drummed the back of Brew's seat. "Yes, you are my friend. Every hero needs a sidekick, and you are mine."

"Get it straight, you guys are helping me, right?" Tom asked. "That makes you my sidekicks for the day."

"You need to rethink your position," Curry said. "I will have so much free gear, you guys will never have to buy another skate again in your lives. Bow to your master."

"Bow to yourself," Brew said.

"Don't begrudge your benevolent master."

"Driving makes me the leader," Tom said. "We just need to stop and get some supplies. Give me all your money."

"Um. No way," Brew lifted his cheek. "You know I don't get an allowance since I took out my parents garage door."

"No denero aqui," Curry said. "I'm a poor boy."

"You ain't poor, Curry," Tom held his hand out. "Cough it up. We'll need it."

"Why should we?" Curry asked.

"Why are we going to the beach anyway, since Curry needs to skate so bad?" asked Brew.

"Yea, I need to get discovered. I'm going to be a superstar."

"I'll get you a treat, now shut up and listen." Tom turned the music down. He wasn't sure how he should tell them why they were going to the beach. If his dad was right he'd be a laughing stock, but if he didn't tell them, they wouldn't go. His gut told him to take the chance.

"Dudes, it wasn't a tsunami that took our class."

Brew nodded in disbelief. "Uh yea, like sure. How hard were you hit in the head?"

"At the beach," Tom explained. "It wasn't a Tsunami, it was mermen. They came out of the ocean and took my class."

Curry hit the back of Tom's seat. "Your whacked, it was on the news. They even had an info-graphic and a little cartoon showing how it happened."

Tom reached back and tried to swat Curry. "I have proof. We just need to find it. The dreams I had at the hospital were too real. I don't know how I know, but it's something bigger than me. My dad didn't want me to tell you. I was on another planet!"

"Having proof isn't needing to find it." Curry slapped Toms hand. "And what the hell are mermen? A pirate band? Sorry dude, but the whole class trip tidal wave experience warped you. Let me out of the car. I'll skate back."

"He feels bad about losing your camera," Brew said.

"There goes the feelings-n-shit stuff again, stop it."

"Since when were you a chicken, Curry?" Tom asked. "Once you had the fortitude of a great skater able to Ollie over any problem in a single bound. But now. . . I don't know."

"Shut up, little mermaid!" Curry hit Tom's seat. "No one calls me chicken."

"Mermen?" Brew asked. "Like mermaids? The ones who wrecked ships, like when Stacey stands out on the island in the middle of the skate park and calls to you, Curry, and you totally trip up?"

Curry threw trash from the back at Tom and Brew. "That's sirens, knucklehead. Shut up, both of you. I've got a training schedule to maintain."

"Don't hit the driver," Tom said. "What's the rule?"

"Safety third," they said in unison.

"On the other hand, Tom," Brew said with a smile, "what if you are some deranged killer now? Dragging us little lambs to the beach for the slaughter. Is that why you are going to the shrink today?"

"Hardly," Tom said. "You knew them too, they weren't our friends but we owe it to them to find out the truth."

"They were dumb jocks, sheeple, and bims," Curry said. "Since when did you start to care? They never did anything but give us grief."

"Yea, what about Bonnie," Brew said. "I wasn't sure if he was an alien or not."

"Maybe they are just as dumb as ever and nothing has changed for them, but by letting them know what happened we can change them."

"Dude, people only change if they have no other choice. It's not going to work. They will never give a rat's ass about you or what you have done. They will never understand, it's beyond their ability. They don't know how to face their fears. They don't skate. That's one of the things I plan on saying when I give motivational speeches."

"We're going, and you're helping," Tom said. "You owe it to me as my friends. Friends help each other out, and if you don't, Brew, I'm telling your parents how their car got dented. They'll spend your college money at the casino. And, Curry, don't make me drag your skeletons out of the closet about your sister's friend during the sleep over she had."

"Ah, man," Curry said. "I was just kidding. If I didn't give you mireda dude, you would know I wasn't your friend or something like that."

Brew broke into laughter and shook his hand up and down. "Dude, Curry sauce. Wax on. Wax off."

"It was nothing like that," Tom broke in. "Right, selfie boy?"

"It's a subject we don't talk about, remember?" Curry blushed.

"The selfie you sent your sister's friend," Brew said. "Didn't she show your sister?"

"Maybe she likes me," Curry hit Brew in the back of the head. "Now shut up. I'm only going along for the entertainment value. Someone has to watch after you dumb asses in case you fall and can't get up."

"I wear my helmet," Tom said.

"Always wear a helmet." Brew pulled his hoodie tight. "Never expect the unexpected."

"Your brain is on the fritz again." Curry thumped Brew in the back of his head. "You didn't even get the expression right."

Tires chirped, Tom pulled the car into a convenience store parking lot.

"What are we getting?" Curry asked.

"Supplies. Wait here. I can leave you two alone, right?"

Curry flipped Tom off with both hands. "Behold, the happy unicorns!"

## CHAPTER TEN
## HA!

Beach access was blocked; soldiers in combat fatigues stood behind sandbags and cement road dividers, and big green trucks were parked in a semi-circle like a wagon train waiting for an attack.

"The sign says beach closed," Brew said.

"Ha!" Tom laughed. "It wasn't a tsunami. They are blocking the beach, I ain't crazy."

"Doesn't mean anything," Curry said. "They have it blocked off because it's a disaster area, and they are protecting people from getting hurt in a hazardous setting. See the signs, Disaster and Hazard."

"Army trucks," Brew said. "Make it bad."

Tom shook his head. "It's where we are going. Like I said, you are my sidekicks for the day."

Curry ducked down. "Don't be stupid. The fact of the matter is those dudes are blocking the beach. And when the army blocks the beach, it's a good indication we should not go there. Like employees only."

Brew shook an elbow pad in his teeth and growled like a dog. "I think Curry is right."

Curry patted Brew's head. "Hear the wisdom in my words. Seek ye not stupidity, my son."

"If we find what I think we will," Tom said. "You'll see the soldiers only have a little bite. We're going."

Curry leaned into the front and pointed. "Not cool. It says Department of Homeland Security on the trucks. They disappear people for a living. My cousin would tell you all about it, but we haven't seen him in months."

"What cousin is that?" Tom asked. "I thought all of your family was in Mexico."

Brew held up his skate, blocking his face. "Aren't the DHS for terrorists. What are they doing at the beach."

"Camping obviously," Curry said. "Tents, marshmallows, and guards walking the perimeter. They got guns too. I don't think you are thinking this through."

"I'm thinking, don't worry; we got it. We are on a mission, and I need to find out if I am crazy or not. The rangers' faces are stuck in my head, and the mermen; they were hideous."

"Tom," Curry said. "As daring as you think you are there's no way we can get in there, the beach is closed. And if there are monsters like you say there are, why are we going to the beach? Just to prove you are not crazy? I think you have to be crazy to want to find out."

Brew spun the wheels on his skate nervously. "It's gonna take a can opener to get in there."

Tom gripped the steering wheel. "We're gonna get in. No problem. I'll park down a couple of miles, they'll never expect us."

"They already saw us," Curry said. "The dude we drove past waved to us. We've been spotted. They're watching us."

Brew punched Tom in the arm. "If we get caught, I'm blaming you for everything."

"Ow!" Tom punched Brew back. "Tell them I am a cult leader, and I brainwashed you into doing my bidding."

"Yeah, right," Curry said. "Ask them if they would like to join an international student group, instead of shooting us. And tell them you're having a meeting at three, downwind on the beach. I ain't going. No way, no how."

"Alright," Tom said. "I'm telling your sister, who I know will go right to your mom."

"We'll never see you again. Boohoo," Brew laughed.

Tom pulled into a turnout and shut the car off. "Put your pads on in case we have to fight."

"That's dumb, we are going to be on sand. Sand is soft," Brew said.

Curry pulled himself up between the seats. "I didn't sign up for any fighting. You can tell my sister all you want. She probably already knows, and my mom, you puta, won't care."

"Your mom will beat you after all the things you have put her through," Brew said. "I know about the marks."

Tom folded the seat forward. "Bwaack, chicken Curry. Come on and get out. If I'm not mistaken it's ladies third."

"Nobody calls me that. If your face wasn't so messed up already. I'd. . ."

Tom put his helmet on. "What? Tell your sister for me?"

Brew made a whistle from the beach grass, and blew. "Dude, remember how to do this?"

Tom flicked Brews ear. "Time to be serious, farm boy."

"Cut it out!" Brew flinched. "Maybe I should go sell some flowers to the soldiers. Like they do on the streets in San Francisco."

"No more bullshit, Hippie," Tom said. "This is the plan. We are going to go down to the water. Then we are going where I found the tooth and the metallic oval. When we see what's there we will decide what we are going to do."

"Your plan sucks," Curry said. "How about we forget all about your little endeavor, and go to the skate park. We don't even know what we will find."

Tom slid back a step as the sand washed over his feet. "This way."

"Man, there's so much trash," Curry remarked. "Who dumps their baby's diapers on the dunes?"

Brew dragged his feet and kicked sand in the air. "Dude, sand slogging sucks and a homeless dude's staying over there. Don't tell me what he's using a pickle bucket for."

"It's only a couple miles," Tom said. "Quit complaining, Brew."

"I'm not complaining. I'm expressing my innermost feelings. Can't you hear how sad I am inside."

"We're skaters and hardly remember how to do this walking

stuff," Curry said. "Without wheels under our feet we are lost."

Brew batted Curry's ear. "Who's expressing their feelings now."

"Curry, you should use that as your excuse for disability so you can get on welfare," Tom said.

"I don't need no welfare."

"The thing about you is," Tom said. "You count on getting sponsored, but if you don't, you won't know how to do anything. What better way to make an unemployment claim. You are totally expert at welfare."

"You might have something there," Curry said. "Check out how stormy my brain is. If I claim to be my cousins, I can collect several checks and never have to work."

"That's like getting sponsored by the government to skate," Brew said. "I'm in too."

"Yeah we gotta figure out how to play the system like everyone else does. There must be whole generations of skaters who do it."

They crested a dune and stopped. Pelicans glided past in a conga line, and seagulls dove into the water around a group of frolicking seals.

"We're almost there," Tom said. "That's surf, Curry, remember?"

"Shut up. It hasn't been that long since I left the skate park. I'm going to get sponsored, you know. Then who will be laughing."

Brew shook Curry's hand. "Congratulations."

"Why, thank you," Curry replied.

"And there's no damage from a tsunami," Tom swung his arms around. "Everything's normal. The lifeguard tower is still there. They are totally lying."

"So where's our treat?" Brew reached for Tom's back pack. "Gimme gimme."

Tom batted Brew's hand away and pulled power bars and drinks from his pack. "Don't grab, dingle berry, it's not polite."

"Dude, eleven tons of sugar, fortified with caffeine," Brew

chortled and chugged.

"The fact here is, all I see is hella sand, trash, and beach grass," Curry said. "I'm quite disappointed. Where's the destruction? Where's the mayhem the news promised me?"

"All fluff and no show," Brew said.

"Dude, this isn't anything like the aerial footage on the news," Tom said.

Surf frothed across the sand, and gulls flew overhead. "What the. . .," Curry said. "Now I'm just mad."

"Ya, where's the damage?" Brew asked. "No screaming children, no picnicking families washing away, no Tsunamageddon, I'm crushed like a little flower."

Curry threw sand at Brew. "Dude, that's panicking."

Brew smacked his lips. "Food."

"I don't know what we'll find when we get there," Tom said. "But if those DHS dudes are about we gotta sneak."

"And not get caught," Curry added. "My mom's got carnitas in the oven for tonight. I can't miss that."

"We're going to down to the rock outcropping," Tom said. "just past it is where Bonnie and I found the wetsuit. Let's do it."

"Watch those waves. I don't want to get wet."

"Man there's hella more trash here," Brew said. "I bet I could build a raft out of it."

"Dude," Curry said. "That's an Armani jacket; my Dad wears those."

Tom stopped. "It's trash from Japan. We might get lucky and find a motorcycle like the dude up in Oregon."

"That bike was radioactive," Curry said. "And the authorities were like, give it up, Comber Dude. Totally lame."

Tom headed up the beach. "Come on, I need to know more."

## CHAPTER ELEVEN
## U WANT THE TRUTH?

The shore line narrowed, sand gave way to rocks, and rocks turned to cliff; they navigated over and around onto Diamond beach. A gull bombed Curry and he ducked. "The fact of the matter," Curry said, "is the tide is coming in. Your plan is failing."

A wave crashed and water sprayed. "Go up the rocks."

They climbed up and squeezed through a split in the rocks.

"I'm not going to fit," Brew grunted.

"If you weren't so big you would fit easy. Suck in your gut."

Tom heaved. "Pull!"

"Forget it, the rocks are scraping my back." Brew pushed himself out of the crack. "Just go ahead and leave me here, I can hang out and watch for whales."

"We're not on a romantic stroll down the beach holding hands, bro," Curry said. "We're spying on the DHS to satisfy this chuckle head's curiosity."

"Dude," Tom said. "Whales don't come in close enough to the shore to see. Try one more time."

"He's a square peg in a round hole," Curry said. "What if he climbs over the rocks, or goes around?"

"Go around or over?" Tom tried to push Brew through the gap again. "That's why I needed you guys to come. Three heads are better than one."

"A real tri-clops," Curry said. "That's what we is. Like the hydra."

"Three heads and one eye?" Brew asked.

"No, you dummy," Curry said. "Now get moving."

Brew grunted as he backed out of the crevice. Halfway around the rock he stopped.

"Don't stop, you'll fall in. The rocks are slippery," Tom said.

"Whale spout!" Brew said. "I knew we would see one."

"Are you even paying attention to what we are doing?" Curry

asked. "You are out in the open. So much for covert action."

Brew took Tom's hand, and he hopped onto the ledge. "The problem with you, Curry, is you are too focused on the task at hand. Stop living in the moment. Relax."

"That's not how it goes," Curry said. "It's a wonder how you ever get out of bed."

"There's another whale jumping." Tom pointed quickly. "I guess they do come close enough to the beach."

Past the rocks above the tide line, a group of silver tents were pitched surrounding a larger one, and black trucks were parked on the side of a dune.

"Change of plans," Tom said. "If I was making it all up. Why are those goons there?"

"I'll be a soulless heathen for not believing," Curry said. "You weren't going to thrill kill us."

"What's with the bubble tent and those guys in space suits?" Brew asked.

"That's just what I said," Tom said. "This is serious. Keep down. Keep quiet. They can't see us from there. We have to get in there."

"I don't like your plan one bit," Curry said. "We need to get out of here."

"You never plan your hairball tricks," Brew said.

Curry backed through the rocks. "I plan everything. That's why I'm going to get sponsored."

"Wait, get back here," Tom said, as a wave crashed, spraying water over them. "You want the truth or not?

"Not from behind bars."

"Life of crime, chicken," Brew said.

"We can figure this out. Watch them. We need to find out what's in there." Tom fell silent, observing. The guards stood around a truck on the far side of the bubble tent. Judging by their body language, they were joking and watching the whales. *No one is serious when whales are jumping.*

"What a boring job," Brew said. "Cold and windy."

Curry threw sand at Tom to get his attention from behind a rock where he hid. "You in there, Tom? Figure what out?"

"How to get in there," Tom replied. "Brew's in. You?"

"Okay, but I didn't say I was in. How many guards do you count?" Brew asked.

"Three," Tom said. "I don't think they are too concerned with intruders being out here. We can get to the tent without being seen if we go around those rocks and bushes."

"Do you even think of this as being a bad idea?" Curry asked.

Brew shrugged and pointed. "What are those dudes doing?"

Curry crept back up to Tom. "What if there's more dudes right on the other side of the tent we can't see? And what about those guys who are coming out of the tent, the ones in the contamination suits?

The tube they are in has a shower, that tells me it's for decontamination. They're trying to keep whatever is in there, in."

"Get down, there's a guard," Tom pulled their coats. "Stay down until he leaves."

Curry backed away. "Yep. Bail on this."

A wave crashed on the rocks below and water splashed up, soaking them. "Don't be dumb," Tom said. "He didn't see us. We need to get into the tent."

"We're not like camo'd," Curry said. "We'll get caught."

"Dudes, it's a whole pod of whales," Brew said. "With all the birds diving for fish, no one is watching for us or anyone."

"He's not coming back. I'm going for it." Tom made a break for it, Brew and Curry followed. Down the rocks and over the sand, they ran.

"What if they shoot us?" Curry asked.

"Dude, we're kids," Tom said. "They wouldn't. Move."

"I can't believe we're doing this," Brew chuckled.

They dove down next to the tent.

"What now?" Curry asked.

Tom pushed on the tent. "It puffed back out."

"The entrance is around front," Curry whispered. "We'll get caught if we try to go way."

"They're all watching the whales. We can make it."

Brew pulled a knife from his fanny pack, flicking the blade open. "We can cut our way in."

Tom nodded. "Do it."

He made a small hole in the side of the tent, air blew out. "It's empty. Just a bunch of science equipment and a smaller tent inside with big tubes going to it. Kinda cool in there. Like a spaceship."

Tom peered in. "Let's do it."

"Wait," Curry said. "Air's coming out. That means it's pressurized in there. They pressurized to keep stuff out."

Brew sliced the tent open, making the hole big enough for them to crawl through. "Well, not us."

"Okay you can wait out here, Curry," Tom said.

Inside, machines beeped and screens glowed and flickered. The smaller tent was made of clear plastic and was supported by metal rods. It housed microscopes and petri dishes in a clear door mini fridge.

"Brew, keep a lookout." Tom went to a laptop perched on top of a stand and tapped the space bar. "This is for the Computational Microbial Genomics Group."

"Yeah, so?" Curry asked.

"No, listen. Changes in marine plankton communities driven by the introduction of Xylocrinebeta dinoflagellates expressed unpredicted results. We review the regulatory mechanisms and discuss their biological significance hence forth. The plankton showed a statistically significant response to four environmental stages.

1. Increase of $CO_2$ rate absorption. Acidification reversal proved remarkable in stage one.

2. The antinuclear antibodies byproduct proteins have demonstrated mobilization in response to the expected genotoxic

stress response to DNA-damaging agents. Whereby affectation is no longer normal.

3. Differential displacement factor fluorescence correlation spectroscopy techniques applied to quantify the kinetics of DNA double strand break repair proteins can be defined as. . .”

"That's some mumbo jumbo," Brew said. "Blah blah blah. This stuff's cool."

"Do your duty," Curry said.

"What the hell?” Tom asked. “It says test subjects are to be fed to the specimens?"

"This is a bad place to be." Curry read over Tom's shoulder. "Just like I said. You need to listen to me, as I am always right."

"I don't get what's so dangerous," Brew said.

"You need to heed, my clumsy friend."

"There's my stuff in there on the table," Tom said. "I can't believe they left it out."

"I don't think they were expecting you to come for it," Curry said.

Brew adjusted a microscope. "Stuff's alive."

"Don't touch anything," Curry said. "I can see you sprouting tentacles already."

"Whatever," Brew picked up a beaker filled with black liquid and swirled it around and smiled. "Dude, drink me."

"Don't be reckless," Curry said. "The facts are a such; you're not smart enough to touch anything in here."

"It's not like I would drink it or anything," Brew put it down. "There's tons of cool sciencey stuff here."

Tom went into the smaller tent.

"Tom, wait," Curry said. "This is like a science tent where viruses are kept. See the ventilators and air filters and those tubes with the stuff in them? We should get out of here. In and out fast."

"It's unreal in here," Brew twisted around. "So many blinky lights."

In the smaller tent Tom picked up the fang and the metallic

oval. "It doesn't get any realer than this."

"Don't get hypnotized, my bullish friend," Curry said.

Brew poked Curry in the ribs with an instrument he got from the table. "Shiny."

Curry flung his hands up in defense. "Dude, don't infect me with something."

Tom knocked on the clear plastic of the inner tent wall. "I got Bonnie's phone. It's the proof I need."

"What about my camera?" Curry asked.

"Dude, give it up," Brew said.

"We only have seconds before they come back," Curry said. "We should go now, we got your proof."

"They're watching the whales. They won't be back anytime soon." Tom pressed play. "People like to live in the moment when whales jump."

"There's you, acting stupid," Brew said. "And what's mutant Bonnie doing?"

"Dude, that's you totally about to get your ass kicked, just like I said."

"You should have been there to back me up."

"Yeah, right."

A large figure appeared on the screen. Bonnie yelped and ran away in the video. Brew jumped "What the hell was that?"

"I told you it wasn't a tsunami."

"Man, it was like a bug eyed seal," Curry said. "That's the fakest video I've ever seen. My animation skills far out match these clowns efforts."

Voices came from outside.

"Whales are boring to watch. Trouble is here," Curry stepped back.

"They're coming. Bail!" Brew warned.

Tom made for the hole with Curry right behind him. "Burgers, let's get out of here."

Brew hesitated as Tom and Curry pushed through the hole. A

guard was right outside the tent.

"Halt," he ordered.

Brew approached the hole as the guard called for back up. It was only a matter of time before he would be caught. He would have to make a break for it and crouched down to sprint out of the hole. *Ready,* he said to himself. He took a deep breath and was grabbed from behind.

"Hold it right there," an authoritative voice barked.

He screamed, grabbed the hand and twisted. A man in a bubble suit went down on his knees. Brew kicked him and made for the hole.

"Wait, you could be infected!" the man said.

Bending down to fit through just on the other side, the guard kicked him; he tumbled to the ground. The guard had his weapon drawn, so Brew threw sand in his face. Blinded, the guard fired, missing. Sand sprayed up next to his head. Brew's ears rang as he tackled the guard and kneed him in the nuts. He ran faster than he ever had in his life towards the rocks.

Other guards had been alerted to the trouble and chased after him. "Halt."

Brew hit the cliff wall and fumbled to find a hand hold. The guards were almost on him. He screamed, "Tom!"

Tom appeared over the ledge, reached down and thrust his hand to Brew. "Take it."

"I thought you left me."

Tom grunted as he pulled. "You need Weight Watchers."

## CHAPTER TWELVE
## U CAN'T HANDLE THE TRUTH

Through the surf and over the dunes to Tom's car, they ran. Their feet pounded silently on the sand.

"Wait," Curry stopped. "I got to catch my breath."

Tom pushed harder through the sand. "Keep going, we're almost there."

"Oh no," Brew said. "A news truck. We're busted."

"Don't be stupid, we're already busted," Curry said.

"Quiet," Tom slid to a stop and knelt behind the tall beach grass. "Those blood suckers, I can't believe they followed us. We can't let them catch us. Where are they?"

Brew couldn't stay still. "We gotta keep running, the soldiers are after us."

Curry prairie dogged to spot the reporter from a large sprout of beach grass. "This sucks, why'd the reporter have to botch our plans up."

"Trapped," Brew said. "Soldiers behind me, reporters in front of me, what am I to do?"

"You're not skating out of this one."

"That's for sure."

"Aren't you glad we parked further down the road," Tom said. "We can just head down the beach, he won't see us behind the dunes. The soldiers aren't on our tails."

"Dude, you can show that blood sucker the video," Curry said. "He'll broadcast it on TV. That's what you want, right?"

"This blood sucker thinks it's a good idea," A voice from behind said. The reporter held out his press ID.

Tom, Curry, and Brew jumped. Curry held up his fists. "Shit, dude, where'd you come from?"

"Hold up there, guys. I'm not here to get you into trouble. Take it easy."

Tom held his arms out, holding Curry and Brew behind him.

"Do you sneak up on people often? Have you been staring in my bedroom window at night?"

"I followed you from your house. You're the boy who survived, everyone wants the story. The networks have offered big bucks for an interview, but your Dad refuses to let let you talk."

"What?" Tom asked.

"That's messed up; you could be rich," Curry said. "Then we'd be skating in the finest money can buy."

"How'd you see us?" Tom asked.

"I parked over there. You stuck out like a sore thumb when you passed by across the dunes. My camera's telephoto lens is better than most binoculars. I have pictures. If you were trying to sneak, you were doing a bad job. Besides, a good reporter always gets the story. You want to tell me what happened on the beach?"

"A whole lot," Brew said. "There were squiggly things under a microscope and an email."

"Brew!" Tom snapped. "He doesn't want to know about the tent."

"Confession time," Curry said. "It's what you want, trust me."

"Do the right thing if you care about getting the truth out," the reporter said.

"Play the video." Tom gave him the cell, tooth, and metallic oval. "and I found on these beach."

"Amazing," the reporter said. "A black frog, it must be huge. Eight feet tall by my estimate."

"One angry seal if you ask me," Curry said.

"It was a monster, a merman just like on the Internet," Tom said.

"Internet, huh?" The reporter took the phone. "We better get in my van if the soldiers are after you. You'll be safe there. I'll take pictures of the tooth and disk, and maybe we can get a cell signal to upload your video."

"What if you get busted for having pictures? Trouble with the law is no fun," Curry said. "And the DHS disappears people, like my cousin."

"Yea, we broke into their tent," Brew said. "They were whale watching."

"Don't worry, I won't let them know who has their missing items, if I'm ever asked. I never reveal my sources. You'll have to tell me about your cousin sometime. Take my card, text me or email, it's the best way to get a hold of me."

"What if they arrest you for having pictures?" Tom asked.

"They don't arrest reporters for gathering news. It's called freedom of the press. We're covered under the first amendment."

Tom held the phone up above his head and waved it from side to side. "No reception here. This sucks."

"You should upload the video to an anonymous account as soon as you get reception. Hopefully it'll go viral. It will be the quickest way to get the story out there."

"If we're covered under the first amendment, why an anonymous account?" Tom asked.

"It's incriminating evidence, you stole it right? Ask your friend here. I've seen him at the courthouse. He can to tell you all about our judicial system."

"I'm not talking about that," Curry said. "My lawyer doesn't want me to reveal my secret identity."

"You're living your label," Brew said. "We all know what you are."

The van door slid open. Inside it was littered with fast food wrappers and a sleeping bag was bunched up in the corner. The reporter spread out a black cloth. "Put the tooth and the rock here. Pictures will only take a moment."

"Can't you use this stuff to upload the pictures?" Tom asked.

"Not from a work unit. I'd get fired." His camera snapped. "Is there anything else you can tell me about what happened that day? Did anything you saw stand out? Anything unusual?"

"Trucks coming." Brew ducked around the van. "This is balls."

"Holy moose," Curry said. "We're hamstered. They're after us!"

"You boys better get out of here. Take your stuff, and I'll deal with them," the reporter said. "As soon as you get out of sight, run like hell. These guys are likely to be agitated."

"Thanks," Tom said.

"Go fast. Go now," the reporter said.

Tom, Curry, and Brew hid at the edge of earshot in the tall beach grass. Three trucks pulled up and screeched to a stop. DHS agents swarmed out. They pointed their guns at the reporter.

The lead agent approached. He wore button down body armor and was covered in go get 'em bling. "Freeze," he ordered, "and follow my instructions very carefully. Put your hands up. Now reach down with your left arm, pull your shirt up and turn around slowly."

"What are you doing?" the reporter asked. "This is a public road. I'm not doing anything."

Tom's neck cracked. Something was familiar about the DHS agent.

"No questions!" the lead agent ordered. "Do as I say. Turn around holding your shirt up."

"I don't have any weapons. I haven't done anything wrong."

The DHS agent waved his arm, signaling to the others, who swarmed around the reporter's truck and began to search it. "It is a state maintained road. Owned by the state. You are in the middle of a crime scene investigation."

"I don't know what you are talking about."

"Where have you been for the past half hour?"

Brew pulled Tom. "Get down."

"What investigation?" the reporter said. "How can I be interfering, when I just arrived."

"We'll see if it's true by what's in your van."

"I'm a reporter and a private citizen," the reporter said. "You don't have a warrant."

Tom flipped over on his back and pushed himself into the sand; he was white as sheet. "I know him. He's the shrink from the hospital. He's the guy who asked me all those questions."

"What?" Curry asked. "Shut up. If we get caught, I can't get busted."

"You have no reasonable expectation of privacy in public places," the agent said. "When on a state owned road, you are subject to search for any potential threat."

"A threat? You have no probable cause. Am I being detained?"

"Your vehicle is parked in a turn out and poses a public safety hazard. Are you willfully creating a hazard?"

Tom reached into the pouch of his hoodie and held the tooth and oval tight.

"I'm a reporter. I was taking pictures of the endangered burrowing owl that lives in these dunes. Can I get a quote from you? What it is you are investigating?"

"Recording a government official who is conducting an official investigation is considered spying. Are you spying on the government?"

"This is insane. I know my rights."

"Sir," an agent interrupted. "Pictures."

"Is it here?" the lead agent asked.

"No sir."

"Hey, you can't do that. That's my camera," the reporter said. "You don't have a warrant, and I have my fourth amendment rights."

"The only rights you have are the ones I give you. You were in contact with stolen government property. Where is it now?"

The gravel of the turnout crunched under his feet. "You can't detain me for nothing. I don't have to tell you anything," his voice shook.

"Fleeing a crime scene?" The lead agent hooked his thumbs into his belt.

The agents at the van turned and held their guns on the reporter.

The reporter froze. "Why are you doing this?"

"Questioning authority is dissent, and dissent leads to radical doctrine," the agent cuffed him. "Did you know disruption of a government official conducting official matters of the state is classified as an act of terror under the patriot act? I can have you detained and held indefinitely without judicial review. Get down on your knees."

The reporter dropped to one knee. "Some one's gotta to stop you."

The lead agent stepped around to face the reporter. "Are you threatening me?"

"No, I was just saying-"

"Saying what? Someone should stop me? Take me out? Stop me from serving my country?"

"Well yes. . . Eh, no not exactly."

"Tell me?" the agent asked. "Which would you prefer? An incompetent force that protects the guilty and fails the innocent or an efficient force that protects the innocent and hounds the guilty?"

The reporter's voice cracked, "Efficient. Please, I'm cuffed, put the gun down."

"You know putting an agent of the DHS in imminent danger makes you an enemy combatant. My number one priority is to protect this great nation of ours."

"I'm cuffed. . ."

The agent's gun popped. The reporter fell to the ground limply.

Brew screamed.

Tom jumped on him.

Curry held his hand over Brew's mouth.

Brew struggled to get away.

"Don't run, they'll kill us," Tom hissed.

The agent shook his head. "Call it in, we have a terror threat here. Have the area sealed off a mile in each direction, a drone in the air, and someone to clean up the mess."

"Yes, sir."

*Why?* Tom screamed to himself. *Was what he had found worth killing for?* His heart pounded in his head. *Why was he at the hospital pretending to be a doctor?*

"What are we going to do?" Curry asked. "They'll kill us and make it look like gang violence or something stupid like that."

"We gotta turn ourselves in," Brew cowered. "They don't kill kids. They'll understand."

"No way, man. You don't know like I do. You're not Mexican," Curry said.

"We can't get caught," Tom said. "They are willing to kill for the video. Who knows what they will do to us. It's too important. We have to get the truth out."

Brew struggled to stand up. "I'm gonna give up right now."

Tom and Curry held him down.

"Truth?" Curry asked Tom. "The truth is they'll shoot us? Is the truth so important we should die over it? This is your trip. Not mine. I'm not risking it over some stupid video."

"We need a new plan," Tom said.

"I have a plan," Curry said. "It's very simple to follow. Get the hell out of here before they kill us."

"We gotta get to your car," Brew choked. "We can drive away. Pretend we were never here."

"Crawl." Tom moved.

Three hundred feet away, they ran for their lives.

Eric Johnson

## CHAPTER THIRTEEN
## I TOUCHED EVERYTHING

The thousand yard dash tore at their lungs and burned their muscles. The flesh on Tom's face bounced with each stride, pulling at his stitches. The "what ifs" crept into his mind. Topping a dune, he half screamed and half laughed; in the distance his car was still there. At one hundred feet, he pressed the unlock button. At fifty, the radio lifeline of the key connected and the locks beeped and cha-chunked, to his relief. "Get in! Get in!"

Doors whipped open. Brew jammed in back. Curry white knuckled the oh shit bar. Tom buckled his belt. A ticket pressed under the wiper fluttered in the wind as Tom turned the key. Solar power to battery. Wind up car to speed. Zero to sixty in eight, his wheels kicked up sand silently.

Tom nearly lost control of the car when a tractor hauling strawberries pulled out from behind an organic produce stand.

Past the strawberries and around the artichoke fields, straight on through the endless blueberry field rows they flew.

Brew's nose bled. "This isn't a joke. What are we going to do?"

Curry pounded the dash. "Oh man. We're so. . . I can't believe it. We need a good plan, a really good plan. Cause if we don't, that dude is going to put us away."

Tom came to a stop at a light. "Calm down. We can't panic."

"Don't stop," Brew said at the same time Curry spoke.

"I can't calm down. He killed the reporter," Curry said. "I'm not going down for you. I can't. They'll put me away forever."

Tom grabbed Curry by the collar and pulled him across the seat. "If you get caught, just tell them I dropped you off at the skate park on the way to school. Tell them I didn't say where I was going and no one saw you. You were just skipping. That's your story."

"You can't just dump us at the skate park and take off," Curry said. "It's a guaranteed fail. We need to come up with a cohesive

87

plan. Not some third grade 'um and uh' story."

"Take us to the skate park," Brew's chest heaved. "We'll pretend nothing happened, that we were never here, I got it. If only my parents were more involved, I'd never have been led astray by you guys."

"So it's out fault. Right," Curry said. "Dude, I got dirt on you going back to the second grade."

Tom hit the dashboard. "Shut up! We stole from the DHS. We're together now, like it or not."

"That dude's some serious shit," Curry said. "We'll be boiled in acid or chopped up and tossed into the sea like chum if we get caught."

In the rear view mirror, anxiety gripped Brew's face. "Calm down," Tom said. "I'm going home, just like my dad expects. Then we'll meet at the bridge where we skated the irrigation ditch. No one knows about our place except us. You guys have to do what I say. Sidekicks, got it?"

"Chopped up like chum?" Brew wailed from back. "My blood staining the water, sharks circling, bits of me bobbing; what if the plan fails and they don't believe us? My parents are out of town, and they'll never know what happened to me. I'm going to puke."

The light turned; Tom floored it across the street and pulled over.

"They're not going to figure it out," Tom said, as Brew pushed past Curry out of the car and heaved. "We were like shadows on the wall. He's totally freaking out, and, Curry, you need to knock it off."

Brew got back into the car and intentionally breathed on Curry. "See what you made me do."

"It's still your fault I have to keep you in line. Otherwise, we would have been caught by now."

"Curry, not now!"

"My prints are all over everything in there," Brew pushed his hands in Tom's face. "I touched everything. The microscope, the thing that went beep, the slide with those little things attacking each other. It was so cool."

"Man, I told you not to touch anything," Curry said. "If you weren't such a dumb ass, we'd be squeaky clean."

"Curry! Knock it off," Tom barked.

"I couldn't help it," Brew went on. "The stuff was like in science class. When we did the pond water thing."

"The class you never go to?" Tom asked. "If you guys hadn't skipped, and had actually backed me up on the field trip like I asked, we wouldn't be in this mess. So stop worrying."

"We'd be dead, that's where we would be," Brew said. "We were destined to die on the beach, and this is some cruel extension of our lives being played out for the amusement of a cruel god for skipping school."

"I would beg you not to worry," Curry said. "But there isn't enough time in the world for me to chastise you for leaving evidence. So let me ask you. What inspired your misplaced educational needs for that shiny moment? The one that will ultimately get us put in jail or worse?"

Tears rolled down Brew's face. "I wish I went to school more."

"Dude, going to school has nothing to do with getting into trouble, because there is no book capable of helping you. It's what you choose to do. And you chose not to listen to me."

"We gotta run and hide," Brew's face trembled. "Going to the skate park is stupid. We gotta go to the mountains. Live like whoever lives there."

"Enough!" Tom pointed out his window. "The mountains are only thirty minutes away. That's not far enough. We got to stick to our plan. They have no idea who we are. The reporter said he wouldn't tell."

Curry checked the road behind. "Dead men, bro. Dead men."

Brew grabbed his chest he started to hyperventilate. "Dead men? I think I'm having a heart attack. What if I never get to go to La Brea? I feel like I'm starring into a mirror with my life reflecting back at me. I don't want to die. We gotta call the police and tell them."

"And tell them we committed a crime?" Tom asked.

"We can't tell anyone," Curry said. "Secrets are only secrets if no one talks."

Brew squeezed his face in his hands. "The dude said it was terrorists. They'll bring in the army. Like they did for the Summer Olympics in Alaska. We're screwed."

Curry held his hands to his face like he was playing peek-a-boo. "We're not terrorists. Am I scary to you? Do you see a ski mask?"

"Kids can be terrorists, too," Brew said.

"Get it off your mind, Brew." Tom sped up. "Talk it through. We will make it."

"Okay, let's think it through," Curry said. "If that's what helps you. The crazy dude wants to kill us. Prompting us to run away. What would I do, if I were a crazy dude who wanted to kill me?"

"How can you be so calm," Brew asked.

"I'm not. I'm freaking out. My naturally calm demeanor is deceiving."

Tom stopped a block from the skate park, Brew and Curry got out. "Remember, stick to the plan. Don't forget."

## CHAPTER FOURTEEN
## WHAT'S IN MONTANA?

Tom drove away, turned the corner out of sight, leaving Brew and Curry. Down the street a construction crew was working on the new pool at the skate park. A few skaters were there.

"I don't like this one bit," Curry said. "Leaving us here alone is cold. I'm in charge now. It's up to me to make the decisions."

"What are we going to do? Tom said we needed to go to our hang out."

"Come on, we can't stand here out in the open. I know what he said, but he ain't here, and we are on our own. I have examined the facts, added them up, and they equal to we are fuckeroo'd, boys and girls."

"I don't know how we are going to get away. They're gonna kill us just like the reporter. What if we turned ourselves into the police and told them?"

"Man, law enforcement sticks together. They would lock us up. Call those DHS goons. Then they'd show up, and say 'thank you, boys, we'll take it from here.' With handcuffs and black bags over our heads, they would take us down to LA, throw us in a parking lot and shoot us in the head. End of story for Brew and Curry. Understand?"

Brew stared blankly down the street, his face drained of all color. "Okay, I'm calm now. They're going to kill us. I can deal with that. Expecting the expected is better than the unexpected."

"Yeah they are going to kill us, but not if they can't find us. This is a life or death scenario. The inevitability of it means we need to change how we are thinking about the whole thing. Be adaptable, like flowing water. The first thing to remember is don't panic."

"What am I supposed to do?"

"You shouldn't panic. Like I said, it's what they want you to do. That's when you make mistakes, like turning yourself in or trying to hide in plain sight."

"What if we get some camping gear from my house?" Brew asked. "We could pretend to be like homeless kids and do just what Tom said."

"What would that get us? No bathroom. No TV. No place to skate. We need luxury items like a toilet and a fridge."

"An RV! Get one and go to Canada or Montana."

"Montana? What's in Montana? And Canada has extradition laws. The fact is, it's lunch time, we're skipping school, and we don't have any money. How far do you think we will get? Maybe I can sell you at truck stops along the way for money."

"You didn't just say that. If anyone gets sold, it will be you. You're the supple one."

"Supple? I'm rugged, and I ain't no lot lizard."

Brew pulled out his phone and texted. "Then what do we do?"

Curry grabbed the phone and pulled the battery out. "You can't use that, dude. I bet your parents have parent tracking activated, so the police can track you if you are kidnapped. You know, under the stored communication act, the police don't even need a warrant."

"They don't even know who we are. They didn't see us."

"Didn't you pay any attention to the reporter. He said he spotted us with his camera. He took pictures of us on the beach. We have been ID'd."

Brew's mouth watered like he was going to hurl again. "We really need to go to Montana."

"I have other plans. Plans to make us safe. We gotta organize, and our soldiers are over there at the park."

"Organize? Soldiers? They kill everyone who stands for anything. MLK, Gandhi, Malcolm X, Harvey Milk, Tupac, and John Lennon, even George Carlin. They said it was a heart attack, but I know he spoke the truth."

"Where do you get all this nonsense? We're going to do it different. Hold on while I think."

"But if they get Tom, they'll water-board him and he'll give us away," Brew said. "No one can resist water boarding. Remember the leaked videos from Guantanamo? They even use electrodes to shock them."

"Oligarchy backed Democracy is a common carrier of ill ideas." Curry got on his skate. "The way I see it, that's a risk we have to take. We're going to go to my house, but first we need to skate."

"Skate?" Brew asked. "We can't tell anyone. They'll tell everyone and give us away."

"But if we don't go over there they'll know somethings up. We can tell them, and they'll mobilize to our aide. We'll fight fire with skate board. Every blow, every move will be calculated and merciless. The government will witness the savagery of an angered people who ride above on the wheels of freedom, and skate them down like fire from the heavens. And if we turn back now, the world will never know the power I offer them. It's a conundrum. I'm faced by certain death. Bound to the park to skate forever. Destined to lead the masses to freedom."

"After what happened, how can you think about skating?"

"In life, things happen that are beyond our control. If they don't immediately affect us, we can choose whether or not to care. That's some zen wisdom I intend on using in a speech I wrote."

"The reporter's brains were splattered all over the road. We talked to him. We have his card. How is it not immediate?"

"Calm down, you are freaking out. We will fight our way through, eye of the tiger style."

"And you are delusional."

"At the risk of sounding cold, I must say the bad guy is really only after Tom. He took the stuff, not us. All we have to do is step out of the way for a while."

"You're hella stupid. You don't even know what you just said." Brew hopped on his board and skated away.

"I'm speaking for real, not from some doorstep pamphlet.

Think about it! Dude? Wait!"

Eric Johnson

## CHAPTER FIFTEEN
## SPIT FLEW

Reporters pooled together as he rolled up to the driveway in the car. The crack of the gun and the image of the reporter falling to the ground hung in his mind. A broken cantaloupe soaked in red paint, spraying across the gravel, he shuddered and his throat tightened. *Could they know what killed their friend was following him? What will they do when he doesn't show up? What will they do when they find out he is dead?*

Holding back the over flowing juices in his stomach, he turned the car into the driveway.

"Tom!" the reporters cried out, and rushed to him. Their faces all looked the same, like the reporter on the side of the road. His eyes fluttered, and his mouth watered uncontrollably. He fumbled with the door handle and leaned out, spewing power bar froth onto the pavement.

A drool thread hung from his mouth as he got out of the car and went to his front door.

A reporter approached. "Tom, are you alright?"

He kicked off his shoes as the door clicked shut. The hall was dark; his dad kept the lights off during the day. Clanking came from the kitchen, and he froze like an escaping prisoner in a spot light. "Dad, I'm home."

The dishwasher's signature clunk and grind started, and his dad's voice came from the kitchen. "You're home early."

"I didn't feel well." He couldn't stop shaking, and put his hands in his pockets to steady himself. "School was too much."

His dad stepped around the corner from the kitchen. "Lets get ready. We'll go have lunch somewhere before your appointment." His dad stepped close and felt his forehead. "You look awful. School was too much, I'm sorry."

Tom started for his room. "Yeah, Dad. I need to lay down."

"Want me to postpone your appointment?"

"Yeah, good idea," Tom said, relieved his dad brought it up. "I think I really need to lay down."

"Can I get you anything? Something to drink?"

"I'm fine. I just need to rest. School was too hard for me. So many people wanted to talk to me, it was overwhelming."

"Sorry, Tom. My advice isn't always bad; sometimes it's right on, sometimes not."

Tom dropped his bag on the bedroom floor. His eyes darted around the room. He had to hide the tooth, Bonnie's phone, and the oval. If they came and searched his house they would rip apart the walls and pull up the rug. He held the metallic oval tight and searched his room for a spot to hit it. The A/C vent, closet, under the carpet, nothing was good enough.

"What are you?" he asked the metallic oval. "Why are you so important?"

The oval was cold and smooth in his hand. He turned it over, and a needle popped up from the depression, rotating in a slow circle as it extended out four inches. Tiny barbs protruded from the shaft as it waved like grass in the wind, then suddenly it plunged into his finger.

He muffled his scream and tried to pull the hook out. The needle started to spin. The oval began to pulse, it turned blood red. He flailed his hand to get it off, but it stayed tight and the needle twisted in deeper.

"Tom?" came a knock at his door. "I brought you something to drink."

He gritted his teeth. "Yeah, Dad?"

"We need to talk right now!"

"Not now!"

"What about your drink?"

"Don't come in."

The door knob twisted; he jumped onto his bed and quickly hid his hands under the covers behind him.

The door flung open. "Tom, there's sand in your shoes." He

took a deep breath. "I know you didn't go to school. Tell me why you went to the beach."

Sweat ran down his face. He could barely stay still. "It's not a good time to talk, Dad. I can't tell you."

The oval burrowed deeper, he squirmed.

"Let me guess. You were curious, and those two friends of yours wanted to see the beach. They pressured you into showing them. How you are going to treat me? By lying to me?"

Tom's face twisted from the pain. If he spoke, he would scream. The needle was wrapping around his bone, sweat ran down his face.

His dad stared at him waiting for a reply. Then spoke. "You can say no. Do you understand it was a bad idea for you to do anything like this? You need to talk to me first. I'm calling their parents to let them know you are forbidden from seeing them until I decide otherwise."

The pain stopped. Tom let out a deep sigh of relief.

"Good, I'm glad you agree with me." His dad shut the door.

Tom opened his hand, it was bruised and bloody. The metallic oval was now solid red. He held it out, examining it. It vibrated slightly and he gasped, expecting it to stab him again. But it glowed brightly for a second, then changed color back to the dull gray it was when he had found it.

It had taken his blood. What was going to happen? He held his breath and inspected his body, feeling with his mind, listening to his heart. If something was going to happen, it wasn't now.

Out in the hall, his dad was nearly yelling, as he left a message at Brew's house when the land line in the kitchen rang.

"Mrs. Martinez, I was just about to call you."

Tom's body tensed. Curry's mom was one intense lady. The phone smashed down on the receiver, the bell rang. "Bye!"

The floorboards practically snapped as his dad stomped down the hall and pounded on his door. He wished he hadn't left his shoes by the door. There were a million things he could say, but nothing was going to stop his dad.

"Tom!" The door smashed open and books from the shelf fell to the floor. "Curry's mom just called. Guess what she said? She said, the police were at her house. She said he was in school. She said they are coming here to talk to you about him. You want to tell me what's going on before they get here?"

Tom gulped. "Dad?"

His dad's finger came across his room at him then drew back into a fist. "Don't deny anything to me. We are past that point."

"Okay," Tom gave in. "We went to the beach. There were DHS agents blocking the entrance."

Spit flew. "DHS? Have you broken the law? What did you do? What kind of trouble have those boys gotten you into?"

Tom held the tooth and the oval out. "Dad, listen to me, they didn't get me into trouble! I got them into trouble. I got the tooth back and the metallic oval. It's real, see the design?"

His dad's eyes widened and his hands balled up at his sides. "You stole from the DHS? Oh Jesus, Tom, the tooth could be from a fish."

"No, Dad, it's not. Here."

"For a hunk of metal and a fish tooth, you stole from the DHS?"

"They killed a reporter, Dad."

His dad's arms flew up and slammed down at his sides. His legs shook. He didn't know what to do. "Killed a reporter?"

Tom's voice cracked. "They shot him."

"Did you witness a murder?" His eyes nearly popped out of his head and his voice cracked. "Is that why they want to talk to you, for questioning?"

"It was the DHS! They shot him. The reporter was protecting us, and they shot him!" Tom put the metallic oval in his dad's hand. "Feel. It's warm."

"You've been holding it, of course it's warm." He sat on Tom's bed.

Eric Johnson

"I have Bonnie's phone. He made a video."

"Of the reporter getting killed? We'll have to turn it into the police immediately. It's very important we do."

"Dad, you're not even listening to me."

"I'll call our lawyer." His voice was distant. "He'll advise us of the steps we need to take. . . What have you gotten yourself into?"

"Watch! The video is of the mermen. I told you they were real, and you didn't believe me, so I went to get proof. You always say I need to have proof for my arguments. Evidence or irrefutable logic. I got it. I did just what you taught me to do."

"So it's my fault you are in trouble?"

"No, but yes, yes it is. I followed through and made my case, because it's what you taught me to do. That's what adults do. Sound familiar?"

"Tom, slow down. I suppose I did say that, but it's not the point."

"Just watch, please."

His dad stood cold and still as he watched the video. "You're joking, right? But you couldn't be because you are wanted by the police."

"Dad, that was the monster."

"It could have been a seal. Did you make it in video art class? It doesn't make any sense to me."

"Seals aren't seven feet tall, Dad."

Outside the sound of screeching tires and shouting came. Police in combat uniforms piled out of trucks and pushed the reporters back, clubbing them with night sticks. Men in black uniforms ran thick yellow tape across the street, blocking it off from traffic.

Tom pulled the blinds shut. "They're closing off the area."

"This isn't right," his dad said, and opened the blinds. "It seems a bit extreme."

"I told you they have gone crazy." Tom pulled them shut again.

His dad took out his phone and dialed. Sweat ran down his

face. "You broke into a DHS tent and stole from a government facility. That's a federal crime. Do you understand why I'm calling our lawyer?"

"I do, but the stuff was mine to begin with. Now do you believe me?"

"With what's going on outside? I think something happened." He pulled his phone away from his head. "There's no signal."

Tom pushed his phone in his Dad's face. "Those are the monsters that killed my class."

"And these DHS agents are out to cover up the truth," his dad said. "It's a typical government thing to do, is that it? And you expect me to believe?"

"Yes. You believe me then?"

"What I see is the police are finally responding to my complaints about the reporters occupying our lawn. Maybe the neighbors complained enough too. Almost serves them right for not listening to me telling them to get out of here in the first place."

"They're not police."

The doorbell rang.

Tom held onto his arm, their eyes stayed together for a second. "They'll arrest me, and disappear me forever."

He straightened his shirt and smoothed his hair. "Not if I can help it. Hang tight here. I'll send them away. Then we'll call our lawyer, don't worry."

Tom remembered, the reporter had said to do, upload the video on an anonymous account. Was there time? He sent it to all from the phone. There was no signal. Where was the power cord? Did he have the right adapter? He swept the junk off his desk, poured the contents of his desk drawer onto the floor and dropped to his knees to dig through a spaghetti of cords. In one motion he plugged it in and hit upload. The Internet was still up; no one gets to tech support, not even the DHS.

His dad was speaking louder than usual, almost shouting. He

was warning him. "No he's not here, officer. I haven't seen him since this morning when he went to school. What are you inquiring about?"

Tom peered out from his blinds; soldiers were moving the neighbors back into their houses. They were ordering them to shelter in place though a megaphone. He could read fear and suspicion across their faces. They were witnessing what the Jews in Germany must have been through. The Stasi, raiding an undesirables house.

"You can't come in here," his dad said audibly. "This is private property."

The officer's voice was muffled, but it didn't matter what was said, they were after him, and his dad was covering for him. He had to hurry.

"Do you have a warrant?" his dad asked.

The officer became louder. Now he could hear him clearly. His throat tightened and his guts spasmed. He fought for control. He could never forget the voice. His ears pulled back fixed in place towards the danger.

"You know I'm a family man." The smile in Ortega's words cur through the wall. "I have kids too. And there isn't a thing in the world I wouldn't do to protect them."

"What?" his dad stammered, taken back by the shift in conversation.

"Under the 2013 ruling of Salinas v. Texas, silence is an admission of guilt. I know you are not telling the truth. Are you guilty of harboring a known fugitive?"

"Fugitive?" his dad was confused. "No. I understand you want to talk to my son, but what's this about? Why is he a fugitive? He is a minor, you understand. Don't you need some kind of warrant?"

The upload was 64%.

"Questioning authority is direct interference with justice, and impedes due process. Are you interfering with the serving of justice?"

"No I. . ."

"I, what? Are you a disruptor? Disruption of an investigation constitutes a willful act of aggression. Aggression towards an officer of the US government is an act of hostility. Are you declaring a hostile act? War? Detain him!"

There was a crash, and his dad cried out. "Get off me," he struggled. "You can't come in without a warrant!"

He shook the phone the video was almost done uploading. How much time did he have? 92%. Connections are never fast enough when you need them to be. If he stayed, they were going to disappear him. And to protect his dad, he had to leave.

Boots stormed into the house. He had to get the truth out there to save himself, and now, to save his dad.

99%.

Plates and glasses crashed in the kitchen.

Book shelves thudded to the floor.

He tucked the phone behind the computer. Good enough. It would finish uploading if he was lucky. He grabbed the tooth and the oval, then dove across the hall into his dad's room. Lifting the window as quickly and quietly as he could, he took off running. *I'll save you, Dad.*

## CHAPTER SIXTEEN
## DUDE, THAT'S FANTASY

At the top of Curry's block, Curry grabbed Brew and pulled him to a stop. Red and blue lights flashed in front of his house. "Man, there's like a dozen soldiers," Curry said. "The one in my driveway's got binoculars, and past those SUVs the fools are going door to door. Ah man, my mom's home too. She should be at the hospital working. They're gonna harass her, and she's gonna turn her wrath on me. Now we're really screwed."

The blood drained from Brew's face. "You said they are after Tom, not us. My parents are out of town. We'd have free reign of the place for a few days, but you insisted we come here."

"No way," Curry sneered. "The DHS dude has made us directly involved, everything has changed. Let me explain to you, this is a fight I intend to win."

"We gotta get out of sight."

"That's for sure, but the funny thing is we should have expected it. Always expect the unexpected. There's a foreclosed-on house we can break into it and wait for the cops to leave, then go get my stuff."

They pulled their pads tight and, picking up their skateboards, crept down the street to the house.

Brew kept an eye out. "We'll never get in."

"These pop up houses they built are easy to get into," Curry said. "Take my word for it. And the realtor lady who haunts them is drunk half the time. And, as expected, she left the gate unlocked. I hope she forgot the back door, too."

"What about alarms?"

Around back, the windows and door were locked. Curry climbed up the gutter to check if any of the upstairs windows had been forgotten, then jumped down. "Fruitless. Now listen to the master. Behold my twelve steps to B&E program. The fuse box and cable phone are both on the outside of the house. Smart planning, huh?"

"Even I wouldn't do that," Brew said. "That's dumb. It's home invasion ready."

"Step one. Ready the stage for home invasion. Make sure the power's off. Two, be careful, I don't want to leave evidence, and three, we gotta find the perfect spot to get in. Here comes four, you're gonna like this one. You hoist me up onto the garage roof, maybe a window's open up there."

"You don't want to add another thing to your rap sheet. Observe as student becomes master," Brew said, and pushed past Curry, popped the sliding door open with his skateboard and went in.

"I should take you out with me more often." Curry followed Brew. "That's some mad skills. Skills to make us a fortune."

Brew wiped his feet on a mat. "Not if you want to get sponsored. You're gonna have to change your ways, remember."

Curry's nostrils flared. Inside, the house smelled of new carpet and lemon.

"Dude, you are a natural, following step two to the tee of the law. Leave no trace behind."

"Who cleans a foreclosed house?" Brew asked. "I'm minding my manners."

Curry flipped the lights on and off. "Dude, it's on the market. Realtors come here all the time."

"If they come here all the time." Brew closed the door. "it doesn't make it a great place to hide. We should head to my place."

"This is serious." Curry opened the cupboards in the kitchen. "If they are already at my house, you know they went to yours and Tom's."

"What if they are different cops?" Brew asked.

Curry slid the door shut and closed the blinds. He sat on his skate board against the wall. "What do you mean?"

"I mean, what if those cops are after you for something else?"

Eric Johnson

Brew asked. "We were just at the beach. Cops aren't fast, right? And who cares about monsters in the ocean. COEXIST right?"

"Can you stay focused for a minute?" Curry asked. "Coexist? Dude that's fantasy. It's survival of the fittest. Like Darwin said, *The very essence of instinct is that it's followed independently of reason.* You don't understand how much I get harassed."

"I get harassed too," Brew said.

"No you don't, not like I do. Your chalky ass always gets left alone. They're at my house right now. If that's not being harassed, I don't know what is."

Brew paced. "Both of your parents are doctors. You have no room to complain about anything."

"When they moved here from Mexico. They had it tough."

"No they didn't," Brew said. "They went to Stanford. Boohoo, they had it so tough."

"I should beat you down right now."

"Because both your parents are doctors? And you have everything you ever wanted?"

"Forget it, man. Shut up. This really isn't the time for us to fight."

"You started it."

"See how the authorities work. They have penetrated our minds to pit us against each other. Drive a wedge. It's tactics to trip us up."

"You're pitted against yourself."

They fell into silence, an hour passed. "Man, I'm hungry," Curry said. "I can't wait to get some carnitas."

"After what we saw, how can you be hungry?" Brew asked. "Dude, out the window! They are coming up the walk."

"Get down."

A radio crackled outside the window. Brew and Curry pressed against the wall. They held their breath.

"Dude, my skateboard is right where he can see it." Brew reached out with his foot.

Curry grabbed Brew's arm and squeezed tight. His eyes peeled wide, shaking his head no.

The crackle of the radio moved off, Brew glanced quickly at the door and grabbed for his skateboard. "We gotta move, he's coming around the back."

Curry sprung to his feet. "Upstairs!"

Standing back from the upstairs window, Brew waited for the police to move away. "They aren't going away, they know we are in here."

"A watched cop never leaves, relax," Curry said. "You know, it just occurred to me. How did they know to come to my house?"

"They must have gotten Tom."

Curry moved close to the window. "We're not going to be here long. Come over here and look. The cops left. But they have a dude parked over there watching. They should know no one in my hood drives cheap shit like that, it's a dead give away. We'll go around the block and take the back way in."

## CHAPTER SEVENTEEN
## WORMS

Tom jumped over the backyard fence; his foot caught. Landing in the neighbor's bush, he tumbled out onto his knees. Sweetpea, the neighbor's dog, lunged at him, teeth bared. He raised his skateboard, deflecting the bite, and knocking the dog back. Sweetpea, more agile, jumped forward and bit into a meaty spot on his leg, sinking its teeth in. Tom held back a scream and brought his skateboard down on the dog's head, clobbering it. Stunned by the power of the blow, the dog sank down, but readied to bite again. Tom smacked it on the nose with every ounce of strength he had. Sweetpea's eyes rolled up. For a moment, all Tom could see were the whites of it's eyes, before it collapsed. Tom squeezed his leg in agony. Through the holes in his pants little dots of blood appeared.

Voices from his yard pulled him back. Move. If he didn't, he'd be caught. Scrambling free, pushing the dog off him, he ran through the yard, across the street, and cut through to the next block. Using cars and trash cans for cover, he made it to the corner. Down the street, DHS agents were blocking off his street, and black trucks rolled by towards his house.

Tom zipped up his hoodie, pulled the strings tight, and ran. He flew across the street and down the block; he had to find a place to hide. Leaving the chaos of his street, the closest place he could think of was a foreclosed house with a peanut shaped pool where everyone skated. He needed help. He needed a ride.

In the alley behind the house, he hopped over the fence into the backyard and collapsed, gasping for breath. He unzipped his hoodie, and held his feet. They were beaten and bloody, he hadn't had time for his shoes.

"Look what the pit bull dragged in," a familiar voice said. "A barefoot wild man. Damn, Tommy, what are you running from? We heard those sirens all the way across town."

"Worms," Tom gasped. Worms got his name from the way he wiggled when he skated.

Two skaters popped up out of the pool and landed next to Tom, one said, "Skater friends unite. Damn. Your face is messed up, dude. Rumors said it was bad, but jeez. When did you get out of the hospital?"

Worms spoke, "You remember Skater Clayton, and Skater Shane?"

"What's going on?" Skater Shane asked. "Why the hard entry?"

"Yeah, like what's happening?" Skater Clayton asked. "I heard the accident killed your brain."

It was hard to speak. Tom's heart was pounding in his chest. His whole body shook. "They came to my house," Tom said.

"Calm down bro, get it out when it comes," Skater Clayton said.

"Tom," Worms said. "Did you get lucky or what. That's one awesome scar."

"No, dude," Skater Clayton said to Worms. "Look at him."

Tom was too out of breath to answer. He held his foot and wiped away the blood with an old newspaper.

"Ah dang, dude, your feet are hella messed up," Skater Shane said. "You need some heavy bandages."

"Don't be a poser, tell us what you did," Worms said.

"You do some crimes, bro?" Skater Clayton asked.

Worms popped his head over the fence. "We're gonna have to bail if the pigs are after you."

"Shut up," Tom gasped. "All of you. This isn't the time."

"What time is it?" Worms asked. "You're totally bogarting our spot. Here we are, peacefully skating to our hearts' content, and you trounce in on us like a freak of nature."

"Listen to me. I need your help. They arrested my dad, and they are after me."

"What? And become an accomplice to your shenanigans? Nuh uh," Worms replied. "I'm too smart to fall for the tricks of madness. With all honesty, maybe you should review the actions you took to lead you up to this point in your life. What did you do to make this happen?"

"You rob a bank or something like that?" Skater Clayton asked.

"I have a special aversion to crime. And going to jail," Skater Shane said.

"They're after me," Tom said. "Not you."

"We got that, dude," Worms said. "I'm all for helping a fellow skater, but when it's the law, that's something else. I intend to go to college, and if I'm behind bars, that, my friend, is no bueno."

"You don't understand. I'm serious." Tom slapped his skate on the ground. "Listen. It's not the cops, it's the DHS."

"Oh dude. You're a terrorist?" Skater Clayton kicked his skate up and tucked it under his arm. "I'm outta here."

"No. They killed a reporter," Tom said and held up the tooth. "We were at the beach where my class got killed. We found a DHS tent and got my stuff. I found it on the beach."

Skater Shane held his fist up. "That's hard core. What is it?"

"That's an awesome fang," Worms said. "You make it in art class?"

"No, from the creatures."

Worms grabbed the tooth from Tom. "Creatures? Let me see it. It's sharp, and it feels weird. Like nothing I have ever felt before. So the DHS is after you?"

"Yes, creatures. Mermen. They came out of the sea and killed my class."

"I don't know about that," Worms said. "The news said it was a tsunami, and their video was pretty convincing. Are you really running from the cops, because you escaped the loony bin? Perhaps your experience has driven you to madness?"

"Gnarly Ninja," Skater Clayton said. "Your lunacy wins our spot. We're bailing so you can hide here. Undisturbed. Let's get out of here."

"You better hang onto it," Worms said. "When you are old it'll make one nice trophy."

In the distance sirens sounded.

"That's not it at all." Tom held out his hand. "Give me your phone. I can prove it. I'll show you."

"Nah, man, we gotta bail," Worms said. "I'm not getting tangled up in your shit."

"They got my dad, and they'll kill me if they catch me."

"All the more reason to bail. Sorry, son," Worms said.

"You gotta help me. I gotta save my dad. Skaters stick together. Just give me your phone, and I'll show you why."

"You need to turtle somewhere," Skater Shane said.

"Show us what?" Worms asked.

"You're safe here," Skater Clayton said.

"I can't hide here," Tom said. "They'll figure it out."

"What do you want us to do about your problem?" Worms asked.

"Give me your phone!" Tom demanded.

"Yeah, like what are you going to do?" Clayton said and handed Tom his phone.

"I don't know. I have to come up with a plan," Tom said. "If they think like us, and use Google maps to find the foreclosed houses, it won't be long before they say, '*Hey that place has a pool what a great place to skate. Let's go check it out.* And wham, they'll be here lickety-split."

Tom held up the phone. Worms, Shane, and Clayton crowded around.

"They haven't pulled it down yet," Tom said.

"Pulled what, Mr. Wanted Skater?" Worms asked.

"I'm not sure I'm old enough to watch," Clayton said.

The video played.

Worms laughed. "Right on, Tommy. You're having a romantic walk on the beach with Bonnie."

"That's like love, isn't it?" Skater Shane said.

"Just watch, it's serious. I am going out into the water where I found the tooth. The douches come, Bonnie screams like a freak and runs."

"What the hell was that?" Worms pulled his head back. "Play it again."

"It's why they are after me." Tom handed the phone back to Clayton. "It wasn't a tsunami, there were dozens of those monsters."

"How come there are dozens. People would know if there were," Clayton said.

"And you are the sole survivor," Worms said. "How cool, you lived to tell the tale, bro. That's like out of a book."

"Worms, when do you ever read?" Clayton asked.

"Get the video out there to everyone you know," Shane said.

"I read all the time. That shows you don't know much about me," Worms replied. "I've never seen a seal as big, ever."

"That's the fakest video I've ever seen," Clayton said.

"Bro, that was a monster-sure-enough," Shane spoke through his fingers. "I mean, is it real? It, like, appeared out of nowhere, stepped out of darkness."

"I know what I saw," Tom said. "My memory is blurry, but real. I was gonna die, and somehow I didn't. Now my class is gone, and I am the only survivor."

"That's the question; what are we going to do about it? What can we do?" Worms asked. "This needs to be told. Uncensored."

Shane picked up his bag. "I don't know about that. We're messing with the big fish. We don't want too much heat on us."

"Sometimes you gotta look life right in eye the, and kick it in the nuts," Worms said. "That's what you do. Total balls out. A divine wind. So what say ye? Do we help Tommy or do we turn our backs on him?"

"What good would it do us to help him if we get in trouble with the police?" Shane asked.

"We need to ask ourselves, as we always do," Worms said. "Will it bring pleasure or pain? And if it is a mild discomfort leading us to greater pleasure, is it worth it? The pleasure of helping a fellow skater? For what is pleasure if you do not know pain? Who's in?"

Shane and Clayton nodded.

"We are in," Clayton spoke. "What do you need us to do?"

Tom stepped in close. "I need someone to find out what the DHS are doing, go by my street, and make some noise; see if you can see my dad. Tell them you saw me at the skate park if you are questioned," Tom pushed on his torn toenail and winced. "You guys can maybe head to the old cement factory and shred it up there after."

"We live outside the law, off the land," Skater Clayton said. "Those hounds will get a whiff of our skunk, and they'll track the scent for sure."

"Skaters stick together when times are tough, bro." Skater Shane tightened his pads. "We gotta fight our problems, it's the only way to learn how to deal with life."

The unmistakable chopping of a helicopter's rotors sliced the air. "They got a chopper in the air beading down on you. Our situation becomes a touch more complicated," Worms said. "We're gonna have to move sooner than I expected. I know where we can hide you until things cool down."

"Thanks, Worms."

"No worries, Tommy," Worms said, and turned to Clayton and Shane. "You guys switch hoodies with Tom. Best to fool the fools."

Shane pulled his hoodie off and put on Tom's. "This is way too small. But anything for the cause."

"I'll catch you bros later," Worms said

Clayton wiggled his fingers like he was putting a hex on the world. "Run some total random chaos."

Shane looked up at the sky. "Yeah, howl at the moon. Later."

Worms spoke to Tom quietly. "We'll go to the record store, my bro works there. Get you some help. Just keep your hoodie zipped up. We'll get there no problemo. But first we gotta do something about your feet. Take this bike tire and duct tape. We can make you some shoes real quick. I saw it on TV." Worms pulled out a knife and cut the tire into segments. "Times of war are tough. We can't just go to the station and say, 'Hey, I'm a fugitive, is my dad here?' But since it's the DHS, they probably have a special containment truck or spot for their own purposes."

"We have to go there. I have to know if my dad is all right."

"Hey you don't want to be like, oh no, Mario Koopa got me. Think about it. You don't stick your head into the mouth of a lion unless you got a jack to keep it open. And you ain't got jack. Now tie these here." Worms handed him the bike tire shoes, and they climbed over the fence. "We can't, like, skate right there. They'll know something is up if we don't act like typical skaters, and head right down the street to the mall. Can your feet make it?"

"Worms, the mall is crowded. I'll be seen."

"Nah. Best place to hide a skater is in a mall. Everyone knows we ain't got no money, so it's the last place they'll look. Besides, I do it all the time."

## CHAPTER EIGHTEEN
## UH, HI, MRS. MARTINEZ

Curry's stomach rumbled, and Brew drew in deeply through his nose as the door opened. The smell of home cooking wafted out.

"Cool, the alarm isn't set," Curry whispered. "We gotta ninja it up the back stairs to my room. But first, we grab some comida."

Slow roasted meat, homemade salsa and fresh tortillas were spread out on the black marble counter. "Damn, I always forget how big your house is. And, your mom makes food."

"That's the one thing I'll give her. She makes up a bunch of burritos and leaves them in the fridge for me."

"Ignacio, is that you?"

Curry pulled Brew back by the shirt and took point. "Hold on, here comes the fire." He faced the hallway and answered. "Yeah, it's me."

His mom stomped into the kitchen. Her face was stern, her long flying waved in the air like the Medusa. She batted a strand to the side and puffed up. "The police were here again. What have you done now, Ignacio? Do you know what they said? They said they would revoke our citizenship if you don't turn yourself in."

"Mom. Hold on. They can't say things like that. It's just a threat and doesn't mean anything."

"Then what does it mean?"

"How am I supposed to know?"

"Why weren't you in school? I'm going to call them right now. I'm sick of your behavior."

"I didn't do anything. Don't call them."

Brew stepped away from Curry. "Uh, hi, Mrs. Martinez."

"Get out, Richard. Go home!"

"Okay." Brew backed up to the door.

"Don't lie to me, Ignacio. I know you're guilty. I don't know what of, but you are."

Curry moved around the kitchen island, her words pushed him to seek safety. "Tone it down, Mom, you're causing me psychological damage. And we've covered this ground before. You know all my excuses. Stop playing the inquisition."

She snatched up a kitchen spoon and waved in the air. "Tone it down? In front of your friend? It's not rocket science, Ignacio. You are always at the damn skate park. It's all you talk about, how you're going to get sponsored. You should stop all the wanna be crap, go to school, and get an education. Your father and I struggled to get our degrees. Do you know what your actions do to us? You're going to be locked up one day, and there will be nothing we can do about it."

Curry bumped into the stove. It was hot, and he pulled away quickly. "Put the spoon down, Mom. Did you tell them where I was?"

He looked to Brew for help.

She swung the spoon in his direction. "He can't help you, and if I have to I'll beat him too!"

Brew wedged himself against the wall in the corner next to the door.

"Man, I mean Mom, school is like a suppository of information. They cram you full of useless things. I'm sick of going, you know that."

Curry's mom's arm shot out to her side. She pointed a single bony finger. "You go home, Brewster. I need to have a talk with Ignacio."

"I think I'll go now." Brew opened the door without turning his back to her. His shoulders relaxed, relieved she was sending him away but fearful for what might happen to Curry. "Alright, bye, Mrs. Martinez, but did the cops mention me?"

Her head twisted. "You're in on it too? Both of you go sit down in the living room, now. I need to get this straight before I call our lawyer. Whatever you did, you are going to turn yourself in today."

"Mom, you can't. They'll kill us," Curry said.

The spoon in her hand flew from side to side. She used it to emphasize her points "Don't worry about them, I'll do it first if you don't go sit down."

Brew took a step out of the door. "Me and Curry gotta get out of here."

The spoon snapped as it hit the counter top. "His name is Ignacio. You have to face your problems. No running away anymore. The next place you go isn't the cakewalk you think it is."

"Mom, we gotta hide," Curry pleaded. "You don't understand what's going on."

She grabbed him by the arm. "I understand you can't run. You're already on probation, remember the two strikes? The judge will put you away for five years."

"Mom!" Curry tried to shake her off in defense. He knew what she was capable of doing. The last time she had a bar of soap in his mouth before he could blink. "Remember what the counselor said. The intense anger you have when you think I am out of line has affects on me too."

"Take those shoes off and put them by the door." She ushered him into the living room.

Brew stared bewildered. "Really, I should go."

"You too, Brewster. Sit on the couch before I snap."

The cushion of the recliner barely indented as she sat on the edge, her spine rigid, straight as an arrow, she took a deep breath. Her head shook slowly from side to side. "Start from the beginning. I'll know if you are lying, too. I spoke to Tom's dad, so don't even try."

"But what did you tell the cops, Mom? What did they say?"

"They wanted to know if you were with Tom today. They wanted to know if you had gone to the beach. What did Tom do, I thought he was still in the hospital?"

Curry sat forward, and Brew sank back into the couch,

relieved. The cops didn't tell her what happened. "We went to his house to take him to school, but he was acting all weird and crazy. Maybe it was trauma from the accident. I don't know how I would act if I were him, so we left."

"Really, he's gone crazy, and you were no where near him."

"Mom." He pulled at the cuffs of his shorts and smiled. "I know you won't believe me, but we didn't do anything. We skipped only to go skating."

She crossed her arms and leaned forward. "And?"

"We need to hide for a while, but we gotta eat first."

Brew's eyes misted with joy; they were getting away.

## CHAPTER NINETEEN
## WE'LL RIDE DINOSAURS TO VICTORY

Down the ramp into the underground parking lot, the wheels of their skate boards click-clacked over the grooves in the pavement. Cars filled the parking spaces near the entrance. Muzak blared under the bright lights. The smell of lemon-scented chlorinated water came from the fountains, giving an illusion of cleanliness.

They skated down the hall past gawking shoppers, stroller carts of screaming kids, and soccer moms in yoga pants.

"Thirsty, Tommy? Worms asked. "I got a babe who works in the slushy shop, she'll hook us up."

"Dude, I don't like this one bit. We'll be caught is we don't hide."

The shop doorbell rang as Worms pulled the door open. Red tile floors, blackened grout, the place smelled deep fried. "Money's no object when you are with the Worms."

Tom's stomach growled, he bowed his head to avoid the security camera. Several people were in the store; he didn't like it. Anyone of them could be an upright citizen, ready to turn him in. "We gotta make it quick I don't like being in here."

A girl behind the counter smiled and wiggled her shoulders. "Worms, how ya doing?"

She wore a red and white checked apron and a hat shaped like a slushy cup, complete with fuzzy straw sticking off to the side. Worms slid over to the counter. "Hey, Baby Z. Que pasa? Can you hook up a couple of hungry skaters?"

"What you need, my Sweet Worms?"

"I love it when you talk culinary to me," Worms twisted around, leaning on the counter and winking at Tom. "She approves of comics."

"Skater special, times two?" Baby Z asked.

Worms patted his stomach. "Hits the spot, don't it. I'll hook you up later with an after-work visit."

Tom grabbed a seat furthest back and sat with his back to the door. Worms threw a hand full of ketchup packs on the table and sat down. "It's risky to stay in here, Worms. How long is she going to take to get the food. We have to keep moving."

"Bro, when fast food ain't fast enough," Worms squeezed a ketchup pack into his mouth. "it ain't the end of the world. Eat, relax a moment. If life is full of pain, why not sample some of its pleasures? Smell the french fries. No hero should ever be on an empty stomach, it's not right."

"I'm not a hero. I'm a fugitive. One they are looking to disappear."

"America still has laws; it's not Brazil, bro."

Baby Z set down Chili cheese fries stacked on top of beef patties with jalapeños. "Here ya go, Worms, baby."

"Just like a picture in a magazine, pure deliciousness. Thanks, luscious."

Baby Z cooed and squeezed his shoulder with affection. "You know me. I'm treated right, you treated right."

"Every time," Worms said.

"Who he?" Baby Z asked. "Don't talk much."

"Ah, just a skater friend. We gotta power up. Gonna hit the park."

The mountain of food teetered on the tray, threatening to fall over. A chili bean slid down on a wave of nacho cheese, and Worms snatched it up.

Baby Z left, and Tom's face dripped with sweat. "Don't talk to anyone. What if she calls the cops?"

Worms pushed the cheese fries over to Tom. "Ain't gonna happen. You're in good hands, so don't freak out; you'll attract attention. Now come on, Tommy, talk to me. What's going on inside that hoodie of yours?"

Tom pulled his hoodie tight and leaned forward. He spoke softly. His voice shook. "Worms, what I expect is you're going to get me to the record store. Your friend will know how to get me to where I need to go without you knowing. So if you get caught you won't give me away. And if you are lucky, they won't kill you. I also need to find out what happened to my dad. They took him. What if they kill him?"

"Whoa, so serious, Tommy, vengeance is joy divine. Have a fry." Worms leaned back in his seat, rested his arm across the bench, and slurped his slushy. "I got all that when I agreed to take you here. I am in full compliance with the things needing to be done to get you to the record store."

"Please can we just eat and get out of here?" Tom begged.

Worms set his slushy down, drummed his fists on the table and shot his index fingers at Tom. "So the way I see it, Tommy, you are on a quest with your dad being taken hostage by the pigs and all. Your situation is like deliverance trapped inside revenge for the death of a kinsman. You are the unfortunate, the pigs threaten you, and I'm like your rescuer. I'm gonna call me Bravepart."

Tom pulled back his hoodie. He stuck the tooth in Worms' face. "This is serious. You see my scar. One of those things in the video gave it to me. You're totally insane. How can you say they killed my dad? I don't even know where they took him, or if they did at all? The only thing I heard was the crazy DHS dude giving the order to detain him, then the fight. I had to take off."

Worms slapped Tom's hand down. "Put it down, dude. Don't forsake your savior. I was just kidding, anyway. I didn't mean actual death, so don't be so sensitive. I'll get you there incognito, no problemo."

"Did something happen to you as a kid, or did you do too many drugs today? I gotta find out what happened to my dad and save him."

Worms looked over Tom's shoulder then leaned forward and whispered. "While it's all noble, Tommy, how do you know he needs your help? He could be sitting at home wondering where you are. All the while, you are here eating awesome chili cheese fries. Maybe you should call him."

Tom shifted in his seat. "Risk calling? They'll find me."

"Bummer, pay phones went the way of the dinosaur," Worms said. "Tommy, you gotta follow what's in your heart. If they captured your dad, where would he be? The police station? A DHS facility? Think about it, ole lion heart is out there to get you. Don't stick your head into the mouth of a lion unless you got a jack to keep it open. And right now, you ain't got jack."

"Just get me to the record store, and I will find him from there," Tom said.

Worms stuffed a handful of fries in his mouth. Drips of chili squeezed out of the sides of his smile and down his chin. "That's the adventure talking. Sally forth, my wayward son."

After slushies were slurped and words were minced, they went out into the mall. Tom had every reason to believe something would go wrong, even staying in the mall as long as they had was risky. Worms was a fool, a magnet for trouble.

Shoppers gawked, taken by Worm's enthusiasm. He hopped on his skate, rail-sliding down the escalator, parting clusters of the unexpecting. "Don't be afraid, dude, that's my number one rule. The sun is burning off a fog covered battlefield. We'll ride dinosaurs to victory!"

Tom ran after him. "We have to leave the mall."

"I'm just trying to get you to have a clear head by addressing all the things irrelevant to your situation. So you can insert your own ideas, and make sense of what befalls you. Go with your gut, Tommy."

"My gut says let's get out of here and stop this messing around."

Worms spun 360s. "I'm no druid king, but I'm waiting for a special feeling to wash over me. It's all part of the plan."

"Your plan is like following a carnival horoscope. We have to get out of here."

"That's the illusion you perceive. We are not on an out of control merry-go-round. This isn't chaos, we are seeking a quieter perspective to let us know when the time is right."

"When?"

"Skate like a skater, don't be a wuss. Act like you are in control and control will follow. Sorry to disappoint you, but this is my way."

"Is the record store even real, or is it part of your fantasy? How many fingers am I holding up."

"Worms!" A security guard yelled. "You can't skate here."

"Jack boot dude says it's time," Worms said.

Tom jumped up seeking a direction to run, but it was too late, the security guard was on them.

Worms sighed. "Stopped by the king's highwayman. Hey we're just passing through, rent a bro. Take no worry."

"I don't have time for your crap, Worms."

"He knows you?" Tom's legs trembled and he felt the Chili cheese fries make a move to come up.

Shoppers stopped and stared.

Worms patted him on the back. "Yeah, long time buds, we go way back, but not to worry. We have an understanding, bro."

The security guard reached for his radio. "How many times do I have to tell you?"

"Not many. I know you don't want the hassle with the cops, you get paperwork, too, bro. So, let me make you a deal. Something you're going to like."

"I don't want any of your deals, and stay out of here on my shift. Go home and play video games."

"It's not like we're vandalizing," Worms stared at shoppers' in yoga pants as they walked by. He shook his head in an *mm mm good* way.

The security guard moved in close, his nostrils flared as he smelled the air around Worms. "Eyes here, Worms. Baggy jeans, gangster beanies, I can tell you are up to no good. You smoking something?"

"Ah, come on. This isn't pleasurable, dude. We can make it

happy for everyone."

The security guard turned to Tom. "Show me your face, kid."

Tom shook. "We're not doing anything, sir. Just ate some lunch, and we are leaving right now."

"Go on, turn around. I want to see what one of Worms' buddies looks like."

Tom turned around.

"Go on, kid, unzip your hoodie."

Tom pulled on the zipper.

The security guard stepped back. Like he had never seen anything gross before. "Jesus, kid, what happened to your face? You get slashed or something?"

Worms stepped in front of Tom, pointing a thumb at his chest. "Don't disrespect this taxpayer."

"The only taxes you know about is the taxing on me. Get out, before I change my mind."

"Alright, no paperwork wins the day." Worms' voice trailed off. Over the security guards shoulder, TV lights flickered in electronics store window. "Hey, what's going in there."

"Worms!" the security guard pulled his cuffs out.

Worms clapped his hands together and laughed. "Dude, on the TVs over there! It's Clayton and Shane. They got the pigs attention. Way to get a helicopter chase as your claim to fame."

"Worms!" The security guard barked again. "I'm not done with you. You gotta go, or I have to call you in for trespassing."

Tom pulled Worms away from the TVs. "We're going. Don't call us in. I'll get him out now."

"Worms, you hear? Go with your friend, right now!"

He shook Tom off. "Yeah, one sec, rent-a-dude, our buds made it on TV," Worms said.

Tom watched through store window, the KVTU 2 live chase scene gave them a birds eye view. His plan was working. Shane and Clayton had successfully gotten the attention of the DHS, but they couldn't see what Tom and Worms could. "Oh man, they're going to get it. The cops blocked off the road. They're skating right into it. Dude, they're gonna get caught. We'll be hunted next."

"Yeah, we gotta go," Worms said. "As cool as it is to watch our heroes at large, we have to get out of the shire. Come on, the time is now."

## CHAPTER TWENTY
## CALL ME CURRY

Suddenly, an explosion blasted open the front door. Three canisters bounced in and flash banged, stunning Curry, Brew and his mom. A team of armored DHS agents stormed into the smoke-filled the living room. Curry and his mom stood defiantly, Brew dove under the coffee table.

The DHS agents held their guns on everybody, one aimed directly at Curry's mom's head.

As the smoke settled, the man Curry and Brew recognized as the lead agent from the beach stepped between the DHS agents. He spoke into his radio, "Begin the search."

A dozen men rushed into the house behind him, and broke off into groups of two. He smiled, his voice soft with false compassion. "How hard is it to admit the truth?"

Curry's ears were still ringing from the stun grenade. He lowered his arms sat and leaned back into the couch. His initial horror and fear past, he laughed aloud. "Now you've pissed my Mom off."

Sounds of smashing dishes and cupboard doors opening and slamming shut came from the kitchen. "Mrs. Martinez, sorry to trouble you," the agent said. "In case your son doesn't know who I am, I'm special Agent Ortega. Do you understand what it means to lie to an agent of the United States who is conducting an investigation of espionage and treason?"

Mrs. Martinez glanced in the direction of her kitchen. "Officer Ortega, you can't come in here like Federales. This is America, you have no right."

"We do when dealing with domestic terrorism."

"Terrorism?" Her fists balled at her sides. "We aren't terrorists. I'm a doctor, and my son is a teenager. You were just here, and you said you were a police officer asking if I knew where Tom Stinson was, because he is wanted for questioning. You lied."

"I spoke to Mr. Stinson. He wasn't very cooperative."

Heavy footsteps stomped above their heads, and the sound of furniture being overturned thudded. Mrs. Martinez stepped forward. "Get your men out of my house!" she said, but stopped after one step as the DHS agents all trained their guns on her. "How dare you destroy my property."

"Watch yourself," Ortega said. "My men are authorized to use deadly force."

With a gesture from Ortega the guards lined Mrs. Martinez, Brew and Curry against the wall. The men who were conducting the search entered the room, cut open the couch cushions and pulled the books off the shelves.

Mrs. Martinez, now more mad than scared, shook her arms in defiance at Ortega. "What are you looking for?"

He tapped Mrs. Martinez' chin with his index finger. "Are you aware of Mr. Stinson's recent dealings with companies in China?"

"Don't touch me, I barely know him. What does that have to do with you storming in here?"

A guard shoved Curry to the floor. "Mom, don't say anything, he'll disappear us like they did with cousin Oscar."

Ortega turned. "Don't worry Ignacio. You are already disappeared, as you say. Aiding and abetting a known terrorist is a serious offense. The video from the beach alone is enough to put you away forever."

He puffed his chest. "Call me Curry."

One of the searchers entered the room. "Sir, the object isn't here."

Ortega's gritted his teeth. "Return to command and wait for further instructions."

"Yes sir," the agent said.

The twelve men exited, leaving the house destroyed. Ortega moved to Curry, stopped an inch from his face. "Tell me where Tom went. I can make it easy on you."

"What object?" Mrs. Martinez asked.

"I don't negotiate with terrorists," Curry said. "Especially bad breathed little ones like you."

"Shut up, Curry," Brew panicked. "He's the one with the guns."

"It's okay, my friend," Curry smirked. "The way I see it, I have him just where I want him."

"Ignacio, cooperate," his mom said. "Tell him what he wants to know."

Ortega raised his taser and smiled. "Didn't anyone ever tell you to listen to your mother? Tell me, what are we going to do about locating Tom?"

"You need to let us go," Brew said.

"That simple?" Ortega shook his head, and buzzed the taser close to Curry's face.

"He's a child!" Mrs. Martinez yelled. "Don't you dare."

Ortega turned to Mrs. Martinez. "As much as I hate to harm a child, the security of our great nation takes precedence. You understand don't you?"

"Tell him, Curry," Brew shook.

Ortega pushed Mrs. Martinez down onto her knees, and held the taser up to her face.

"Tell him, Ignacio," she pleaded.

"Listen here," Curry said. "We've made our mistakes. I'll cooperate. Just don't harm my mom. It's time. Eye of the skater, dude."

"Eye of the skater?" Ortega stepped over to Curry. "What do you mean?"

Beads of sweat formed on Curry's forehead.

"What are you doing?" Brew asked.

"I'm going to tell him."

"It's the right choice," Ortega said, his eyes shifting suspiciously.

In a flash Curry hit Ortega's wrist, and pulled the taser from him. Ortega responded; he sidestepped, punching Curry in the throat. "Shoot them."

Curry reeled backwards, and dropped to a knee, gasping for breath.

"No!" Mrs. Martinez hands flew out as she rushed to shield Curry.

Brew dove behind the couch as an agent fired at him, and slipped away into the next room.

"After him!" Ortega yelled, and turned to kick Curry, but Mrs. Martinez blocked him. "Move away from Ignacio, Mrs. Martinez."

The room fell silent from the echo of a single gun shot and a thud.

Mrs. Martinez bent at the knees, hitting the floor, reeling in disbelief. "You killed a child!"

Ortega's eyes creased in satisfaction. "Move away from Ignacio. Let's not end this poorly."

She wrapped her arms around Curry. "You have to kill me before that will ever happen."

"As you wish Mrs. Martinez."

Curry choked out, "It's okay Mom. My plan."

Ortega pulled her off Curry by the hair and threw her aside. Curry took the opportunity grabbed the taser and shocked Ortega in the leg. He convulsed as he collapsed and Curry fell on top of him, jamming the taser into his mouth.

The agents rushed forward.

"Tell them to back off." Curry pushed the taser in deeper.

They stopped and one spoke, "Let him go, you'll only be in more trouble."

"I'll do it!" Curry rasped holding them at bay. "Tell them."

Unable to speak, Ortega used his eyes to tell the agents not to move. The agents hesitated.

"I'll fry him," Curry said.

Regaining her composure Mrs. Martinez stood between Curry and the DHS agents. "You will not shoot me or my son. Put those guns down."

Brew appeared behind the agents and clubbed the closest one with his skateboard, then swung at the next, dropping both.

The remaining three agents turned, and at the same time Mrs. Martinez grabbed Ortega's gun. The agents fired. Brew dodged, but wasn't fast enough. The impact spun him around, blood splattered the wall and he hit the floor holding his arm.

Mrs. Martinez fired and emptied the entire magazine into the DHS agents.

Ortega put up an intense struggle. He had the look of a hunted predator who feared they might not be strong enough to escape. The years of his training, kicked in, he shouted, "Quick or dead!" And like an eel he flipped over.

Curry lost his grip on Ortega, but in his effort to hold him he pulled the trigger of the taser. Ortega's body tensed bolt straight, and he lay still, unconscious.

Mrs. Martinez pulled Curry to his feet and stuffed her car keys into his hand. "Get out of here." Then she moved to Brew. "Help me get him up."

On quick examination she said, "He's not bad. Go now. Go!"

Curry and Brew entered the garage and got in his mom's car. Curry jammed the car into reverse, crashing through the garage door and smashed into a DHS SUV, pushing it out of driveway.

The agents dove out of the way. Curry stomped the accelerator pedal to the floor and sped away.

Bullets pocked the car.

"I'm bleeding," Brew cried. "They shot me. We gotta go to the hospital."

"We can't!" Curry checked to see if they were being followed. "The bullet went clean through, put pressure on it."

"Hospital," Brew said. "I gotta go to the hospital. They won't be able to take us, not with all the witnesses there."

"I know what I'm talking about. You are fine. And don't fool yourself they have the law on their side. If we go there we are dead."

"I'm not fine. Don't let me die."

"What do you think my family talks about at dinner? My parents are doctors. I know what I'm talking about."

"It hurts so bad."

"Dude, I know it does." Curry reached into his pocket. "Smoke this. We gotta get far away and ditch the car."

"Where did you get that?"

"Medical companies give samples to my dad."

"You stole it?"

"This is an emergency!"

"Curry!"

## CHAPTER TWENTY-ONE
## IT'S THE SEWERS

Down the stairs and past the fountain, the parking lot entrance doors slid open. Worms kick-flipped over the bus bench and on to the asphalt, passing Tom. Worms called back, "How're the feet doing, Tommy?"

"Good," he replied, but not just good. They didn't hurt at all. How?"

An SUV backed out of a space quickly, almost hitting Worms. He ollied into a front axle grind across the SUV's rear bumper and grabbed the rear window wiper, snapping it off. "Look before you tweak, asshole!"

The brakes slammed on. "My car!"

Worms threw the wiper on the ground and sped away. "Watch where you're going, road rage dude."

The man in the SUV got out and ran after Worms. "Get over here, punk!"

"Not today, I gave at the office."

Tom kept his distance, road rage dude was on a mission. He would pound whoever he got a hold of first. This was a bad scene. This was Worms' fault.

Worms ollied over a fallen shopping cart into the street, and froggered across traffic; tires screeched. The road rage dude stopped chasing. He stood on the corner and yelled at them to stop.

"This way; short cut," Worms called back. "He's not following us."

From down the street, road rage dude whipped around the corner in his planet killing guzzler. His tires chirped. A hubcap broke free and bounced off the curb. Tom pointed. "Yeah, he is."

"Time for evasive maneuvers." Worms skated down an alley. Past a dumpster he bumper jumped off a parked car, and grabbed onto the end of a fire escape ladder.

As Tom and Worms stood on the hood of the car, the road rage dude appeared at the end of the alley. He revved his engine and barreled down on them as the fire escape lowered.

Worms yelled victoriously, "Fuck you!" And jumped, scaling the ladder like he had done it a million times before. Tom followed, he held tight to his skate board, climbing one handed.

Near the top, Worms slipped on a rung, his board fell straight down and bounced off the car below. His skate board landed truck's flush to the pavement unharmed; he cheered. They topped the ladder and got onto the roof. He leaned over the rail. "We gotta get Melanie, I can't leave her behind."

"You named your board?"

"Whether it be land or sea, they name all good ships, Tommy."

The road rage dude barreled down the alley towards Worms' board. There was nothing they could do. He ran it over, dead center. The wood flexed, the trucks bent, it snapped in two. Worms wailed, fell to his knees. "It's as if a thousand skaters cried out, then were suddenly silenced. Melanie!"

"Dude, we gotta get going, he's going to come up the ladder."

"They promised us flying cars, Tommy. If I had one right now I would fly over Road Rage dude and shit right on his head."

The road rage dude got out of his car, picked up the pieces, and waved them in the air. "Like that, punk!"

Worms flipped the road rage dude off. "You better be worth saving, Tommy. Road rage dude has gone too far."

Road rage dude threw down the pieces of Worms' skate board and started to climb the ladder.

"I'm sorry, Worms," Tom said, sincere as he could. "No one messes with a skater's skate board, but we gotta go."

Worms hocked a loogie down at the road rage dude. "Go F-yourself!"

A helicopter passed overhead, then circled back, rotors flashing in the afternoon sunlight.

"What if it's the copter that was after Brother Clayton and

Brother Shane?" Tom asked. "If they saw us?"

Tom and Worms ran to the roof access door, it was locked. "We're boxed in like a fart in a jar," Worms said.

Tom pulled the handle, the door rattled. He kicked the door. "Damn it."

"Tommy, locked. We gotta go back the way we came," Worms said.

Tom ran to the edge. "He's not coming up, like, he's on his phone."

"Gads, the jerk is calling the cops," Worms said. "You may think we're really trapped now, Tommy. But fear not. There's always a way out."

Black SUVs roared down the alley from both ends and screeched to a stop on the street below, pinning in the road rage dudes car. Men in black body armor rushed out, one pointed up his gun up at them, and spoke into a radio. The others pushed the road rage dude onto the ground and cuffed him, in a hail of fists.

"Any other ideas?"

"Yeah, back the way we came, but into the building. No one is safe today."

On the street side of the building Worms went over the edge, down a drain pipe. One floor down, he broke out the window and went in. Tom was right behind him.

"Okay, now what?" Tom asked as he, sought an exit.

"Know your town history, this was a hotel in the 1920s."

"So?"

Worms snapped a door open with a swift kick. "Out here."

Radios popped and crackled as boot stomping agents entered the building. Worms went to the end of the hall and pulled a picture down. "I hate corporate art."

"Hide, we need to hide. They are coming up the stairs."

He put his ear to the wall, then hit it with his fist. Worms kicked the wall, and his foot sank in. "Right here, we are in luck."

"What?"

"Dumbwaiters. We ride them to the basement and find the tunnel to the Speakeasy."

"What the hell are you talking about?"

Worms pulled at the drywall. "I'm a student of many disciplines. I know it's here."

"They are almost up the stairs, there's no waiter."

Worms reached into the hole and pulled a rope out. "Get in and hold on tight," Worms squeezed in to the hole and made room for Tom to climb in. "Time for some subterfuge."

With one arm, he reached out and hung the picture back over the hole. Their shoes squeaked against the wall of the shaft as they slid down. Near the bottom, a light shown on them from above. A man spoke into his radio, "They're headed to the basement."

"Shoot to kill." Crackled over the radio.

Silenced shots followed by the tap of hot metal punching through the shaft walls.

Worms let go. "Drop, Tom. Drop!"

Tom felt the bullets pull at his hoodie and he let go, falling down the shaft. He hit the top of a table and bounced off into a stack of boxes. Worms was already up and pulled him to his feet. "The door's somewhere around here. Help me find it."

Tom stuck his fingers through a hole in his hoodie. "They shot me."

Worms felt along the wall. "You're talking, you're all right. Help me."

"We're dead if you are wrong."

Worms kicked boxes out of the way, and pushed a shelf over. Office supplies spilled across the floor. "It's gotta be along this wall somewhere. In great halls, they tell legends of heroes, Tommy. Think like a drunk."

Across the basement the elevator bell dinged. "Get down," Tom said. "They're here."

"Sorry, bro, I tried."

The elevator door opened across the room. DHS agents rushed

into the basement. "Stay frosty, they are armed and dangerous," one shouted.

Tom crouched behind a storage crate. "Think like a drunk? What the hell is that supposed to mean?"

"Pretend you are a drunk escaping from a prohibition raid."

"Drunk. Okay, drunk. I've never been drunk."

Worms stood and swayed, and then stumbled, hanging his head down. "Follow my lead."

Tom hung his head down. "Worms."

"What? Sway back and forth like me."

"It isn't a door, it's right here."

"Oh ho, a hatch."

Rusted hinges creaked and a waft of sewage rose out. "Go first," Worms gagged. "They are after you."

Tom swung his legs down, grabbed onto a rung, and climbed down. "Thanks."

Worms closed the hatch and dropped down. "See I was right. Smarter than your average, something or other."

"It's not a speakeasy tunnel."

Worms gagged and spit.

"Correct," Tom said. "There's no way we can stay down here, there are dead rats everywhere, and the air is toxic."

"This place is familiar."

Tom held his nose. "Yeah, it's the sewers."

"No," Worms said. "Like back in the 70's there was an expedition of boarders looking for the ultimate adventure who came down here and were never heard from again."

Tom pushed a dead rat with his foot. "Shut up, Worms. We need a way out of here."

"Using my knowledge of the city plans, I think if we go down the tunnel approximately a hundred feet we should be under the record store."

## CHAPTER TWENTY-TWO
### DUBSTEP DROPS

The record store dude glanced up from a stack of CDs as Worms pushed the basement door open. "What are you doing in the basement, Worms?"

"Coming in hot. Skater hater called the cops on us."

"What? Again?" the record store dude asked. "Worms, you got to stop showing up here bringing trouble with you. They'll catch on one day, come in here and ruin the business."

"Worry about it when it happens, but for now we need a place to hide."

The record store dude took a bite of an apple and tossed his keys to Worms. "Safe house room is ready, respect it."

Tom collapsed on the floor next to the safe-room door. He smelled his shirt and gagged.

"Man, where you been?" The record store dude's face scrunch up. "You stink like the lower pits of hell."

"We've been down in the sewers," Worms one-hand twerked. "Hey, that's some hella cool steps you got on. Makes my loins go mad."

"Stop that, Worms, it's hurting my eyes," he turned his head. Sirens dopplered past outside. "That siren for you?"

Worms hung back in the shadows of the back hall. "Is the store empty?"

"Yeah. As always. Who's this dude?"

"Him?" Worms thumbed over his shoulder at Tom. "He's the dude who surfed the tsunami down at Diamond beach. Sole survivor."

"No shit." The record store dude held out his hand to Tom. "Damn, man, what was that like? Your face got messed up, but I guess you got gills or something."

Tom pulled his hoodie off. "I got lucky."

"The skater that lived to tell," the record store dude said. "And all he says is he got lucky. It ain't right."

"Hey, he's one of the bravest dudes I know," Worms said. "He needs to hang out for a bit, like quiet."

"Ain't they after you too, Worms?"

"Yeah, but, I got a date."

"Right, then. You know me. I don't know nothing. I don't see anything. There's a couch and a TV back there. Just don't mess anything up, and if the boss comes, tell him I said to hire you, and you should be alright."

"Mission accomplished." Worms gave Tom a high five. "I got a date with sweet Baby Z."

"Sorry about your skate, Worms," Tom said. "Thanks for getting me here."

"In loving memory of Melanie." He frowned for a second, then smiled his pain forgotten. "Better to have skated and loved, than not to have skated at all."

"You know those dudes I hang with, Brew and Curry," Tom said to Worms. "If you see them tell them to meet at our spot. They'll know what you're talking about."

"Roger, wilco Tommy," Worms said. "I need some new dubstep before I take off. Got any Loud DJ Hush?"

"Thanks," Tom replied.

"So, what are you running from anyway?" The record store dude asked. "Obviously the cops, but what's the root of your troubles? Your parents? They don't understand, and you need a place to unbend for a while? Or is it not that simple?"

Tom told the record store dude about the reporter. His jaw dropped. Worms thumbed through the used CDs and nodded, interjecting with a few yups and uh huhs.

"Shit, Worms, you brought me some fucker who is hot. Not just with the police, but Homeland? Motherfucker!"

"Listen to him," Worms said. "It's all important. Hear what he has to say. Tell him about the other stuff, Tommy."

The record store dude played the video on his phone. "Dude,

your video has gone viral. That's one angry seal. Maybe it's mutation from some experiment. I read about these things before. Alright, I know what to do. Let me make a phone call, I have some friends who might be able to help. But you, Mr. Tsunami, need to follow my advice, because you don't even have real shoes."

"Read about it? Where?" Tom asked.

"On the net of course. There's the couch in the back you can crash on for a bit. Be sure not to open the fridge."

The taste of slushy skaters delight and grease hung in the back of Tom's throat. "I couldn't eat."

Boxes and trash were piled up in the corners and an old TV sat on top of a filing cabinet. The record store dude drew the curtains and fiddled with something in the corner. He held up a thumb drive, dropped it on the floor, and stomped on it. "It's camera footage of you."

"What do I do now?"

"You wait until dark, then get out of here. For now, take this tee, you smell like shit, and use the first aid kit to fix those feet up. There might even be some old shoes left by former victims of this hell hole in those boxes. Now I gotta mind the store. Keep quiet."

Worms' head poked in the door, he signed unicorn. "Later, dudes."

"Wait up," the record store dude said.

The door shut, tumblers clicked. The energy sucked from Tom's legs. He collapsed onto the couch, a spring popped out near his head and it smelled of cat, it was the most comfortable thing he had ever sat on. Behind the locked door, he closed his eyes and relaxed to the steady beat of the music. He kicked his makeshift shoes off. His torn toe nail fell off; wetting his thumb he wiped it clean. Underneath the dirt, the skin was pink like a newly healed cut. Why was he healing so fast?

The back door's buzzer sounded and through the door. The

record store dude spoke. "Can I help you, officers?"

Their muffled voices seeped through the door. He could feel them standing there. "We're looking for two suspects. Both between five and six feet tall, both wearing dark hoodies and have skateboards."

The record store dude stammered. "Uh, I, uh."

Tom's heart pounded; he went to the window. Sweat covered his forehead. He peered through a crack in the curtains. A cop car was parked just outside, lights flashing. There was only door in the room. The window latch was painted shut. A car pulled into the lot, the driver saw the cop car and backed out quickly. He was trapped.

"Pigs gotta die!" Worms yelled from the front of the store.

"There's one now!" a cop yelled. "Hold it right there!"

"Shoot to stun!" The other ordered.

"Screw you, pigs!" Worms yelled. "Bravepart! Never surrender!"

Tom froze, there was no where to go. The music stopped, and moments later the door opened. The record store dude rushed in carrying a backpack stuffed full of CD's. He went to the safe and opened it. "The cops are gone. I called the boss, he said it was okay if I put the gone fishing sign up a little early. I turned out the lights too, so no one will come and bother us. Let me give you the details, little buddy."

"Isn't he coming down here? Didn't you tell him about the cops and Worms?"

"Who? My boss? No way. That'd be crazy. He gets hot, like destructive weapons of the atomic age."

"Thanks," Tom said.

"Those cops are everywhere; they even have a picture of you. They're putting the whole town on lock down until you are caught."

"Are they coming back?"

"I closed the store. They have no reason. Never give a cop a reason."

"You got any food?"

"Just green growth in the employee fridge. Eat at your own risk."

The record store dude turned the TV on. The five o'clock KVTU 2 News was on. They had a picture of him, Brew, and Curry on the Breaking News. "See, that's you. You are wanted in connection with the murder of the reporter and the theft of government property. You a terrorist?

Tom was speechless; they had the picture of him from his living room. He laughed in disbelief.

"I guess it's serious," the record dude turned off the TV. "They are swarming like ants searching for you. Did you do it? If you did, you gotta get out of here. You know what happened in Alaska. Even though they were right for trying to stop the slaughter of the polar bears. Those activists didn't have to release polar bears into a crowded stadium."

"I didn't do it," Tom said. "How can they call me a terrorist when I am innocent?"

"They can do what ever they like. The dude who is after you is crafty. He's using the ultimate tool against you. The law. What better way to get at someone."

"What law? How can they do this?"

"Because they make the laws, that's why. Don't think that when you vote it counts for anything. It's all a stage show, man. Corporations have our country in their pocket. It's a system of careful checks and balances. The corporations write the checks, and the senators check their balances."

Tom rubbed the metallic oval between his fingers and examined the tooth, then held them up for the record store dude to see. "They are after these. If I hadn't gone to the beach, none of this would have happened. How can these things be so important?"

"Hey, I don't want to see that shit. No fate but what we make.

Your decisions have brought you nothing but a world of hurt, and I don't want to be involved anymore than I already am. You should stash your stuff somewhere and forget about it. Then make it to LA. Lot's of kids go to LA. It's easy to get lost there."

"You said you knew what to do," Tom said.

"I did before they pegged a murder on you and your buds."

"What about the friends you called. The ones who can help?"

"Yeah, that call, I thought the dudes on the website could help you. Apparently they ghost out and vanish when the tin foil gets too real. Sorry, little dude."

"Why did I think I could count on you?" Tom yelled. "Worms said you could help. I just met you, and I don't even know your name. Worms, he's probably arrested. What if he talks? What then?"

"Worms is a good kid, but he's talking. Everyone talks eventually."

"What am I going to do?" Tom stood. "They have a helicopter, and cops are everywhere."

"Fear of the future is your real enemy. Use your senses, take precautions. Plan for it. When you leave, watch out for the traffic cameras. They say they aren't hooked up to anything, but it's a lie. They are watching every intersection, and with the face recognition shit the spooks use, they'll know where you are, fast."

Tom opened the fridge. Foil wrapped balls of half eaten burritos and a tub of moldy beans fell on the floor. His nostrils flared. "How am I supposed to know where the cameras are when I am running?"

"If it has a traffic light, it's bugged. I never go near traffic lights."

"Don't you have a car? I could hide in the back."

"No car here, broham. You have to register your presence for a license, and that's almost as good as having a tracking chip implanted in your forehead."

Tom found a pair of socks and pulled them on. "You're

whacked."

"Listen here, I ain't running the underground rail road, and you came to me for help. Take these boots and here's a five, it's all I can spare. There's a taco place a couple blocks from here. Just watch out, the cops like to eat there."

Tom nodded.

"In the element of self interest, where are you going to go?" the record store dude asked.

Tom pulled the boot laces tight. "If I tell you, and they find out I was here, they'll kill you like the reporter."

"I knew I shouldn't have helped, color me burdened," the record store dude said. "You gotta go now, man. I gotta get out of town. Across the tracks, you know."

Tom followed him out into the store. The record store dude ran to the cash register, opened it, and grabbed the cash out, then hit the alarm system on. He pushed Tom to the back door, got on his bicycle, and took off down the street.

## CHAPTER TWENTY-THREE
### STACEY

Alone, Tom skated down the street. The boots the record store dude had given him were way too big, they were like clown feet. He needed a place to hide until dark. An alley, a doorway, anything to keep him out of sight. He had to get to Brew and Curry.

The sky was emptying of light, turning from coastal hues of pink and winter gray to the dingy yellow of street light. A car pulled up alongside him and honked. The passenger window rolled down. "Hey, skater boy, where ya going?"

Tom's body lurched. "Stacey? Get away from me, you're nothing but trouble. Out of all the times I've had to deal with you since you puked on me, what are you doing here now?

"My hair's pink again, you know what that means."

"Don't," Tom said.

"When I met you you were just an innocent Midwest boy. Now look at you, a fugitive. Sexy meow meow."

Tom skated faster and cut around a corner. "Go away."

He had met her at a punk rock show when they were fourteen. Her parents gave him a ride home because it was late. They sat in the back of her parents car together. She was like no other girl he had met.

He told her about everything on the ride home, things he never told anyone before. Everything he said cracked her up. They laughed uncontrollably, and her dad wanted to know if they were okay riding in the back together.

There was a moment of silence as he tried to catch his breath. She made a face, and started to laugh again. His eyes were drawn to hers. She was so hot. His body quivered at her touch, like electricity flowing through him.

He wanted to kiss her, but he couldn't risk it. Her dad eyeballed him in the rear view mirror. He was the big and scary type Tom imagined would beat you with a hammer. Time blurred, it was forever and only a second at the same time.

When they pulled up to his house, they got out together to say good bye. She twisted her hair with a stray finger, blinked, and smiled, and tugged on his shirt. "My dad's not looking."

He had to go for it, it was what he wanted, what she wanted. Her dad was watching, but he didn't care anymore, he had to kiss her. He tilted his head towards hers and moved in with grace he thought not possible.

Suddenly, her shoulders heaved forward, she made a gurgle gag sound, and puke sprayed across his chest, on his face, and down his legs. Romance turned to nightmare. The burning desire ignited in the back seat of the car was extinguished. Her puking made him puke too. They lurched over, facing each other and retched together all over his lawn. Their puke intermingled in a way no puke should ever. Her bile, his soda; he knew they would never be. She had been drinking. Her dad was pissed. He was guilty in her dad's eyes.

Ever since that night she'd creepered him. Everywhere he went she was sure to follow. Maybe it was out of embarrassment, maybe it was love, but who was he to say. He just wanted her to go away.

Stacey pulled up along side and paced him. "Come on, Tom, I saw you on the TV. You need a ride."

Tom slowed. "Don't seem so excited. Your enthusiasm is like a vampire in heat."

"You are so sweet."

"Get out of here. They're after me." He continued to skate. "You don't want to get caught up in my mess."

"Sometimes you need a little help from friends, Mr. Lone-wolf. I'm your friend."

Tom stopped. "Lone-wolf? I was with Curry and Brew."

"Did you do it?"

She was thin, he didn't remember her being so thin. "Stacey.

Please. Go away, and get some help for your disorder."

She brushed a lock of hair away from her eyes and stared at him. "I can hide you. We can go to my house. You can stay in the tool shed in my back yard. No one ever uses it."

"Talking to you is like lying on a bed of thorns. Only a fool would fall for your tricks. I'm not going to hide in your shed. You'd keep me like a prisoner. Probably experiment on me when I was sleeping."

"I would never do that," Stacey giggled. "Did you ever imagine us running into each other?"

"How did you find me?" Tom leaned into the passenger window. "You show up at the worst times. Can't you just leave me alone?"

"I know where you are at all times. Call it a psychic LoJack. Call it a girl's intuition."

"Stop stalking me, Stacey, you don't know what you are getting yourself into." He pushed away from the car.

"I like the word into." She put her car into park, leaned over, and opened the passenger door. "Don't be a coward, share the excitement."

"The road is calling me," Tom said.

Stacey knocked on the steering wheel. "I'm not a mystery or an unsolvable puzzle, you know. I'm crazy, driven, and full of secret plans that I'll never reveal. Get in."

Her enthusiasm waned when he stepped back, and the gloom she put around him dissipated. She gripped the steering wheel and bit her lip. He could feel her desire to wreck his life strengthening. "Can't you ever forgive me?" she asked.

"I can't ever forgive you." He turned, putting his foot on his skateboard.

"You need me."

She was trickier than two skaters in a pool skating tandem. "Why is that?"

"I'm like friends with benefits," she said with a hopeful smile.

"I got a car. You have nothing. The way you're limping reminds me of a wounded animal who needs the gentle hand of a master."

"There's no way I'm gonna risk myself with you. You might think we are dating."

"You care, how sweet," she beamed. "Get in and find out."

"I can't do that, you're crazier than a tweaker on bath salts. Go home and take your meds."

She slid into the passenger seat and hung her arms out of the window. "Get in before a cop comes if you're so worried. You know they are telling everyone to shelter in place, you're a terrorist."

"Hardly, I can't believe I went from sole survivor to terrorist in a day. When all I want is the truth."

"Hey, Earth to Tom. Take your helmet off and get in. Or you going to skate to LA all by your lonesome?"

"LA?"

"It's where everyone runs to."

There really was no alternative. Resigned to a fate probably worse than actual death, Tom got in the back seat and sank down. His mind filled with unpleasant possibilities of what might happen. "Don't try anything crazy."

Stacy reached back to touch him. "So, where we going, lover?"

"Not we, me. You're dropping me off at the old bridge."

Stacey tossed him a pack of pills.

"What are these for?" he asked.

"You look like you could use them. Take the edge off your limp."

"Date rape much?" Tom tossed the pills back at her. "I'm not falling for your tricks."

"Aw, Tom Tom," she said. "Pull the blanket over you and stay down, The cops are everywhere."

They followed a bumpy farm road out into the strawberry fields.

"You guys hangout all the way out here?" Stacey adjusted her mirror to see him. "I always wanted to know where your secret hideout was, it's not what I expected. It's totally lame. There's nothing here."

"After you drop me off, you have to forget you saw me. Tell no one."

She pouted in the reflection of the mirror. "Tom. You know I have to come with you. There's never any excitement around here, and if it's with you. Think of it this way, I'm your worst enemy and your best friend. Who knows who I could call. You need me, Tom."

The last rays of sun fell below the horizon. "It's over there. Stop here," Tom said.

Gravel crunched under the wheels as they pulled onto the shoulder. "There's nothing out here except for artichokes and strawberries."

Winter fog rolled over the field, and Tom rubbed the window. "Curry and Brew should be here. If they didn't get caught."

Stacey's hair glowed pink in the dome light as she got out. The hatch opened. She pulled out an emergency road kit and turned on a flashlight. "Get out. You'll need the light, I wouldn't want you to slip into the drainage canal."

Tom grabbed for the flashlight. "Turn the light off. I don't need it, and someone might see."

"There's no one out here."

"They closed off the entire town and are going from door to door searching for me."

"I'm like an usher at the movies. Taking you to your seat."

"Quit playing around. Someone will see the light."

The hatch slammed shut. "Then why did you drag me out here?"

"Drag you? You threatened to turn me in."

"Helping you is the only way to keep your dark secret," Stacey laughed. "What's going on in that criminal mind of yours, Mr. Bad-boy-on-the-run? You're so nice and sweet on the outside. Let me in to find out what makes you work."

"You never change, Stacey. Why do you always have to manipulate everything? It's always about you."

Stacey put her hand on his shoulder, pulled his hood off, smacked her lips, and leaned in for a kiss. "Girl's gotta do."

Tom stepped back just in time. "Whatever happens to you from now on is your fault."

"Fine, don't thank me for helping you."

"Don't worry, I won't."

Loose rocks tumbled down the embankment and dust rose. "I don't know what's worse, choking on the dust or gagging from the stench of fertilizer. It smells like death."

"If you can't stomach it, it's not too late to leave."

"I can take it."

"Quiet. I need to listen. Brew and Curry should be here."

Stacey slipped on the gravel and yelped. She turned her flashlight on and shone it under the bridge.

Tom spun around. "I said keep it off."

"Tom?" Curry called out from the dark. "We thought you guys were the DHS. They are everywhere."

"Dude, you made it," Brew said. "We've been here for hours waiting. Check out my arm, I got shot."

"Shot?"

"It hurts like hell."

Curry emerged from the dark. "He's just crying. It ain't that bad. I fixed him up with a little medical mota."

"They took my dad. They took him and arrested all of the reporters. That DHS agent has gone mad. He's pinning the reporter's death on us."

"They got my mom," Curry said. "She shot three of them. We need to, like, twang out and get us some six shooters."

"Then what?" Brew asked. "Die in a shootout? We gotta get out of here."

"How'd you guys get here?" Tom asked.

"I took my mom's car, and dumped it in an irrigation ditch way out with the strawberries," Curry said.

"Hi, guys." Stacey held the light under her chin and smiled.

"No way, we were on the run," Brew said. "She'll slow us down."

"Hi, Curry."

"Hey, Stace," Curry smiled.

"Don't look so happy," Brew snapped.

Tom held up the metallic oval. "Stacey, I need your light. Shine it here. I have to show you guys what the DHS is really after."

"See, you need me," Stacey said. "What's that? It's pretty."

"When I was at home. This totally stuck a needle into my hand and drained my blood. Curry, touch it and see."

"Draws blood? No way I'm not touching it."

Brew shook his head.

"I'll do it," Stacey said. "But aren't you guys like 'We're all about pushing the human potential to see how much a skater can take?' Especially you, Curry, but I guess not."

"Okay, give it to me." Curry took it from Tom and turned it over in his hand. "It doesn't do anything. It's just a hunk of metal."

"Give it a second."

The oval buzzed and then the needle shot out, plunging in. Curry screamed and shook his hand. "Get it off me."

Brew shone his light on Curry as he hopped around in pain. "Sucker."

"Hang in there, dude. It'll stop in a second."

"Not so tough now, are you," Stacey said.

"Shut up," Curry replied.

"Glad it wasn't me who fell for that," Brew said.

Curry sighed in relief, and Tom took the metallic oval from him. "Now watch it." He held it out in the palm of his hand. The oval glowed bright red and vibrated. "You see that?"

"It hurt like hell, you douche. That's what."

Stacey stepped in between the three of them. "So it sucks your blood. But what does it really do?"

Brew laughed at Curry. "You fell for her trick."

Curry fumed. "Okay, we need to think about this logically. It's made of metal, and it takes blood. Turns red and vibrates."

"It's a lost vampire stone," Brew said. "And it drinks our blood, so it can like, summon a demon."

"That's dumb." Tom turned it over in his hand. "It's from outer space, that's why the government is after it. It might give the holder some great power, like makes you able to burst stuff into flames with your mind, or go invisible."

"Stacey is here," Brew said. "Prove me wrong."

"Maybe it can make you fly," Stacey said to Brew. "Try jumping off the bridge."

"Nah, his mental capacity isn't strong enough to make it work," Curry said.

"Let Stacey jump," Brew suggested.

"You don't have any idea what it is," Stacey said. "And you're not going to either. That's as logical as it gets."

Tom took the flashlight from Stacey. "You guys have camping gear here?"

Stacey took the flashlight back. "So, you guys' plan is to stay here until the psycho DHS agent gives up on finding you? Not very sound."

"I'm glad someone thinks like I do," Curry said.

"You have a better plan?" Brew asked. "They won't look for us out here."

"Yes, they will," Stacey said. "Some one will see you sooner or later."

"You need to get away, Stacey," Brew said. "You are not involved."

"I'm not leaving until you guys really tell me what's going on. Besides you will have a loose end if I leave. You should dispose of any loose ends or take them with you."

"What?" Curry asked. "I take it back, you don't think like me."

"Give me your phone." Tom held out his hand. "I'll show you."

The video played, and Stacy said, "That's a. . ."

"A giant seal." Tom held up the fang. "Everyone says that, but it's not. Seals don't have fangs."

"They don't?" Stacey sneered and crossed her eyes. "If you're going to figure it out. I think you guys should start with the boat."

"Boat?" Tom asked.

"Duh? The one in the video, didn't you see it? It's plain as day." She hit play again. "Here, see."

"Not available in your country?" Tom read the screen. "Damn, they are on to it already."

Stacey put her phone away. "You're going to have to take my word for it."

"The boat was there, but it doesn't matter," Brew said. "It's like, way out there. Even if it exists we would never find it."

"You got the tooth and the metal thing from a diver's bag, right?" Stacey asked. "That's where the diver must have come from. So where would the boat end up?"

"The current would carry it away," Curry said. "But it's been over a week, it would be gone. Towed in as a derelict or sunk."

"It hasn't been on the news." Stacey stared into Tom's eyes. "Not one word about it. I've been watching."

"More like stalking the newscaster," Brew said.

"It might be hung up at Razor Point," Curry suggested. "The currents go south, and no one goes there this time of year it's too cold."

"And the trails suck," Brew said.

"We should start there," Stacey said. "Before the DHS figures it out. It's where the answers will be."

"You can't come," Brew said. "You shouldn't get involved."

"I just figured out what you need to do," Stacey snapped. "You can't tell me I can't come."

"I can, and I did," Brew replied. "You'll mess things up."

151

"We need her," Tom said.

Stacey patted Tom's cheek. "You're so sweet."

"No way," Brew said. "She's like princess goody three toes the way she hangs around and clings to other people's fun."

"But she has a car, and we need her if we're going to find the boat."

Stacey jingled her car keys. "Leave the gear. We'll come back for it."

Brew handed Tom a burrito. "You might need this."

Tom peeled back the foil. "We'll take the back roads to Razor Point."

## CHAPTER TWENTY-FOUR
## RAZOR POINT

Razor point, known for bird watching, abalone diving, and a multitude of party spots. Hidden coves dotted the trails that followed the shore and rolling meadows topped the cliffs. Around the bay to the beach was twenty miles. The gate to the beach was open. Stacey pulled into the parking lot and shut the car off.

"This better not be a waste of time," Brew said. "We could be out of state by now."

Curry pushed on the seat. "Get out, this car is way too small for normal humans."

Brew pushed out of the car. "I can't see anything."

A wind whipped up, chilling them through their clothes. Stacey opened the trunk and grabbed a heavy coat and flashlight. She shone her light along the trail.

"Yeah, me neither. Got an extra flashlight?" Curry asked.

"The flashlight makes me the leader and you my side kicks. Trail head is over here."

"I'm staying in the back, so if you go over the cliff I will know to stop in time," Curry said.

Brew stepped behind Curry. "Don't lead us over the edge."

Up stairs, down stairs, around a bend, and past a memorial bench. Parts of the trail were too close to the cliff, only yellow tape tied to trees was used to mark where trail ended and cliff began.

"Watch out, the path is narrow and slippery." Brew stumbled into Curry.

"I can see the moonlight on the waves down there," Curry said. "Falling would splatter you."

"Narrow and slippery. You talking dirty to me, Brew?" Stacey asked.

"Down there, a campfire in the cove," Tom called out. "We should avoid them."

"The matter of fact is," Curry said. "It's dark and we are on a narrow, uneven sea cliff path with roots and loose rocks sticking out everywhere. We need to take it easy."

Stacey threw a pine cone over the cliff edge and picked up the pace. "Curry, most people see a chair and think sit. I think lion tamer. That's the difference with me."

"Lions eat you, and I think keep them in a cage. That's the difference with me."

"Except when it's skating," Brew held onto Curry's shoulder. "You do some crazy shit."

"Only when unleashed in my element."

The trail split, one path turning away from the cliff to the ridge and the other winding down the sidewalls of the cove to the shore.

"There's the fire," Tom said. "Turn off the light. There's people around it."

"What are they doing?" Brew asked.

"Having a party," Stacey said. "We gonna crash it?"

"We gotta find the boat," Tom said.

"The likelihood of it being here is next to nothing," Curry pointed out. "And even if it was magically floating in one of these mini coves, we wouldn't see it."

Stacey went down the stairs. "Let's see if we can get a drink from them."

"We should hang back," Tom said. "Nothing worse than being sneaked up on when you think you are alone, and are altered."

Stacey made it to the bottom of the stairs, and approached the party. The figures around the fire jumped when they saw her.

"See?" Brew laughed. "No one expects Stacey The Stalker."

"She's some fine shit," Curry said.

Brew flicked Curry's ear. "Don't play with crazy."

Three figures crowded around her. Their laughter rose up the cliff side over the crash of the waves. Brew bounced out of his shoes. "Dude, they're not partiers, they're babes."

"Yeah, and what are you going to do with them, Richard?

Show them your skate board?" Curry asked.

"It's a bad idea," Tom said. "We don't have time for fun. We're here to find the boat."

"Stacey's waving to us. I think we should join her," Curry said.

"Dudes, we are on the run, remember?"

"They ain't looking for us out here. We may as well have some fun. No one will expect us to be partying on the beach. If you're not living dangerously. . ."

"You're not living at all," Brew finished.

Brew and Curry went down the stairs towards the fire. The stairs were so steep they had to crab-walk. Tom held the metallic oval tight and watched them run to the fire. Plans fail by not keeping focused on the goal and not adapting when the situation changes. "Screw you guys."

Rocks bounced down the cliff as he followed the path to his favorite place; the old coastal artillery position from World War 2. It was slow going with only the moonlight to guide him. It gave a perfect view of the bay to the south of Razor Point.

Up the trail, he crested the ridge. Yellow rope and a fence cordoned off the stairs to keep people out, but you could climb over the rocks and jump out to a tree to shimmy down. Once the moon came up he could get a good look at the bay. Maybe he would get lucky and spot the boat.

Pine needles and lichen made it slippery on the rocks. The crash of the waves below were muffled by the lush undergrowth, and the smell of salt mixed with the scent of the pines. The cold night wind bit into him; he wrapped his arms around himself and rubbed them. He edged his toes over the lip of the cliff, and sized up the distance. The tree seemed further in the dark. He jumped. Bark shredded and new growth branches snapped. Splinters slid into his hands and he hit the ground hard.

From the battlements, he watched as lights blinked out on the ocean. Probably cargo ships headed to China with recycling. He sat and piled fallen pine needles over his legs; anything to keep warm.

Lights flickered on the horizon. *Damn Stacey,* Tom thought, *it was stupid to think they would ever find the imagined boat in the video. Come to think of it, whatever Stacey saw was probably the crest of a wave. She had manipulated them, again. Curry was blind to it, so was Brew.*

He leaned against a tree and pulled more needles in, covering his legs. Looking for the boat was getting him nowhere. This was a waste of time; he needed to prioritize. How was he going to find his dad? He had to go home to see if they had taken him. Stacey owed him, she could drive by his house.

Tom kicked a rock over the edge of the cliff. The oval vibrated and he reached into his pocket to run his fingers over it. Out on the water a boat was coming towards the shore; from above it a light shone down on the water. Helicopter. He ran.

Tripping on a root he tumbled down the stairs to the cove. His descent stopped abruptly at a crook in the stairs, where he hit his head hard and bashed his knees. Dazed, but alright, he stumbled on a rock as he came into the light of the fire. "They're coming!"

Stacey handed him a beer. Brew stood up. Curry laughed and slapped his knee. They were cozy around the fire. Startled, the partiers fell back from the fire, "Who are you? What happened to your face? It's so messed up."

"He's my boyfriend," Stacey slurred. "He's lost his boat."

"You guys are going to have to take off if you can't be mellow."

Tom pulled Curry to his feet. "We gotta go now."

"Don't kill my vibe, Tom," Curry protested. "Meet Kim, she's really nice."

"Yeah relax, no one is coming," Kim said.

"You have no idea." Tom pointed to the cliff. "You have to get out of here and never tell anyone you saw us."

"Where are we going to go?" Brew asked.

"Move!" Tom said. "We only have a few seconds before they get here. Stacey, you stay here, they don't know you are with us.

When we are out of sight go to your car."

"Come on, guys." Stacey threw her beer into the fire. "You need me. Don't leave me. Its a lame party. "

A partier waved a piece of burning driftwood at Stacey. "Speak for yourself, little girl. We were having a good time until you showed up."

The helicopter came over the top of the cliff, lowered down, and hovered above them. Lights shone down, blinding them. Reflexively they crouched and shielded their eyes. The noise was deafening. Sparks from the fire flew around them, singeing their hair.

"Stay where you are," a voice from the helicopter boomed. "You are in violation of state code 602."

One of the party goer's clapped a flying spark out of her hair. "What the hell? We didn't do anything."

"How did they find us?" Stacey yelled.

"Worms," Tom shouted back over the chop of the helicopter. Don't show your face. It's not you they're after. Run!"

"Do they know it's us?" Curry asked.

Brew patted his pants and took out his cell phone. "I left it on."

Tom grabbed the phone from Brew and threw it into the water. "You idiot!"

"I told him they could track us if he left it on," Curry said. "I even took the battery."

"I had an extra."

Curry hit Brew in the back of the head. "That's the dumbest thing you have ever done."

Stacey spat sand. "They have no idea who we are. Just wave them on."

"We're staying," one of the girls said. "We'll just get a ticket and call it done. It's only like sixty bucks."

"The only way out of here is up the stairs and back to the parking lot," Curry said. "The fact is, running along cliffs at night is stupid. We can fight them here, we can't fight falling off a cliff."

Brew grabbed Tom's arm and shouted into his ear. "What about the sea cave in the cliff wall?"

"Sorry, this is none of our business, we're out of here," one of the girls said.

The light from the helicopter seemed to intensify. Tom shielded his face as sand whipped up, biting his eyes. The partiers were running for the stairs when one fell flat, face down in the sand. The other two turned back to pick her up. Another girl's head snapped to the side and she fell, the other turned with her hands held out. Tom could see, but not hear the scream on her lips. Several flashes of light erupted from the helicopter. He looked back to the girls, they lay in a heap.

"Stay where you are!" the voice boomed again.

"They know it's us," Brew said.

"Ding dong, hello." Stacey said, and ran to the water. "Out there?"

Didn't she see, didn't she understand? Tom lunged for her and pulled her back. "Are you brain dead? They killed those people."

Bouncing lights appeared on the ridge above, they were moving fast towards the stairs.

"The boat!" Brew shouted. "I can't believe it. It's real!"

Two hundred feet offshore the diving boat rocked silently with the waves. Stacey thrust her fist in the air and cheered. "Do you believe me now, my doubting followers? If it wasn't for the lights on the helicopter, we would have never seen it."

Tom drew them into a huddle. "We have to go out to the boat."

"What good is it to us now?" Curry asked. "It's way out there. We'll never make it."

"We gotta swim out there."

"But they'll shoot us," Brew said.

"The fact is, it's January," Curry said despairingly. "We're gonna freeze and drown before we get there."

Brew fell to his knees. "We're dead."

"We can't give up." Tom pulled Brew to his feet. "Even if we die. We gotta try."

"Call of duty says no way to your shit," Curry said. "There is a limit to how much BS a human can absorb before they call it quits."

"Give up and just die?" Tom pulled Curry in close by his shirt. "Don't you want to get sponsored? If you give up, it will never happen."

"Yeah, come on, you plebeian skater!" Stacey laughed. "You can't give up."

"Don't you care that we'll die?" Brew asked.

"No, she doesn't," Tom said. "It's what I've been telling you for years. She's bat shit crazy."

"Bat shit crazy!" Stacey yelled. "That's me! Come on, we only get one chance at life. Make it happen!"

The soldiers amassed at the top of the stairs. The beams from their flashlight trained on Tom. They bounded down the stairs with amazing speed.

"Swimming equals death. They'll shoot us too," Curry said.

"A bullet is certain, drowning is without a doubt. If you can choose your death which would you have?" Tom asked.

"We'll freeze to death in a minute."

"Hurry, they're almost down the stairs," Tom said. "We have to do this together."

"Why haven't they shot us yet?" Brew asked.

Tom kicked off his boots, threw his hoodie down and held up the metallic oval as he waded out into the water. "They want this and I'm not giving it up. I'm swimming out to the boat. They think we'll die in the water so they won't waste the bullets. Come on, we have to try!"

"I'm taking my chances with them," Brew said. "I don't want to drown."

Stacey took off her shoes and waded into the water. "He's right. Don't let the fear in. We will live forever."

Brew smashed at the sand and followed her out into the water.

"This is so stupid, come on, Curry."

Eric Johnson

## CHAPTER TWENTY-FIVE
## YOU KILLED BREW

Black in the night, the salt water bit at their limbs. It was cold and sweet. They bobbed their way out to the boat. Soldiers kicked up sand as they ran and gathered at the waters edge. The helicopter hovered over. The voice from the loudspeaker called. "Turn back now. You are in serious danger!"

"We gotta swim faster, I'm freezing!" Brew spit water. "My legs are cramping!"

"I can't feel my arms." Stacey fought to stay afloat.

Curry gulped for breath as he trod water. "I didn't know I could swim."

Back on the beach, more than twenty soldiers stood, waiting for their return.

"Keep going," Tom said. "Don't listen to them."

"I can't," Brew gasped for air. "I can't feel my legs."

"We're almost to the boat."

"I can't make it," Brew croaked. "So cold!"

"Don't give up," Tom said. "It's not that cold, you can make it."

"Stop complaining," Curry bobbed.

"Turn back!" the man in the helicopter ordered.

"Help," Stacey gasped, and went under.

"Tom! Something. . . Touched my. . ." Brew went down.

"Get them!" Tom shouted, and went after Brew without a thought.

By the light of the helicopter's search beams, Tom and Curry searched for Stacey and Brew. They hadn't sunk as deep as feared. Stacey's pink hair waved like ribbons in the water. Brew's skate pads floated at his side. Their arms and legs stretched out, caught in the seaweed of the cove.

Tom grabbed Stacey and Curry took hold of Brew, pulling them towards the boat. The light from the helicopter moved off.

Above them the bottom of the boat appeared. Surfacing, they gulped for air to ease burning lungs.

Tom held on to the side fender and pulled Stacey in tightly.

Curry surfaced holding Brew. "He's not breathing."

"Get in the boat! I don't think she is either."

They worked their way around the boat. It had to be more than sixty feet long. A diving platform hung off the stern. Tom pulled Stacey aboard first and lay her on the deck.

"Help me," Curry said. "Brew is hella heavy. Pull, I can barely move my hands."

They rolled Brew onto deck. "Man, he's not breathing," Tom said. "What are we going to do. Your mom's a doctor; what do we do?"

Curry turned Brew on his side, water came out of his mouth. "We gotta breath for him. Get him breathing."

"I don't know how," Tom said.

"Man, he drowned." Curry listened to his chest. "He has no pulse."

"What should I do?" Tom panicked.

Curry blew air into Brew's mouth and started chest compressions. "Don't tell no one I put my mouth on Brew." He counted to fifteen as he pumped his friend's chest, then gave more three short breaths. "Find blankets. We have to get them warm."

Scuba gear and electronics stacked the shelves of the ship's cabin. There were no blankets to use. Tom grabbed a pile of wetsuits and ran back on deck. "All I could find were these."

"Cover Stacey, and check if she's breathing."

The wet suits were clumsy, making it hard to cover her. Her neck was ice cold as he felt for a pulse. "She is!"

"Dude, help me. I need you to do the compressions. My arms are hella tired." Curry blew more air into Brew's lungs. "Okay, go."

"Tell me when to stop?"

Between giving breaths Curry said, "Didn't they see us? We

swam hella far under the water."

"I don't know how we did it," Tom said. "We need to get the boat started and get out of here."

"Come on, Brew! Breathe!" Curry blew more air into Brew's lungs. He pushed Tom to the side and hit Brew hard in the chest. "Breathe!"

Tom fell back, landing on Stacey.

"He's not going to make it," Curry said. "If he isn't conscious by now, he's not coming back."

Tom learned in to start compressions again. "Do it again. Don't stop trying."

"Man, he's dead." Curry pushed Tom back. "I'm done."

"No!" Tom shoved Curry, pounded Brews chest, and blew air into his lungs. "We can't let him die."

"He's dead," Curry said. "We tried. It's is your fault. You killed Brew."

"Don't you think I know?" Tom rested his hands on Brew's body. "I made you guys help me. I'm sorry. I'm so sorry."

"Tom, saying you're sorry isn't going to bring him back. You killed us."

"We're not dead yet."

"We will be once those DHS dudes get us."

"Damn it!" Tom cried, and hit Brews chest, before blowing into his lungs again. "Live!"

Curry held Tom's arms stopping him. "Tom! It's no good. He's dead."

"I can't give up, if I do I've failed you."

"Man, it's over!"

"We're not a quitters!" Tom squeezed Brew's shirt. "And I'm not going to sit here and go without a fight. I vowed to win. Get a suit on, swim away, and hide. Just leave. If I fail, I will be responsible for your death too."

"You already are responsible." Curry knocked Tom's hand away. "Don't think it makes you special. If we give up now, then you are doubly responsible."

"I was willing to risk my life, and yours to find the truth."

"So now I have to save you," Curry said. "Is that it? Don't make me have to save you. We were your sidekicks remember? You were the leader. So act like it. Why is it always up to me?"

Tom took out the metallic oval, put it on Brew's chest and sobbed. "This has to do something, otherwise they wouldn't want it so bad."

"What are you doing?" Curry asked.

"How do you think we were able to swim so far?"

"Because we are superior sportsmen. Our endurance is way above average from skating pools. Our bodies are learn mean skating machines."

"Think about it. I was right. The oval is alien technology."

The oval buzzed and its hooks shot out, sinking into Brew's flesh. It glowed red. Suddenly, his body convulsed. He threw up water, balled up, and rolled on to his side gasping for air.

Tom jumped. "He's alive!"

They dragged Brew and Stacey down into the cabin, and laid them out on a double bunk together.

"Man, they are frozen," Curry said. "We need to get some blankets on them. I think they are hypothermic. Damn it, my mom would know what to do."

"You knew CPR." Tom picked up Stacey. "She's barely breathing now."

"I'm not an EMT." Curry dragged Brew to the crew cabin. "I just listened to dinner conversation."

Tom tore open the cabinets, searching for anything he could use. "We have to figure it out. How do we keep them keep warm?"

"Use your body heat," Curry said. "My mom always joked that if we were trapped in the woods in winter, I would have to get naked and huddle up with my cousin under sticks and leaves."

"Then we have to get their clothes off," Tom said.

"No way, dude."

"I'm not asking again." Tom unfastened Stacey's clothes.

"You get Brew." Curry stopped Tom. "I can use it as insurance you won't tell anyone I did CPR on him."

Tom nodded and pulled Brew's shirt off. "They don't have to be totally naked. Do they?"

"Yeah, and Brew's going to be so pissed," Curry smiled.

"Dude, we're saving his life. He'll forgive us."

"There has to be a heater somewhere."

"The copter's way over there above the cliffs."

"They're on to us. There's a boat approaching."

Tom pushed Brew on top of Stacey and grimaced. "That's got to be the boat I saw from the cliff."

Curry took a spear gun off the wall and handed it to Tom. "Here, take it."

"They have guns; a spear gun's no match."

"Take it, No-beard, we're up to some pirate shit. We'll ambush them when they board us."

"You're fantasizing. What if we start the engine and drive away?"

"You know how to drive a boat?"

"It can't be hard. Just throttle forward and don't hit anything."

Tom and Curry climbed up to the helm. The Coast Guard entered the cove, gliding across the water at amazing speed.

Curry pulled at Tom. "Dude, they are going to ram us. Hurry!"

## CHAPTER TWENTY-SIX
## DON'T SHOOT

A siren wailed as blue and red lights started to flash. Floodlights illuminated the cabin, blinding Tom and Curry as the Coast Guard patrol boat pulled along side. Shielding his eyes, Tom fumbled to find the ignition. Power lit the console, and the radio hissed static. He jammed the throttle lever all the way forward. The engines roared, churning the water and pushing the boat forward with unexpected force.

Curry fell backwards and Tom grappled with the wheel to keep control. He turned the boat hard to starboard, pointing it out towards open sea.

"This is the Coast Guard. Power down and hold for instructions," came over the radio.

Curry climbed to his feet. "We can't let them on board."

The chopper flew in a tight circle overhead, shining its light down on them.

"Prepare to surrender. This is a law enforcement operation. Failure to comply will result in the immediate seizure of your vessel."

"Get us out of here!" Curry screamed.

"Power down immediately and prepare to be boarded. You will not be asked again!" the Coast Guard warned.

"I'm trying," Tom yelled. "They're cutting me off. We're going to hit them. Hold on!"

Flashes of light erupted from the bow of the other boat, and the windows in the helm room shattered. Tom and Curry ducked away from the splintering glass.

"I can't see where we are going."

The boat came to a sudden stop with a boom. Metal screeched against metal as the two vessels collided and crunched together. Tom and Curry were thrown against the wall of the helm as the boat's stern rose up and fishtailed to port.

Dazed, Tom fumbled to get his hands on the wheel. He pulled himself up, but it didn't feel like the boat was going anywhere. The engine had stopped.

Curry rolled on the floor, he held his head in the flickering light. A gash crossed his forehead and blood flowed down his face. "Get us out of here."

Tom turned the key; the engine whirred. "Come on. Come on."

Nothing. He tried again and again. Outside the helm room, boots hit the deck, and voices shouted to secure a line and pull the boat in.

Light flooded into the helm. "Get up Curry, I need you."

"You have ten seconds to come out with your hands up," the guard ordered from the deck of the other ship.

"What do we do?"

The helicopter backed off and circled high above.

"Eight."

Curry clamped his hand to cover his wound. "If they arrest us we are dead."

"Six."

"We can't give up."

"I'm hurt. Maybe they won't kill us. What if we've been wrong?"

"Four."

"After all we have seen?" Tom gazed at Curry. He was suddenly filled with doubt. He looked around, trying not to let his emotions register on his face. What if he was wrong, his dad was at home like Worms said, and nothing was what he thought. He didn't see a way out.

"Two."

"Wait!" Tom yelled. "Were coming out."

Tom helped Curry up. The light from the patrol boat was blinding, making it hard to see. He opened the cabin door. "Don't shoot. I'm just a kid. Don't shoot!"

"Move slowly down onto the deck, do it now!" the guard

behind the light ordered.

"My friend is hurt, he hit his head real bad." Tom held Curry and stepped down. "I don't think he can make it without help."

"Don't stop, or I will shoot. Come down the stairs slowly," the guard said.

Tom stepped cautiously down onto the deck. "Okay. My friend's hurt. Don't shoot."

"Get down on your knees. Now!" the guard ordered.

Two men stood on deck; one trained his gun on Tom as the other approached. "Where is the artifact?" the guard demanded.

Tom sank down. "I don't know what you are talking about."

The guard kicked him in the chest, sending him onto his back. Before he could react, he was flipped over onto his stomach. A knee pressed into his back. "The tooth, and the oval. Where are they?"

Tom strained to speak. "I lost them in the water when I swam out here."

"Don't lie to me, kid." He pressed his gun to the back of Tom's head, holding him down by the barrel and searching him. He pulled the oval out of Tom's pocket. "You've been more trouble than you are worth, kid. Now it's time to say goodbye."

Brew's defiant cry came from the passenger cabin, and a red object blurred past. A clunk and a yelp came from behind Tom and a fire extinguisher clattered across the deck, rolling past him.

The guard who had pinned him slackened his grip, distracted by Brew's attack. He wasn't going to be a victim. He flailed his arms free and did the hardest push up of his life and twisted over onto his back, punching him in the jaw to knock him over. He failed.

"Make this easy on yourself," the man grunted. He scythed his hand, clamping it around Tom's neck, and raised his gun at Brew.

Tom gasped for breath, strained his head forward, and sank his teeth into the hand around his throat.

Brew burst out from below the deck cabin, leaped through the air and tackled the man, knocking him off Tom before he could get a shot off.

Tom crawled away towards the cabin, kicking as hard and fast as he could in the direction of his assailants crotch, narrowly missing Brew. He hit true. The man's eyes bugged out and his face went pale.

The guard who had been hit by the extinguisher was holding his head; he staggered, and fell overboard.

Shots were fired from the cutter and Tom dove, rolling towards the cabin hatch. A bullet impacted just above his head sparking off the metal frame as he dropped down into the cabin. If they were going to kill him he was going to kill them first. All his life he'd been told to be good. Don't fight, don't get mad, talk about it. Listen to authority. Enough! Find a peaceful solution. Bullshit! If peace worked, then how come there were so many wars? He scrambled for the spear gun. It was under the wetsuits next to Stacey. He took it and ran to the hatch. Kneeling on the stairs, he took aim at a third man who jumped onto the deck, moving to stop Brew. Tom fired.

The spear pierced the third man's neck, sticking right through. Blood sprayed. The third man's eyes bugged out of his head as he grappled with the spear, trying to pull it free. He cried out, but choked a sickening gurgle deep in his throat as his face paled, and collapsed and convulsed on the deck.

Tom felt dizzy, almost sick. He couldn't believe it.

Brew and the first guard continued to wrestle, and he darted across the deck after the fire extinguisher.

The man now held a knife in his hand. Brew in his weakened state was no match for him. Tom raised the fire extinguisher to strike, but he pinned Brew to the deck and put the knife to his throat. "It's over," he panted. "Make a wrong move and he's dead."

"Okay, you win," Tom said, but charged forward, catching him off guard, swinging the fire extinguisher like he was in a batting

169

cage, hitting him square in the head. He collapsed and lay still on the deck.

"Start the engine, Curry. Start it!" Tom yelled, and took the metallic oval from the man's pocket.

A flash and bang grenade went off next to him, he staggered and couldn't see. His ears rang and something ripped across his arm. Through searing pain, he yelled, "Go, Curry!"

Brew stood up as Tom fell to the deck. "Get down!"

Brew wobbled with the rock of the ship. A rapid pop of shots came from the cutter; Brew took a hit. He stood almost unaware of what had happened, but as he stepped forward he fell. The bullet had been aimed for his head, but had gone astray, catching him in the leg. The movement of the two vessels on the waves saved him. Tom scrambled across the deck, dove for Brew, and pulled him down. Curry rammed the boat into the Coast Guards, pushing it out of the way. The helicopter maneuvered above. Flashes of light erupted from its side and splinters of wood danced around them. Tom pulled Brew across the deck and down below into the cabin.

Eric Johnson

CHAPTER TWENTY-SEVEN
CURRY AND BOOZE?


The staccato thud and ricochet of bullets against the wood and metal of the ship's deck halted. The engine roared. Blood slicked the floor around Brew. Tom didn't know how to tell if an artery was hit or not. There was more blood than he'd ever seen. He squeezed Brew's leg, trying to stop the bleeding. "Stay with me!"

Brew screamed and kicked and tried to sit up, "Did I get him?"

"Hold still. I need to see if the bullet went through." He felt the back of Brew's leg for an exit, his finger found a hole. He grabbed a wetsuit and tied one of its legs around his tight. "Stay down."

Brew tried to high five Tom. "I totally battled naked!"

"Effective, but not pretty my friend. Stay still, you've been shot again,"

"Dude, your arm's totally bleeding." Brew smiled. "You've been shot too. Now we really are bros."

Tom vaguely remembered the sting, and now it started to hurt. "Shut up, you're delirious. It's only a graze."

"What happened?" Brew asked.

"You saved me."

"Last I remember I was going under. Then I'm naked covered in a bunch of wet suits next to Stacey, and they were going to kill you. I don't know which of those was worse!"

"We had a few problems, but don't worry about that. And just forget about the Stacey thing."

"My leg hurts like hell."

"Stacey has pills, she always has pills. I need you to hold your leg tight."

"What about booze? They used it in the olden days."

"I don't think it's a good idea right now."

Tom put Brew's hands on the wet suit. "Squeeze here. I mean it. If we are lucky, you won't bleed to death."

"Righteousness. I live to skate another day!"

"Were you worried I would let you die? Hold tight while I search for something better."

"Dude, the pain," Brew relaxed his grip, and blood welled up.

"Brew, you need to hold that leg tight. It's more important to stop the bleeding." A first aid kit hung on the wall. There was nothing useful for a gunshot in it. He searched the compartments and came up with some clothes. They would have to do.

"What should we do with her?" Brew asked.

Tom tore a shirt into strips. "You have to listen to me. Put your hands here and press hard while I tie it off with these. When the bleeding slows, check to see if she's alive, and get her dressed." He pulled the makeshift bandage tightly, and the bleeding almost stopped. "I gotta go check Curry. Can you manage? Keep the pressure here and here."

"What happened to him?"

"He was hit in the head. Holler if you start to bleed again, okay?"

Brew nodded, and Tom went out of the hatch. The helicopter was following them at a distance. The man on the deck lay motionless and would be a problem if he woke up. He grabbed a rope to tie him up, but his body was unusually cold. He checked for a pulse. Nothing. His jaw tensed, he had killed two people, although it was in self defense, in one day. The body rocked back and forth with the rolling of the waves. How could he have done it? What was he to do?

City lights glowed on the horizon, they were heading out to sea. He had to push his feelings aside and get the job done. The man had taken what he called the artifact. He searched the body and pulled it out from the front pocket. He had a knife, extra ammunition, zip ties, and mace. He took all of it.

First things first; Curry needed attention. Tom was the only one who could help him. He climbed up the stairs to the helm. Broken glass crunched under his feet. Curry lay bleeding on the floor under the wheel. Tom held a rag against his head. "Let me stop the bleeding. How many fingers am I holding up?"

"One, you fucker. Those men weren't Coast Guard. The Coast Guard doesn't just start shooting."

"We got one on the deck. He's dead."

"How?"

"Doesn't matter. It was Brew who saved us, but he got shot in the leg."

"Again? Is it bad?"

"I stopped the bleeding. I think he'll be okay. He beaned one guy, and I got the other two."

"Was that psycho DHS agent on the boat?"

"I don't know. Just his lackeys, I think. You got us out of there. That's what matters."

"He's not going to stop. I mean like he can't until he gets us. We are the only witnesses to the reporter's execution except for his men, and they probably think he was right."

"Here's the first aid kit. I gotta go take care of the man on the deck. I need you to steer."

"Wait," Curry said, pointing out the window. "There's another boat coming our way."

"We'll deal with that when it gets here."

Tom went down to the deck. The man's body was gone. He ran back up to the wheelhouse. "He's gone."

"You said he was dead."

Tom ran down to the crew cabin. "He's gone."

"Who?" Brew asked.

"The man on the deck is gone. His body is gone. We gotta find him. Stay here."

Tom combed the ship. He wasn't anywhere to be found. He went back to the wheelhouse.

"Did you find him?" Curry asked. "I can't see anything from here. It's too dark."

"He's not on the boat unless there's a secret compartment we don't know about. I checked every hatch I could find."

"Then where did he go, overboard?"

"What if he slipped past you."

" I have a feeling we are not alone."

They barreled down the stairs, through the hatch and into the cabin. "Brew! Stacey!"

"What?"

"Did you find him?" Brew asked.

"He's gone," Tom said.

"He's nowhere," Curry said.

Stacey sat up. "I'm freezing."

Tom and Brew stared at Stacey.

"You almost drowned," Curry said.

"Where are my clothes?" She stood up. "There better be a good reason why I'm naked. Hey, what did you guys do?"

Brew blushed. "Nothing like that. Put the wetsuit on."

Curry stared at Stacey as she got into a wet suit. Brew turned his back. Tom searched the cabin.

"See what happens when I'm not around to take care of you," Stacey said.

"Who saved who?" Curry asked her. "If I remember it was you who almost drowned. We saved you."

"I knew we could make it to the boat. So where are we?"

"We're in the ocean," Brew said.

"Where are we going?" Stacey asked.

"How should I know? No one is steering," Curry replied.

Tom and Curry ran to the helm. Stacey faced Brew. "So, why am I naked?"

Brew blushed even more. "Don't worry, I was naked next to you."

"You naughty boy."

"F-for warmth," Brew stammered. "We were both out cold, and totally frozen. They thought it would warm us up."

She took a step towards Brew. "Really?"

## CHAPTER TWENTY-EIGHT
## FIRE IN THE HOLE

The radio blared another message to power down and wait for instructions. The light from the controls illuminated Tom. He grabbed the wheel. "It must be prerecorded."

Curry hit the radio off. "Lucky there isn't anything to hit out here."

The ship jolted. Tom jumped. "What was that?"

"I spoke too soon."

"Don't jinx us," Tom said. "It was a wave. We need to go faster, but I got the boat full throttle.

Curry pointed aft. "The helicopter will be here any second, and the boat is right behind. We're almost out of gas too. We need some place to go."

"I can't see the lights on the coast anymore." Brew strained his eyes. "Do you know how to navigate?"

Tom looked at a compass on the dash. "Nope. I could use the GPS, but it has a bullet hole in the screen. I don't think it matters, they will catch us again."

Brew hopped into the wheelhouse with Stacey's help. "We got a problem."

"Tell me about it." Curry dug through cabinets. "The fact is we are lost at sea, have a boat closing in on us, and our navigation instruments are dead."

"No, dude. It's worse," Brew said.

"Worse? How could it be worse?"

"We're sinking. That's why the boat is slowing down."

Tom pushed the throttle forward.

Stacey put her hand on Tom's shoulder. "We aren't sinking fast, we can make it to shore."

"You didn't hear me, did you," Curry said. "Our navigation equipment is broken."

"That's the north star." Stacey pointed Curry. "If you steer the ship toward it and a little to the right we will hit land."

"How would you know when we are totally lost?" Curry asked.

Stacey arced her hand outlining the coastline. "Don't you ever look at a map to see where you are? Right coast Atlantic. Left Pacific. The coast curves eastward from Razor Point."

"How long do we have before we sink?" Brew asked.

"I'm a skater, not a sailor. How should I know?" Curry shrugged.

Brew took a deep breath. "That's trouble."

"Stacey." Tom stepped towards the door. "You search the front of the ship, I'll search the back. We need to find anything we can to defend ourselves with. The other ship is getting close. Curry, I need you to steer north.

Brew looked at Tom. "What do I do?"

"Nothing." Tom frowned. "I don't want you to start bleeding again. We'd have to take time away from getting the defenses ready."

Curry opened a case attached to the wall. "Flare gun and four rounds. Here."

"Give it to Brew," Tom said. "Brew, your job is to shoot the helicopter. It has to be open for them to shoot us. So we can shoot them back."

"Like in a war movie. Aye aye, Sarge!" Brew acknowledged with a salute.

Stacey reached up above the wheelhouse door. "Fire ax!"

"Did the dude drop his gun?" Curry asked.

"I bet there's more spears down in the crew cabin." Brew looked hopeful.

"Stacey, never mind searching." Tom stopped her by the arm. "Help Brew down to the cabin. I'll look for that gun on the deck."

Brew moaned as Stacey helped him down the stairs to the cabins.

"What if I tie off the wheel and help look for the gun?" Curry asked.

"Do it," Tom nodded.

"I want you to know this scares the hell out of me," Curry said.

"Me too."

Tom went down to the deck. He found the gun in a corner. The last time he tried to use one, it was empty. Safety third, he thought, and found the safety catch, pointed the gun away from the cabin, and squeezed the trigger. Nothing. He pushed it back and squeezed. Bang!

"What was that?" Curry called down from the wheelhouse.

"Found it." Tom waved the gun showing Curry.

"As a matter of fact I have used a gun before, and am a better shot. You should give that here." Curry held his hand out.

"Not a chance," Tom replied. "Did you get the wheel tied off? We need to get down to the cabin and barricade it."

Tom and Curry entered the crew cabin. There was three inches of water on the floor.

"We're lucky the engine is still going." Curry kicked the water, splashing Brew. "I would think the engine compartment should have flooded by now."

"Here are more spears." Brew handed them to Tom.

"Brew, try to get into the wetsuit," Tom opened a closet and handed Brew a suit. "In case we have to get in the water. We need to have the tanks ready."

"I can't. I'll bleed out once I get wet."

"Duct tape and plastic bags should keep the wound dry." Curry bandaged him. "Everyone get suits on."

"You know how to scuba dive, Tom?" Brew asked.

"I saw it on a TV show, it didn't look difficult," Tom opened a tool box.

Brew struggled to get his leg into the wetsuit. "We won't last long in the water. It's too cold."

"It still gives us a chance." Tom helped Brew. "The suits will help."

"We're way out to sea." Stacey turned. "She's an unforgiving mistress. Way more than I am."

"Let see how far we can get before they get here." Brew smiled. "If we get close enough to shore, we can swim."

Curry turned the ship east. "Not with your leg like that."

"No." Tom stood. "When the other ship gets here we are going to take it."

"Like pirates?" Brew asked.

"Just like pirates." Tom nodded. "They will never expect it."

"Yeah, they will," Stacey paced. "They killed those girls on the beach. They'll kill us too."

"No, they won't." Curry followed her with his eyes. "We play the "we're just kids" card. No one likes to kill kids. Then we jump them."

"That's not true; look at what they have done." Brew raised his eyebrows. "You're in denial."

"It will work. It has to work." Tom stood straight. "We are out in the Pacific. Where else do we go?"

Stacey stepped back from the hatch. "They're almost here."

"Help me pull the life raft down here," Tom said.

Tom and Curry went onto the deck unfastened the life raft from the mountings.

Curry pulled it below deck. "It says rescue pod not a raft. Pods are small, I don't trust it."

"It works for me. You can swim if you don't like it," Tom said.

Brew dug through a hideaway in the back of the cabin. "I bet they are going to come in shooting."

"Don't be in a place where they can see you if they stand in the hatchway." Tom pulled up a mattress and leaned it against the port window. "Take cover and ambush them when the get on board."

"Yeah, like, hide behind the walls in here," Curry said.

Stacey stepped back. "The water is rising faster; it's going to be up to my knees soon."

"Brew see if you can get a shot at the helicopter from the hatch when it gets here," Tom said.

178

Eric Johnson

"But, if they don't see us." Brew raised his index finger. "They will board and won't be able to shoot from the helicopter."

"Yeah." Curry pulled at the sleeves of his wetsuit. "Turtle the situation."

Stacey searched a cupboard. "Spoken like a true chicken."

"Don't call me chicken, you pink haired freak. This better work," Curry said.

There was no announcement. The Coast Guard rammed into the side of their boat. Wood snapped, the boat jolted, and the engine cut out. Flash bang grenades were tossed onto the deck first, then down into the cabin. They covered their ears and squeezed their eyes shut. The concussion reverberated around the cabin. A canister spewing gas bounced in, stinging their eyes and making them cough.

Tom grabbed the face mask respirator and breathed. He picked the smoking canister up from the water and threw it out of the hatch. "Get the masks on!"

Shadows were cast down into the cabin from up on deck. A man appeared in the doorway. Brew shot. The flare propelled forward. It hit the man in the chest, knocking him down on to the cabin stairs. The cabin glowed red, and the flare billowed gray smoke. Another man appeared in the hatch, shooting his gun. He grabbed the fallen man and pulled the him out onto the deck.

Boots tromped across the deck. "Fire in the hole!" a man cried.

Orange fire bloomed in the hatch way with a roar. Tom looked for a fire extinguisher. It was on deck.

"Burn us out," Curry's eyes narrowed. "Make it look like an accident. How typical. Not very creative, if you ask me."

"We're going to burn to death," Brew said. "I don't want to burn to death, and if I go in the water my leg will bleed. I'll bleed to death."

"They'll shoot us if we go on deck," Curry said. "Even if we make it into the water, the combination of blood and noise will bring sharks. We'll be eaten by sharks after we are burned, shot,

179

and drowned."

"Relax, guys, the boat will sink before it burns," Stacey said. "We can close the door. That'll keep the sharks out. If we are lucky, we will only sink sixty feet. If not, the sea floor drops down 12,000 feet at the Farallon trench. But it depends on where we are in the bay."

"We will be trapped on the boat," Brew said. "We'll be pulled down to the bottom. Our tanks will run out or air, and we will be crushed under the pressure of the ocean."

"This is insane. I'm swimming for it," Curry said.

Fire lit the cabin window, and the Coast Guard boat backed off.

"Shut up and listen," Tom said. "We need rules if we are going to make it out of here alive. Rule number one, don't be afraid. That's is what Stacy is saying. If we go down with the ship, and we use the air tanks, we can wait an hour. When they go away, we swim out, grab the inflatable rescue pod, and use it to get to shore."

"That's not what I meant," Stacey said.

"Only if they go away, and we don't sink 12,000 feet down." Brew breathed rapidly.

"Man, I knew I should have listened to my mother," Curry said. "You're forgetting about the currents. They'll take us back to Razor Point. That's the last place we want to go."

"You just figured that out, Mr. I'm going to get sponsored," Stacey said.

"I'll bleed to death. There's no way I can live through that. I can't swim. I can't do anything."

"The water's coming in faster," Stacey said. "They must have made the hole bigger when they hit."

"Going down with the ship is a bad idea," Curry said. "We need to plug the hole."

"There's two feet of water in here. Do you see the hole? Would you know how to fix it?" Stacey asked.

"Get the tanks on," Tom ordered. "We need to be prepared for when we go under."

"I don't know how to," Brew said.

Tom pulled the wet suit hood over Brew's head and handed him a rebreather. "When the water is over your head, put the regulator in your mouth and breath slowly, don't panic."

A ring of fire lit the cabin hatch.

"The ceiling's blistering," Brew said. "It's smoldering."

"Forget the fire, try to breathe off the roof for as long as you can," Tom said. "We need to conserve the air in our tanks."

"Aren't these suits supposed to keep you warm?" Curry chattered. "I bet we are going to freeze to death. Like when we swam out to this boat."

"You and Tom were fine," Stacey said. "It was me and Brew who couldn't take the cold."

"Yeah, that's because me and Tom are more virulent."

"How did you and Curry make it to the boat? What's different about you?"

Tom held up the metallic oval. "Both Curry and I used it."

"Vindicated, Stacey. The dupe is on you for tricking me into using that."

"I offered to do it first."

Tom gave Stacey the oval. "It's how we saved Brew. We will survive."

Stacey winced as the hooks sank in. "Now what?"

"We go under."

The boat listed and the bow rose up. Water closed over the roof of the cabin forming a pocket of air. They slipped under the surface.

## CHAPTER TWENTY-NINE
## DON'T PANIC

Out of the starlight and into the black of the night sea, the boat sank. Ballasts burst; seams and welds popped, compressed by the increasing pressure. The high water mark grew higher. With a sickening wrenching sound, the crossbar supports crumpled, and water spurted in though newly formed holes. Debris gathered in the center of the swirling water.

Brew flung himself against the wall a shelf collapsed under his weight. "I'm scared."

Capturing Stacey, Brew, and Curry's attention, Tom's voice shook in the dwindling pocket of air, "Push the fear out of your mind. Keep it down. We will make it."

"No one will ever know what happened to us," Brew said mournfully. "My parents will never know I died. Why do they have to travel so much, don't they love me?"

Stacey caressed Brew's cheek with her hand. "Our spirits will be together forever if we die."

"Our souls," Curry said. "Co-mingling together forever in eternity? Not going to happen. Dying on my skateboard is how I'm going to go."

"Is there a promised land?" Brew cried. "Or are we on a journey to nowhere?"

"There's no way we could have foreseen this happening," Tom said. "Everything we did up until now has led us here. We had choices, we made them, and we are still alive."

"Yeah there were choices," Curry said. "Like when you rammed the other boat. Didn't you know when two boats collide in the night like ours did, they sink?"

"They set us on fire," Brew said. "They shot us."

"Shut up, Curry," Tom said. "You were at the wheel."

"That's not the way I remember it."

Tom ignored him. "Listen, Brew. . ."

Eric Johnson

"No," Brew said. "I don't see how are are going to get out of this."

"Just because you are afraid," Curry cut in. "Doesn't mean you have to skate towards death. Pull your pads tight and float backside air off the vert, dude. Live large."

"That's the dumbest philosophy ever, Curry." Stacey splashed water at him.

Brew's face twisted, his eyes shook in their sockets. Stacey held his hand. "We're not floating. We're sinking. I feel so weak. I'm bleeding again."

"Pull yourself together," Tom said. "If you don't calm down, you will bleed faster and use all of our oxygen. Don't doubt for a moment that we'll get out of this. Curry, see what you can do to stop his bleeding."

"In water?"

"Just try."

Through the porthole window, the helicopter's spot light faded as they went under. Brew's teeth chattered. Curry held Brew's leg above the water, keeping pressure on the wound. Stacey held Brew tightly.

Hearing their breathing, feeling the movements of the sinking ship and the pressure of the sea against his body, Tom crossed his fingers. They were out of control, plunging deep into the ocean.

A porthole cracked and water sprayed in. The fragile sanctuary of the cabin came to an end. Brew's head whipped from side to side. Stacey took his head in her hands and stared into his eyes. "We can do it, Brew. You can do it. Do it for me."

Tom looked at Curry, his eyes were closed and he breathed slowly. "Breathe slowly like Curry, Brew. See what he's doing, slow deep breaths."

A mattress floated in the center of the cabin. Their hearts slowed, and their limbs became numb. The cold water sucked at their strength. They held their heads in the dwindling air pocket, waiting to the last moment before they had switch to the air tanks.

Tom's ears popped, and he looked at the depth meter. Seventy feet. "We're going down slowly."

Curry squeezed Tom's arm. "Dude, if we are over the trench."

Tom spat water. "Conserve air."

Curry gave him the middle finger.

Stars sparkled in front of Toms eyes, his chest felt tight, it felt hard to breathe. It was time. "Air tanks now." He bit the rebreather and submerged.

Tom clicked the flashlight from the emergency kit on. He gave the thumbs up sign to Brew, Curry, and Stacey, hoping they would indicate the same. Brew shook his head no, pointing to his ears. He signaled with his hands to Brew for him to hold his nose and blow to regulate his ears.

Stacey pulled his hand to hers and tapped the dive meter on his wrist. It read ninety feet. Her eyes relayed they were over the trench. They had gone too deep. Thoughts flooded his mind. How long would it be until they hit bottom? If they were sinking into the trench, how far down would be too far to swim to the surface? What was the point of no return for their dive? Would the metallic oval give them the ability to survive if it had kept him from freezing and revived Brew? What else did it do?

The deeper they sank, the closer they moved to each other. The flashlight was the only thing keeping them from complete panic. Drawn to it, they found a single a point of hope keeping the madness of their plan. He pulled them tight; he couldn't give into despair.

Curry bumped his face mask against Tom's and pointed to the dive meter. Tom showed him the depth meter, it read 150 feet. He yelled a bubbly, "Don't panic."

The water absorbed the sound, but Curry understood. A burst of bubbles came from Curry's respirator, and he gave Tom the finger. A sure sign he was all right.

They waited for the boat to hit bottom. Nothing. Out the of windows, the pitch black engulfed them. Pressure increased, squeezing their bodies.

Tom checked their air gauges. Stacey was using her oxygen too fast. Tom took hold of her shoulders; she had to calm down. Brew held his leg as tiny wisps of blood rose and swirled around. He moved as if he was crying out.

Tom turned to Brew, steadied his head in his hand and looked into his eyes, then checked his air gauge. Only twenty minutes of air was left in Brew's tank. It couldn't have been full.

Piercing the silence of the sea, a guttural roar vibrated the water around them. Their skin tingled. They could feel it in their bones. The wreck whipped from side to side, slamming them into the walls like eggs in a tin can. The hull snapped and popped with the sounds of wood and tearing metal. The ship was torn in half, leaving them floating in the dark. They were not alone. They twisted around and clung to together. It was the mermen.

Debris drifted off into the black. Tom pulled Stacey close. How did astronauts feel in the dark of space? The flashlight flickered, Tom shone the light in all directions and caught a glimpse of a tail as it sped past, inches from his face.

Another set of reverberations shook their bodies. In the beam of his flashlight he caught sight of a bright yellow bundle. The emergency pod; they had to have it. Curry swam after it and caught it by a straying rope. From above, a merman came out of the darkness and grabbed Curry, swimming away with him and leaving the trio to free fall alone in the dark. Together they retrieved the pod, but there was nothing they could do.

A light shone up from below, and Curry's silhouette appeared tiny in the distance swimming towards them. Above and behind Curry, the ominous figures of mermen glided, encircling him as if to guide him back to them.

Tom couldn't warn Curry, but he couldn't let the mermen take him. He grasped and pulled at the water, kicking with his legs, urging his body forward. Reaching Curry, he grabbed his arm and swam backwards, pulling him away, but without flippers it was an impossible task, and the mermen closed in.

Seeing the mermen, bubbles erupted from Stacey and Brew's respirators. They clung to the life pod and kicked wildly to get away, but the mermen pulled Tom and Curry back to Stacy and Brew. Tom shone the light into a merman's eyes. They were cold and familiar.

Suddenly he felt hands on his shoulders. Legs wrapped around him and squeezed. Stacey had him in a death grip. They clung together facing mask to mask. Unless he did something fast they wouldn't make it to the surface alive. Desperation set in. He didn't have a choice, and no matter how dangerous it might be, they needed a way to rise to the surface quickly. Death was above, and death below, he pulled the inflate cord on the life pod. It burst open and dragged them up from the depths to the surface rising faster and faster.

Clinging to the pod became difficult, and breathing was painful. Tom's legs cramped, and his eyes pushed from their sockets as the pressure inside his body grew from expanding gas bubbles. They were rising too quickly.

Breaking the surface, their lungs burned and they gulped at the air. The dark blue water roiled and boiled and foamed; waves crashed over them. They pulled themselves into the life pod, writhing in pain from the rapid ascent.

Stacey covered her ears and shook. Tom held her, but pulled back. In the flickering light of the pod's emergency beacon, milky black liquid seeped from a gash in her head and ran down her neck. He felt it between his fingers, viscous and icy. "Let me see." He turned her head to look in her eyes. She didn't respond. "Stacey?"

Brew cried and slapped at his arms and legs. "What's crawling on me? Get it off."

"Stacey!" Tom yelled. "Answer me! Why is your blood black?"

"I can't hear!" she screamed.

There was no time to find out, the situation was dire, pulling everyone together to survive was more important.

Curry laughed and shouted excitedly. "We did not just do that! Do I look like a superhero or what!"

Tom lay back. There was nothing he could do for them. Smoke burned his nose. Between the swells, the flaming carcass of the patrol boat was sinking, pieces of debris floated around the life pod. The Helicopter was gone. Bodies bobbed up and down, supported by life vests. Tom swam out to check for survivors. There were none.

"We did it!" Curry yelled from the life-pod. "That was the craziest ever. How far down were we? Two hundred? Three hundred feet?"

Brew screamed. "Get them off me!"

Curry held Brew's arms. "There's nothing there, Brew. Stop!"

Stacey lay quiet in the life pod, holding the blood back with her fingers in her ears.

Tom pulled himself into the life pod, grabbed a long piece of wreckage and paddled. The flaming wreckage of the patrol boat soon disappeared, but he couldn't tell if he was able to control the direction of the pod. It was no good. The current was too strong to make a difference. "Now we get carried wherever the current takes us."

Curry laughed uncontrollably. "Do you believe it?"

"Curry," Tom said. "Don't lose it on me."

"I'm not losing it, dude," Curry cackled. "When the mermen pulled me away and then let me go, all I could think was I'm too hot for them."

"I need to be ready if we make it near to shore. We'll have to swim for it."

"That's going to be a long time from now, Bro. If we don't get eaten by sharks."

The bottom of the raft jolted up, sending it up into the air. It splashed down, and mermen surfaced around them. One peered

187

into the life pod hissing, then dropped back down into the water. Curry screamed. Its face made no sense, hideous and scaly, its mouth a torn hole. The life-pod bobbed silently.

"We're not going to get to shore, are we?" Brew screamed.

Water flooded in as they were pulled under. The pod acted like a bag, trapping them like kittens tossed from a bridge. Helpless.

The depth meter readout flashed in the dark.

Thirty.

Seventy.

Two hundred.

Five hundred.

The pod tore away, leaving them floating in the silent abyss. Pale light enveloped them from behind. Electricity jolted their flesh, seizing their muscles. Flashes of mermen on the edge of sight scattering. Their descent stopped, leaving them drifting alone.

## CHAPTER THIRTY
## SERIOUSLY?

The light pulsed. Tom tapped Curry's face mask and pulled him in its direction, urging him to follow. Curry's expression under his mask was to monstrous to be concealed. He was losing it. The ocean floor came into view between flashes. A part of Tom wondered if he were losing his mind; his eyes felt like they were going to pop. How deep had they gone?

Stacey and Brew followed. They swam towards the light, past corroding metal drums leaking toxic waste, dumped in the depths away from the prying eyes of environmental groups.

As they neared the beacon, flood lights snapped on, an island of light in the vast blackness.

Squinting in the glare, the light exposed a series of gigantic cylinders connected in a mega structure rose from the sea floor. Skeletons of unknown sea creatures littered the area. Eyeless fish picked at clumps of cartilage that floated directionless in the water.

Brew patted his air gauge, then put his hands to this throat; only five minutes of air remained. His only hope was to find a way into the structure for breathable air, if indeed it contained any.

Underneath the structure, a ring of lights illuminated a downward facing hatch. Tom found and pulled a lever; the hatch lowered with a ladder attached to the inside. He pulled them in. On the wall, a series of buttons glowed. Brew clutched Tom desperately. He bucked and thrashed. Bubbles ceased coming from his respirator. Tom jammed his hand against the control panel. The hatch closed, and the water was pumped out of the chamber.

Brew collapsed to the floor, spitting his respirator out. He was confused, terrified, and unable to understand how or why he was alive. "I," he choked. "Ran. Out of air."

Tom held Brew and checked his leg. "You made it. Breath

easy."

"Man, we was like, flushed down a giant toilet," Curry said.

"I feel so dizzy," Brew said.

"That's the spin cycle of being dragged down into the depths by monsters," Curry said.

Stacey shook. "We gotta get out of here."

Rust stains streaked the walls and the air smelled of moldy fish. "What the hell is this place?" Curry gagged.

"Why do our voices sound like mice?" Brew squeaked, rubbing his throat.

"Deep sea explorers mix air with helium to avoid hypoxia. That's what they use for deep sea dives and stations." Tom studied the room.

"It looks old, really old."

"I swore we were dead," Brew said.

"The oval must have changed us more than we imagined," Tom said to Brew.

"Define okay?" Curry dropped his air tanks. "We sound like Alvin and the Chipmunks, and we have no way of getting back to the surface."

"If you are able to complain, you're okay," Tom said. "We can't just sit here, let's explore."

"Where do we go?" Brew asked.

"Through the door to find out what's on the other side," Tom said.

Together they wrenched the door open. The locking wheel groaned louder than they did. The hinges squealed and gave way suddenly, flying open with a bang.

"We got it," Tom said.

Curry peered out from the decompression chamber. "Where the people?"

Brew looked to Tom. "Turn on the lights."

"They must be saving electricity," Curry said.

"Did you want a parade? Just turn on the lights," Brew said.

Stacey pulled back from the open hatchway. "Now we find out if we are in the monster's lair."

Curry helped Brew stand. "Why would mermen need an underwater building?"

They entered. Racks held diving equipment and archaic instruments. Fine powder covered the floor. Brew pointed to a control panel on the wall and almost fell over. "It looks like a WWII submarine in here."

Curry held Brew up. "You don't know what a sub looks like."

"I read, you know," Brew said.

Stacey cleared her throat. "Excuse me? Not all this stuff looks old."

"Yeah, I doubted it to," Curry said. "They had no idea how to build advanced stuff back then. The hatch we came through was electric, it looked newer than that."

"They didn't have electricity back then, either," Brew said. Curry looked at him and shook his head.

"I saw pictures before, it's from the 1800s," Curry said.

It was Tom's turn to shake his head.

"Is that a camera on the wall up in the corner?" Brew waved his hand in front of the lens. "It looks nothing like the cameras at the school. It's so square."

Stacey picked up a piece of equipment and tossed it back onto the shelf. "If anyone is here they know we are too."

"Check every door," Tom said. "And cut the chatter. They'll hear us."

"Who?" Curry asked. "There ain't nobody here."

A speaker mounted in the wall crackled to life. "Go through the door opposite the one you came in and move to the end of the hall."

"Hide!" Brew screeched and ducked between rows of shadowed equipment.

"Do not hide," the voice buzzed and popped. "I can see everywhere in the room. Do as instructed."

"We better do as it says." Tom stepped out from behind the shelf. "We can't hide in here forever."

"No way. Don't trust anyone down here," Curry said.

"Move!" The voice boomed over the speaker.

Down the hall and through another hatch, they stepped into a control room.

Wall-mounted antique TVs were displaying the decompression chamber they had come from, plus the hall outside. The screen views changed from room to room throughout the station.

"How big is this place?" Brew asked.

The view changed again, and they appeared on the monitor. "We're on TV," Curry smiled.

Stacey gasped and turned. "Behind us."

In the shadows, a man stood silently behind a tall table. He wore a black jump suit, and an off-white lab coat. Torn apart electrical equipment lay strewn across the table. He raised a device from the table and pointed it at them. "Who are you?" he asked. "I observed what happened on my view screen when the Venusians pulled you down from the surface. How did you survive?"

"Venusians? Like, from Venus beach?" Brew asked.

The scientist turned his gun on Brew. "Do you have a problem with cranial development?"

Tom moved in front of Brew, shielding him from the scientist. "We were lucky."

"Nobody is lucky at a thousand feet," the scientist said, and stepped out from the shadows.

"Those creatures pulled us down," Stacey said. "Then the light came and hurt us."

"That was a pain beam I developed many years ago. I use it for defense when they get agitated. I see you are scared. I would be too, but there is no need to fear me. I am not going to harm you. What were you doing out on the ocean in the middle of the night?"

"Dude, why are you talking so funny?" Curry stepped forward.

The scientist trained his gun on Curry. "I could ask the same of you, but it is inconsequential to the task at hand."

"Look, creepy dude," Curry said. "What. . ."

"Please hold your questions," the scientist said. "Your confusion is understandable. You wonder what has happened to you? Let me explain. But first you have to remember what you saw under the microscope on the beach to fully understand. The xylocrinebeta dinoflagellates. Those fools on the surface, how I watched their follies. I warned them not to."

"I get it," Brew said. "You're a mad scientist."

"Do tell," Curry said.

"I began work here in 1964, just before they closed this station when the government learned the aliens weren't going to share any more technology. I was a young man then. Against the government's wishes, I stayed on to finish my work by hiding aboard. The government eventually came to see the importance of my work. They have used me as much as I have used them, our underwater friends are not the only occurrence of alien arrival they have needed me for. Together, we have made great advances over the years because of my presence here and help elsewhere."

"Aliens?" Curry laughed. "Quit the mad scientist BS."

"Don't you listen? Aliens. They were on a colonization mission from their home world of Venus. Simple enough, you would think, but we shot them down and they crashed. Here, in the ocean. It was they who caused the battle of Los Angeles. How could they have anticipated we were at war with the Axis? They have been here in the Farallon trench since 1943.

"Look, dude," Tom said. "We gotta get out of here, and now. The Venusians will try again to get us."

"There's no chance of escape. Not when the Venusians are so agitated."

"What?"

"You are trapped here like I am, that's what. A week ago the Venusians started attacking ships and populated sections along the coast. After all these years of being peaceful, the fools played with fire."

"But why would they do that? We left them alone, right?"

"I believe they were provoked into attacking. Under the United Nations Agenda 21, Project Cloverleaf was created. It's a geoforming project to stop global warming. They released aluminum nano particle aerosol from jets in the atmosphere to reflect solar radiation back into space. And in the oceans, Project Neptune, they released genetically modified plankton to stop the acidification caused by excessive $CO_2$. As a result they altered the Venusian's environment, because they require $CO_2$ to live. They are merely trying to save themselves."

"If you have been talking to them for years, why don't you just ask them to stop?" Tom asked. "Can't they just go home?"

"Where would they go? Like us, they destroyed their world. Their planet is uninhabitable, and they do not trust humans to put aside greed. They think we are deceiving and destructive. I tend to agree."

"They killed my class, and we haven't destroyed our world yet," Tom said.

"What did you do to provoke them? But more importantly, how did you kids get in here? You are a thousand feet underneath sea. I find it impossible, but you are here. How did you do it?"

Tom explained.

"You are the thieves!" the scientist said. "We must return the oval at once. The pain beam I used on them only lasts so long."

"No, I found it. It's mine. If it weren't for the oval, we never would have made it."

"How infantile. They are very possessive, too."

"The oval, whatever it is, saved us," Tom said.

The scientist worked a device on his wrist, and a hatch whined open. He pointed down a darkened passageway. "Give it here. We must go to the escape pod. They'll destroy everything I've worked for, follow me, quickly."

"Didn't you hear us, they'll kill us."

"That's a risk you will have to take. I can't jeopardize my life's work. It's too important."

"If it's so important and secret that no one can see it," Tom said. "What's the point? It makes all your work a waste of time."

"You don't understand what it would mean to tell the world that extraterrestrials exist. Imagine the repercussions."

"They would get over it," Tom said. "I think most people are ready to hear and see proof aliens exist."

"I have a special room where they can enter the station. I can return it there. Give me the oval."

"You talk to them?" Curry asked.

"Of course I do," The scientist turned around, exposing a pulsing spiny growth on the back of his head. "They implanted the symbiote into my brain."

"Holy shit," Curry said. "It's sucking on your head. I thought you meant you use the universal language of math to communicate."

"Nothing so mundane," the scientist laughed. "See, I can never return, this is my world now. Breathing a mixture of helium and oxygen stresses humans bodies. One can only endure it for so long. The symbiote has helped keep me alive.'"

Suddenly the station jolted, and they fell to the floor. Equipment flew off shelves across the room in all directions. Twisting metal groaned as the station shook violently.

The scientist crawled through the hatch into the passageway, yellow light glared through holes, steaming black pipes hissed. "Quickly! Before they destroy the station!"

The station was hit again. Creaks and moans lurched through the structure, and sparks flew from electrical conduits. Tom regained his balance. "Did the station just move?"

"The Venusians must be trying to move the station and push it down into the Farallon trench. They must know you are in here."

All around, pipes cracked; water and steam shot out. Their eyes widened and filled with fear. They crawled after the scientist down the passage.

"We're not in the trench?" Brew cried.

"No, we are on a ledge fifty feet from the edge where it drops 11,000 feet to the bottom. Hurry to the escape pod. I'll activate the pain beam, it should give you a head start to get to the surface."

The scientist flipped switches and pulled a lever. Bubbling and gurgling sounds come from behind a hatch. A light on the wall changed from red to green, and a hatch swung open. A spherical pod sat in the middle of the room, suspended over a drop pool.

"That's the escape pod? What a piece of junk," Curry said.

The ceiling imploded behind them. Pipes and splintered support beams crashed down. Water rushed in.

"Get in! Hurry!" The scientist fought for balance against the water. "It should work. I have maintained it over the years."

"Should is the word I'm worried about," Curry said.

"The pod has room for six. Aren't you coming?" Tom asked.

"Like I said, my life is here, I'm not leaving. And if having pink hair is the norm for girls, I don't want any part of it. Now sit down and strap in. Take my gun, I don't need it any more."

Tom held onto the metallic oval. "If we take this with us they will follow, leaving you and the station alone."

"It is a good idea in theory. You have no way of knowing, but we have met before. I was assigned to be your handler when you arrived. One of my easier assignments I must add. I am sure we will meet again. I wish you luck on the trip to the surface."

"Met before?" Tom asked. "Arrived?"

The hatch snapped shut. Tom pressed his face against the view port, the scientist remained in the room as it flooded with water. "What do you mean!"

Released from the research station, the pod drifted out into the darkness. A bolt popped, shooting across the cabin, and a thin mist of water sprayed from the seam.

Stacey pressed against the window. "The mermen are coming. They'll crush us."

The pain beam flashed, illuminating the view port of the pod, but flickered and went out as quickly as it had come on.

"The station is gone," Stacey said.

"Goodbye, everyone," Curry said.

Tom pressed against the view port window. "He died to save us."

"Tom." Stacey put her hands on his shoulders. "I just want to say I am sorry for what happened. I didn't mean to puke on you."

"I guess I can forgive you."

"Oh, lovey dovey," Curry said in a high pitched voice. "Cut the crap, you guys. We are in the middle of some serious shit, here!"

"And I'm sorry, too, Tom," Brew said. "I didn't mean to leave my cell phone on."

"Next time think twice when I tell you what to do," Curry said.

"The oval gave us the ability to survive without the pressure crushing or the cold freezing us, maybe we have the power to breathe water too," Tom said. "Either way, if it does or doesn't, we are going to find out. We can do it by choice, or sit back and let it happen."

"You want to open the hatch to find out?" Curry asked. "What are you, crazy?"

"It doesn't matter. We are dead once the mermen figure out were we are. Open it."

"Do it, Tom!" Stacey urged.

The mermen returned and attacked.

"They are pulling us back into the trench," Brew said. "There's no way out!"

Tom grabbed the door control wheel and turned. "I'm going with my gut."

Curry and Brew lunged at him, but were to late. The door popped outward, water flooded in, and the light of the escape pod shorted out.

Instead of wasting their last breath on final remarks, Brew and Curry both hit him. Tom kicked away, holding his breath. Stacey floated peacefully a few feet away, she reached out and held his hand.

A tickled burned at the back of his throat. A balloon of pressure welled in his stomach. The instinct to breath broke his will. He inhaled.

## CHAPTER THIRTY-ONE
## BONNIE

Echoes of dripping water bounced across darkness. Dried salt and the smell of ammonia stung Tom's eyes and nose. His head throbbed. He couldn't move. He was bound, wrapped tight in something like thick strips of plastic. Through a split in his bonds, he could see dark blue and green phosphorescent algae lighting a cave. His eyes adjusted to the murky glow. Others hung around him, bound in seaweed, like hogs for the slaughter. Working his chin, he bit into his bonds and chewed. The bitter flavor of the seaweed deterred him, and he broke down into violent convulsions to loosen his bonds. Exhausted, the fight worn out of him, he called out. "Brew? Curry?"

"Tom, is that you?" a voice cried.

Tom was able to move his head a fraction of an inch. He recognized the voice. "Bonnie?"

"We are all here," Bonnie replied, but an eerie sound resonated, causing him to pause and whisper. "Quiet, they are coming. Your struggling alerted them."

"They come and kill us," a girl rasped hysterically. "I don't want to die. We have to make noise to scare them."

"Quiet," Bonnie said.

A rush of sound sank right into Tom's bones, deafening him. Something big stepped into view. Its head reared back, jaws stretched wide. Air whistled through slits in its neck. Panicked, his body shook, he couldn't control his breathing. It turned towards him, sniffed the air, then stepped out of view.

Muffled sounds of a struggle erupted behind him. Uncontrolled pleas, curses, all with the same message, not me, echoed in the cave.

Several feet away, gurgling screams pierced his ears. Followed by the sloshing sound of water onto the cave floor, then silence.

Horrified, Tom recoiled into his cocoon. The creature brushed past him, causing his cocoon to swing in a slow circle. He didn't dare to breathe. Through the gap, the creature carried a bloody leg over its shoulder and disappeared into the dim light.

Moments later, his class all cried out at once, echoing, their voices filled with relief.

"Get us out."

"Why can't they just take me?"

"We're all going to die down here."

"Are you free?" someone asked. "Get me down first."

"Where are we? Do you know?"

"I'm as stuck as you." Tom struggled. "Now shut up while I try to get out."

"You'll never get out, no one has," a girl said. "They stand in the darkness waiting."

"I'm not about to give up," Tom said.

"We've been here for so long," the girl said. "It feels like something's moving inside of me."

Curry's muffled voice came from across the cave. "The tooth. Use the tooth to get free."

"You're alive," Tom said.

"Did you doubt it for a second?"

"I think I can reach it. Can you see Brew and Stacey?"

"I can't."

"Brew? Stacey?" Curry called.

"Cut us down. Hurry," a girl said.

"I'm trapped too. When I get free, I'll cut you down."

"We've tried, the seaweed stuff is too strong," another said.

"We need to figure out where we are," Curry said.

"A cave with glowing moss," someone said.

"That's obvious," Curry replied. "I mean like where, where?"

"Deep under the ocean in a place that has air," Tom said.

"That's stupid."

"Maybe we're not at the bottom of the trench. What if they lived closer to the surface or even if they made their home underground. I think I am almost free," Tom said.

Tom fell to the floor with a thud and a crunch, found Curry and cut him down. "Soon as we find Brew and Stacey, we need to get out of here."

"That really cramped my style," Curry said. "Look at all these bones. Sure sets the mood of the cave. A creepy "we're all gonna die" mood."

"Get up," Tom said. "The Venusians could be back at any time."

"It doesn't look like everyone is alive," Curry said. "Talk about a low carb diet for monsters. They made lettuce wraps out of our class. Where's that gun the mad dude gave you?"

"Gone. They took everything else, but didn't find the tooth. I need the oval back."

"Like that's not going to happen."

Brew pushed his fingers through the seaweed and poked his head out. "I don't want to be a California roll, cut me down."

"Brew?" Tom called out and followed his voice. He tore at the seaweed. Brew fell to the floor. "Cut everyone down anyway, Curry."

"What if they need mouth to mouth like Brew did on the boat? I only go so far on the first monster rescue."

Tom tore at another cocoon and a decayed head fell out. "Do it."

Brew backed up. "Who's that?"

Tom reached into the cocoon and felt for a pulse. "I can't tell. I don't feel anything. Go and start unwrapping the others, get them to help. Who ever this was, they're dead. Call out if you find Stacey."

"Tom?" It was Bonnie.

"Bonnie?" Tom ripped the seaweed away, and he fell to the floor.

"Have you been here the whole time?"

"It's complicated. We need to get out of here."

"Shouldn't we wait to see if anybody comes?"

"The four of us are here. We'll have to do."

"How long have we been in here?"

"Two weeks."

Bonnie sobbed. "My parents must think I'm dead."

"They had a big service at school for everyone. They think everyone died."

"Those creatures have been killing us, using us as food."

"Venusians."

"The monsters, Venusians?"

"Tom, Stacey's over here," Curry called.

He left Bonnie on the floor and pushed his way past the cocoons to Curry.

"Help me lower her down." he held onto the cocoon.

Tom eased Stacey to the floor. She was out. Brew limped over. "At least we have our clothes."

"How's your leg?" Curry asked.

"I think the oval healed me."

"Come on Stacey. We have to get moving, wake up." Tom patted her face.

She punched Tom. "That was the dumbest thing anyone has ever done."

"You told me to do it, you agreed."

"I didn't mean try to kill us. Where are we now?

"A cave."

"This is getting old."

"I did what I had to do," Tom said to Stacey, then turned to Curry and Brew. "Keep helping. Get everyone down, then we will get out of here."

Brew and Curry freed the class.

"Would you look here," Curry said. "If it isn't Jackson. Hanging like a country ham, and is that Hernandez too? Tom, check them out."

Jackson wiggled. "Let me down. Let me down."

Tom approached, his fist balled at his sides. "Shut up."

"Tom. Buddy. Get me down."

"I don't think so," Tom said, then asked Curry." Where's Chi?"

"I don't see him."

"The monsters took him," Jackson said. "Please get me down."

Tom stared up at Jackson. "That's a big request for such a small person to ask."

"Come on, Tom, I said please. Be kind, buddy."

"I have no reason to do anything for you." Tom turned. "Leave him."

"What about Hernandez?" Curry asked.

"Especially not him."

Jackson gulped. "We're people. You can't leave us here."

Bonnie stepped into sight. "You said the louder we were, the less chance they would eat us, and you stayed silent."

"I screamed like everyone else, it was our plan. You guys made me leader."

"I didn't want you as leader," Bonnie said.

"Whose side are you on?" Jackson asked.

Stacey approached. "They're total douches, but maybe they can help us get out of here."

Tom spoke sharply. "Help us? What the hell are you talking about."

Stacey smiled in the faint light. "If you let them down, they'll run, because they they can't stand you being the leader. They'll scout out the place for us. Their screams will let us know where the monsters are."

"You're one sick chick," Curry smiled. "One I like more and more. I should have thought of that."

"We won't run," Jackson said.

"Get us down," Hernandez pleaded. "We will help. We can fight."

"We need weapons," Jackson said. "We gotta fight back."

"If I free you, you will fight for us?" Tom asked.

Bonnie moved in front of Tom and stared him in the eyes. "Come on, Tom, don't. You know they lie."

"We need them."

"On the beach you were right, they are only interested in themselves, and I was only for their amusement."

"Don't listen to him," Jackson said. "We treated you right, Bonnie."

"If you were my friend, you'd call me Bonafair. Don't call me Bonnie."

"I call you Bonnie," Tom said.

"The difference is I know who my friends are."

"Cut them down," Tom said.

Curry's head snapped towards Tom. "What?"

"Do it."

Bonnie shouted. "No. You can't."

"We have to fight," Tom said, as Hernandez and Jackson hit the ground. "Their parents care about them. The whole school cared. That has to mean something."

Weak from their bonds, Hernandez and Jackson tried to stand.

"Listen up, douches," Tom said. "If you want to wrestle or tackle the monsters, then stuff them into a locker then please, be my guest. Prove to me I didn't waste my time coming to find you, to see if there was any reason why I should care about you."

"So fierce," Stacy said. "Tell us the truth, hero."

"The creatures brought you here, too," Jackson said. "You're just as much a prisoner as we are."

"Except I'm not a prisoner. I am here trying to find out if you were worth saving."

"We promise. We can change. Honestly."

"You don't get it, you can't just lie and bully your way through These are alien creatures who live by different rules."

Jackson stood. "I should be the leader. You need to sit down."

"I told you," Bonnie said.

Tom bumped Jackson's chest with his. "I'm the one who found

you."

"That's it, tell him like it is, Tom," Curry said.

"You promised you would help us get out of here," Bonnie said.

"How many people are okay? Sound off," Tom said.

"We need food and water," a girl across the cave said. "The Japanese eat seaweed all the time."

She bit into a bulb of seaweed that hung from the ceiling.

"Wait!" Tom tried to stop her. "You can't eat strange plants."

"They're filled with water, it's not salty. It's sweet."

"Don't drink it. We don't know if it's safe."

A second later she buckled over. "Oh god my stomach, it burns."

"Oh god, she crapped everywhere," Curry held his nose. "We'll never make it if this type of shit happens."

Using the distraction, Hernandez and Jackson pushed Tom to the ground and kicked him. "Come on. This loser will get you killed."

Several students ran off with Hernandez and Jackson into the darkness.

Brew helped Tom up. "You okay, man?"

"Tom, let them learn on their own," Stacey said. "I told you they would run off. As for the others, we can use them as human shields on our way out of here. They have no value, they're just sheep. Extras in my movie."

"See, Tom, she's a smart one," Curry said. "Throw them to the monsters."

"I like your idea," Tom said. "But it's not the right thing to do, no matter how satisfying you think it."

"I feel disappointed," Curry said.

Tom counted who could stand. "Everyone who thinks they can walk come over here. If you are too weak, I will assign someone to help you."

"Go get them, my cruise director friend," Curry said.

"If there's a way in, there's gotta be a way out. Let's go," Tom said.

"That simple, right," Bonnie said.

"It ain't gonna be simple. Take a look around. Take a good, long look around."

"A floor covered in bones is what I see."

"That's a sign, Bonnie."

Eric Johnson

## CHAPTER THIRTY-TWO
## SICK SENSE OF HUMOR

Tom gazed into the black of the cave for any sign of movement. "I need someone to watch our rear and two people to watch our flank."

"Whoa! Listen to you, buddy, getting all military," Curry said.

A classmate hurried past Tom.

"Wait," Tom said.

"What?" He turned and stopped. "You don't even know who I am. At least Jackson did. I'm going with the others."

"Tell me your name then? We have to stay together."

"I'm just a nobody with you." He disappeared into the darkness. "Hernandez. Wait up."

"Come back," Tom called after him.

"That's free will for you. His decision," Curry said. "A stupid one if I might add."

Tom led the survivors out of the cave. The shaft tributary opened into a larger two-tier tunnel. They move forward cautiously, huddled together in the faint light. The air was still. The only sound was the crunch of fish and sea mammal bones under their feet.

"A treacherous path, if I do say so," Curry said.

Tom patted the wall. "These walls are too smooth to be natural. If we follow the right hand wall it will lead us out. Everyone hold hands."

In twenty paces, the tunnel ended into a cave. Speckles of glowing algae dotted the high ceiling like stars in the night sky.

A commotion of voices came from his class, and the line halted. Tom jumped and pushed to the back of the line. One of the girls whipped her head around like a cornered animal, her purple face gasping out gut-wrenching sobs. "There!" She pointed.

Dressed in a shredded jump suit, a horribly scarred man reached out from under a pile of bones and collapsed, his arm

207

reaching out to Tom, fingers twitching. "You," he hissed, then became still.

Tom stared at the man dumbfounded, then at the girl. "That's the missing man from the fight on the boat."

"We need a plan," the girl shuddered. "If we go out there, how are we going to protect ourselves?"

"We don't know what's out there." Another held the panicking girl.

Tom bent down and searched the man. "Getting out of here is better than staying."

"We listened to Jackson," a third person spoke up. "And he lied to us, used us to protect him, and you guys joke about using us as shields. That's cold. You're just as bad as he is."

"I don't know what will happen to us," Tom said. "But I have seen those creatures and I'm not waiting for them to come back."

"I'll take my chances," the girl said, and went back the way they had come.

"Curry, say you are sorry, apologize."

"Me?"

"And you too, Stacey. We have to work together."

"Dude."

"Now. Say you're sorry."

"Sorry," Curry and Stacey said in unison.

"And I'm sorry, too," Tom said. "It's their sick sense of humor. I won't let anything happen to you."

"We'll take our chances."

Five more students split off and disappeared into the darkness.

The light from the phosphorescent algae faded. Soon it was pitch black. Steps became smaller; echoes of their shuffling feet bounced around them. They felt their way along the wall.

"It sounds like something is following us," someone said.

"I know they are coming to get us," another panicked. "We have to go back."

"That's the echos playing tricks on your mind," Tom said.

"There's nothing there."

Time disappeared in the dark and after a long while the girl from before spoke, "We need to rest. It's so cold down here."

"The floor feels like it's going up," Stacey said. "It's different here."

"It's lighter over there," Tom said.

Curry pulled on Tom's arm. "You're seeing things. It's just more glowy stuff."

"Seriously." Stacey said. "This place goes on forever."

They kept on. The rock and gravel gave way to an unknown metallic surface. Little ringlets of light illuminated their feet where they stepped. "The path is new. Feel how it slopes up slightly. If we go back, we won't have made progress."

"Define progress?" she asked.

The bare outline of a door etched in the wall glowed purple as they neared. "Vindicated," Tom said. "That's a door. Doors lead to places."

"Open sesame, for sure," Curry said.

The group moved closer together. Strange markings glowed, decorating the walls. The air was cold and dry.

"Everyone quiet," Tom said. "And when I hold my fist over my head. Stop."

"Is this the way out?" a girl asked.

Tom felt for a trigger to open the door. "I'm not sure, but we will find it."

"We've been going around in circle for hours. There is no way out."

An iris spiraled opened. Escaping air shrieked out. Blinding green light throbbed around them. Curry squinted and followed Tom in. Capsules lined the wall of a long corridor. He spoke calmly, "Seems to be the place."

Brew touched a display. Stacey pulled his hand away.

The confinement amplified their breathing. Tom's voice hung heavy in the air. "Everyone in. There's a room there."

Stacey cleared her throat. "It's hard to breathe in here."

Tom held his fist up and went ahead to the room. A helix rose to the ceiling from a hovering table in the center of the room. Tubes pulsing with orange and red liquid spider-webbed around the outside. Soft footsteps approached from behind. Tom held his fist up, stopping the class. "Told you to stay!"

Mist parted at his feet, and the helix pinged faintly. Entranced by the pulse of lights, he tried to comprehend what he saw within the recesses of the helix. Leech-like larvae fed on liquid in honeycomb pockets. Blood jelly frothed at their toothy orifices as they squirmed in their nests. "These look like the thing on the scientist's head."

Stacey stepped behind him, her cheek brushing his shoulder. "Don't touch those, they will hurt you."

Tom ran his fingers across the helix. "If the these helped the scientist, they can help us too. He said the symbiote helped him communicate with the creatures and adapt to living down here."

"It's not a good idea."

"We need to find the way out of here."

"That's just pure stupid, Tom," Curry cut in as he appeared from the entrance. "Now is not the time to experimenting when we have save our asses. See the ring on this wall? It looks like another door."

"You're always complaining how much smarter you are, Curry," Tom said, not taking his eyes off the larvae. "You should agree with me."

Out of the darkness, Jackson appeared with his group, they shoved through the class into the room.

The class cried out in an emotional crescendo at his appearance. Brew and Curry moved next to Tom and squared off with Jackson and Hernandez, fists up.

Stacey laughed, "So predictable."

Tom shook his head darkly. "Enough is enough."

"Get the hell out of my way," Jackson pushed Stacey out of the way, and went for Tom.

Hernandez rushed Brew with a long bone in his hand. It looked like a human femur, broken at one end, sharp.

Tom blocked, only to be hit by a forceful right hook from Jackson, making him reel.

Brew kicked at Hernandez and missed.

Jackson swung around with a back-fist, but Tom blocked it deftly. Then a left hook from Jackson knocked him back again.

Hernandez circled around the helix.

"Get him," Jackson said to his group, and kicked Tom in the back, sending him staggering forward into Hernandez.

Curry was slow to react, but snapped into the fight and one-two'd Hernandez in the side of his head, then side kicked him in the leg, dropping him to his knees as Tom crashed into him.

Tom and Hernandez sprawled across the floor.

A sea of fists and legs crashed like waves around the room, churning and billowing.

Brew mirrored Jackson. "Try it."

"Stop fighting!" Bonnie yelled.

"Don't be a wimp, Bonnie," Stacey said and charged Jackson, jumping on his back.

Jackson spun around, throwing Stacey to the floor.

"You're not getting out of here," Hernandez said, and thrust the bone spear at Curry.

Curry side stepped and chopped Hernandez' hand, forcing him to drop the spear.

Stacey sprung back to her feet and swung at Jackson.

Jackson blocked her punch and grabbed her, locking his arms around her torso.

Unable to use her arms she stomped on his feet and smashed her fist into his groin, squeezing. He let go and shrank back, holding his crotch.

Stacey whirled and snap kicked Jackson in the chest and. He fell down. "Next time I tear them off."

The fight seemed to have come to a halt. Tom held his fists up, expecting more to come. "Have you been following us the whole time?"

Jackson gasped for air and spit. "I can't risk you getting us killed. I'm going to kill you."

"Risk?" Tom asked. "These are creatures from Venus, Jackson. Don't you get it? You need us."

Brew had retrieved the spear. He pushed Hernandez to the ground next to Jackson. Without warning, Jackson sprang to his feet like a coiled snake, rushed to the helix and took a larva. He held a larva up. "It could be the key to get us out of here. We're gonna have to try it."

Hernandez stood next to him, rubbing his jaw

"You don't know what those are," Tom said. "Let me tell you."

Jackson grabbed a girl from his group and put the bug on her head. Tom recognized her as the cheerleader who told him to kill himself. "You don't have to tell me anything."

The cheerleader twisted, trying to break free from Jackson's grasp. At the same time Tom dove to stop him, but it was too late. She fell to her knees and screamed. Her face streaked with tears, she fought to get it off her. She shrieked and collapsed to the floor, dead.

"You killed her!" Tom said.

"Such a douche," Stacey said.

"Better her than me," Jackson said. "I'm not going to die because of your weakness. You said these will help us get out of here."

Hernandez stepped towards Tom, his chest puffed out.

Brew held the spear to Hernandez's neck. "Don't."

"Wait a second!" Curry said. "Let's all just relax for a minute. I want to see you two love birds throw down some more as much as anyone else, but the fact is we are lost in a monster's labyrinth."

"Jackson's right," Tom said.

Faces whipped around.

212

"What?" Curry asked. "Are you out of your mind?"

"Yeah, do what it takes," Jackson's voice hung in the air for a second. "That's what I'm saying."

"We need this to work," Tom said. "If we don't, we will never find the out way out. Think about it, do you really think we are going to make it out of here alive? Since when has any of you helped anyone but yourselves? I help people all the time. I'm not scared to do it either. I'm not a coward. Push the human potential to see how much you can take. Right Curry?"

"You are flat out insane," Curry said. "Whose side are you on?"

Jackson smiled, "Let him. He's right."

"Maybe we are different because of the oval, Curry. I think it has altered us in some way, and I think that's how the scientist was able to use the symbiote."

"What stone?" Jackson asked.

Tom grabbed a symbiote and held it to the back of his head. Spines shot out of its body, it latched on, he screeched and fell to the floor, his body convulsed.

Stacey fell to his side and pulled on the symbiote. "Help me get it off him." The harder she pulled the more Tom's body convulsed. "It's killing him."

"That worked," Hernandez chuckled. "Give one for the team. Problem solved."

"He's dead now," Jackson said. "That's what you get for being selfless. Now we need a real leader, and that's me."

"At least he had the guts to try," Bonnie said. "That's more than you'd ever do."

"Shut up, dude, I'd rescue someone in a heart beat. I always put myself first."

"Then you should try for once, it could save us all." Bonnie spat at Jackson.

"Well I, uh. First to step up. If it weren't for me you'd all be dead by now. I saved you."

Curry knelt at Tom's side and checked his pulse. "He's still breathing. It didn't kill him."

Tom sat up bolt straight. His face was chalk white and the symbiote on the back of his head pulsed. "I will never do that again."

Stacey cringed, more disgusted than afraid. Blood froth oozed down the side of Tom's head. "How do you feel?"

Tom patted his body, tilting his head from side to side, cracking his neck. He stood up. "Good, I guess."

"No, I mean do you feel any different?"

"Maybe. My body feels the same. I can't feel the bug on the back of my head."

Curry stuck out his middle finger. "How many fingers, Tom, how many?"

Tom's eyes were distant. "Lizardmen. I was on Mars."

"No, my friend, we're under the sea and it's Venusians. That thing has messed you up. I wish I had a mirror to show you."

"I remember now." Two seconds passed. "I was on Mars, and my school was destroyed by a space ship. They were using us as food."

"Snap out of it, Tom. That's the bug nibbling on your head talking."

"I was trying to find my Dad. We escaped from Mars. Then the scientist in the research station was there. He said it was a tornado and that no one could ever know. He erased my memories."

"So that's true origins of why they call you Tomnado," Curry said. "Take it easy Dorothy, nobody's making you remember anything more here."

Jackson sneered and shook his head. "What a waste of time. So he remembers some movie. Like that's going to help us."

"You don't get it, do you?" Tom grabbed a symbiote and stepped toward Jackson. "We are trying to get out of here alive. Why don't you help for once?"

"Go on," another cheerleader said. "Help! He's right you know.

All you have done is put yourself first and sacrifice us to live longer."

Tom held out a symbiote. Its spines flexed and it's body quivered. "Try it, I feel smarter already."

"You already did it."

"Scared?"

Jackson stepped back.

Hernandez rushed Tom. Brew and Curry were ready and held him back.

"Go on, try it," Tom said.

"That thing is making you crazy. You can't expect me to try it. Look what it's done to you."

The class formed up behind Jackson; they pushed him forward into Tom. He turned to break through and ran for the door.

Stacey stepped from around the side of the group and kicked the back of his leg, the bone crunched. Jackson screamed and dropped to the floor. He flipped over looked up at Tom, pushing away with his good leg. "You're out of your mind."

"Am I? Let's see. I remember a joke you told. What's green and jumps? Here's mine, what sound does dumb jock make when an alien bug is stuffed into his mouth?"

"Don't," Jackson whimpered.

The class grabbed Jackson's arms, pulled him to his knees and held him. Tom held the symbiote up to Jackson's face. Needles rose up out of its flesh like porcupine spines and tiny arms with hooks extended and pulsed instinctively.

Jackson screamed.

"That's the sound it makes, exactly," Tom smiled, and shoved the symbiote into Jackson's mouth.

Jackson's scream was muffled like a mouth full of marshmallows as he clawed at his face, trying to pull the it free. The harder he pulled on the symbiote, the deeper it dug like a blood hungry tick. With a shuddering snort, he inhaled a last breath as it sealed his wind pipe. His body started to convulse.

Stacey stepped close, poked at him with her foot and smiled as he writhed. "I should say something funny here, but I am at a loss for words."

Brew puffed his cheeks out. "Pudgy bunny."

"Exactly." Stacey kicked Jackson again.

Hernandez begged and fought hard to free himself. "Don't do it to me. I'm sorry! I'm sorry!"

Tom stood over Hernandez. "They have plans for him. Let him go."

Hernandez yelped, "Plans?"

"The Venusians."

"You can't let them take me. I'll do anything."

"What are you talking about?" Curry asked.

"I just know," Tom said. "They have plans for him."

"Don't!"

"The thing on your head isn't right," Curry said. "It's creeping me out."

"Please don't make me go."

"I think something went wrong with your little idea, Tom," Stacey said.

Curry and Brew let Hernandez stand.

"Run away, Hernandez." Tom took another symbiote from the helix. "Or I will test this symbiote on you."

"Pudgy bunny," Stacey whispered and cackled.

Hernandez ran from the room. The class parted, letting him exit out into the cave.

Tom put his hand to his forehead. "Something is happening. I feel it."

Stacey's hands went up to her mouth. "Your head is glowing, Tom."

Tom closed his eyes. "I can see them coming. They know we are here."

"Talk to them. Let them know we are on their side," Curry said.

A guttural roar came from beyond the entrance to the cave.

Hernandez's head flew out of the dark, bounced, and rolled to their feet.

"Typical monsters," Stacey said.

"The symbiotes are their children," Tom said.

A dark figure emerged from the shadows. It hung in the light and pierced their souls with a gaze as cold and pitiless as a midnight sun. Time screeched to a halt. Tom, Brew, Curry, and Stacey took cover, the class stood dumbfounded.

Then without warning, the creature dashed forward, eyes glaring, claws flashing. Lightning fast, its arms, tore holes through those who stood closest. In mere seconds, many of the class lay unconscious or dead across the floor. The creature turned and sliced at Brew.

Stone faced, Tom stepped forward putting himself between the creature and Brew. The symbiote glowed brightly on top of his head. "Stop. Stop now," he commanded.

Brew jumped behind the helix, keeping it between him and the creature.

The creature lashed at Tom, its claw stopping millimeters from his neck.

Tom stood his ground.

Curry grasped for Stacey's hand. "Don't move, Tom. Play dead."

Stacey pressed against the back wall of the room and yelled, "Tom, don't."

Tom pushed his head tight to the creatures. "It's not a bear, Curry."

The creature became still, opened its contorted face to Tom's and spewed slime, engulfing his head in a caul-like mass.

"This is hopeless," Brew said. "It's got us cut off from the cave. You can't control it."

Mist clouded out from tiny holes across its head. The symbiote on Tom's head glowed changing color, it began to purr.

The creature breathed heavily, cooing in response.

Tom wiped slime from his face. "You got any better ideas?"

"I have a plan," Curry said. "Run like hell."

At the same moment Curry spoke, Tom slapped the symbiote he had intended for Hernandez onto the creature's head. The symbiote latched on instinctively and dug into its chitinous exoskeleton. The creature staggered back through the door as it pulled at the symbiote. Tom charged forward and put his hand to the wall; a red circle lit up, and the iris spun closed.

Stacey clutched Curry's arm. "Tom, Curry, we need to run."

"Can we do my plan now?" Curry asked.

Tom stepped away from the door. "There's no other doors."

The iris opened and the creature stepped in, the symbiote gone.

Curry fell back against the far wall as if pulled by invisible gravity. "It looks mad."

Stacey pounded on the wall looking for an exit. "Define mad."

"Didn't you lock the door?" Brew yelped.

Tom faced the creature once again. "Maybe there was a key hidden under the door slime."

The creature advanced, Tom backed away to the far wall. His head glowed, and a second iris twisted open.

"Go!" Tom ushered the remaining class members through.

Sweat poured down Curry's brow; he held arms up in defense. "I knew using the bug was a good idea."

"No you didn't."

## CHAPTER THIRTY-THREE
## GOOD GOING, NEMO

Through the iris and out into the hall, they ran. The door spun closed behind them. They stopped.

Left and right. "Which way?"

"We are rats in a maze," Brew said. "Trapped."

The symbiote on Toms head glowed, he went left. "No monsters this way."

"I know where this is going," Brew said. "They're studying us for spatial learning and memory!"

"Down the hall?" Stacy asked.

"It's not hard to figure out," Tom said. "Forward, or back to the creature."

Doors twirled open and closed as Tom passed.

"Tom, you are like an automatic garage door opener," Curry said. "We should search the rooms."

"We have to keep moving."

Stacey put her hand on Tom's shoulder. "Where are we going?"

"We need alien weapons," Curry said.

"Alien weapons are designed for alien hands," Brew said. "They won't work for us?"

"It's worth a try. We can always use our feet," Curry replied.

The lights dimmed and the corridor glowed purple. Tom held his fist up, stopping the class.

Stacey caught her breath. "What's happening?"

"They aren't saving electricity." Curry looked behind, down the hall. "That's for sure."

Brew's voice shook. "Something tells me they are coming. Monsters love to kill you in the dark."

"This is the ship the scientist told us about," Tom said. "There has to be something here we can use."

"Have you listened to one word I said?" Curry asked. "Aliens have weapons, you know. The really cool ones they use to kill humans. Can we get some?"

"Maybe they have escape pods," Brew said. "We can use one to escape."

"We tried, remember?" Curry looked into a room. "And Tom tried to kill us."

Stacey pulled Curry around and looked him in the eye. "You always have to complain, don't you?"

"Twice submerged, three times pissed off," Curry said. "Yeah."

"Two times is enough for me, too," Brew said.

"Stow it, sidekicks," Tom cut them off. "We are trying to escape."

"We are wandering the halls like a lost dog on a freeway," Curry said. "We could be struck at any time."

"What if the hall leads to their cafeteria," Brew said.

"Test ideas by experiment and observation," Tom said. "Build on those ideas that pass the test. Reject the failures. Follow the evidence wherever it leads, and question everything."

Curry stepped out of one room and said before he ducked into another. "Must be the bug in his head talking. No one thinks like that."

"Curry, come back."

Curry exited the room, his face as white as a sheet. "I did not just see what I think I did. I have been scarred for life. Stay with the group, right."

Stacey poked Curry in the ribs. "What'd you expect, an armory?"

Brew went to look.

"I told you it was a bad idea," Tom said. "Brew, stay out of that room."

"It's empty," he replied.

Tom pushed ahead. "The end of the corridor is there."

The iris ground open. Light flooded out across them. A chill ran down Brew's spine. "A sub?"

"It doesn't look anything like any sub I've seen before," Curry said.

"It's WWII sub," Tom said. "The scientist did say first contact was with the aliens when they crashed here. They must have built the sub base too."

"Then what are all those alien-looking things on it?" Curry observed.

Brew moved towards the sub. "They're doing something to it."

Curry followed. "Would you care to elaborate, genius?"

"What on earth would they want it for when they have a space ship?" Stacey asked.

"They crashed, remember," Tom said. "If they didn't have spare parts. Wouldn't they need to make a ship to go get the materials they needed if they couldn't find them here on earth?"

Curry looked back at Tom. "Now that's even more stupid than your other idea."

Tom ushered the remnants of his class aboard the sub. "That's just what we need. Everyone get on."

"The only experience I've had here is a bad one," Curry said. "I advise we think about this before we go in."

"How big were these people?" Brew asked. "I can barely fit in the hatch. And how do the creatures get aboard?"

A scream came from below. "That's how," Curry said. "Some are smaller than others."

"Sounds like Bonnie," Stacey said.

The four followed the class down into the sub. Bodies of the sub's crew sat in position at their stations.

"Tom, turn your head around to light the room," Curry said. "They look mummified, that means the aliens don't eat humans."

"Yeah, bug light boy, shine for us," Stacey said.

"What if something was wrong with them that made the aliens not want to eat them?" Brew asked.

"Don't be stupid," Tom said. "They were working on the sub, look at all the alien ware in here. We have to figure out how to start it."

Curry moved to a console. "Hold on. Let me pry these dead guys off the controls."

"The button here says start." Brew pointed.

Curry pulled. "How long has it been here? Fifty, Sixty, a hundred years? It can't possibly work."

"They didn't have a how to maintain your sub class in school," Tom said.

"No power," Brew said, and pressed the button. "It's an electric ignition, see."

Curry slumped. "Great, what size batteries does it take? How do you know, anyway?"

Brew flipped switches on and off, quickly. "I never skipped shop."

"It's not like we can run to the drugstore and get a few."

"No, we just need to find the engine room," Tom said. "If we are lucky, the aliens have a power supply or have modified the engines to work."

The corridor to the engine room had been widened, the metal of the door frames bent and crumpled inward as if something had pushed it in.

Stacey crossed her arms. "I still don't get why the aliens would have need of a sub?"

"The ship we are on is unrepairable," Tom said. "And their colonization attempt failed. They want to return home?"

"To what?" Curry asked. "They destroyed their world."

"We don't know that," Stacey said.

"The scientist said so," Brew said.

"Just because he said it doesn't make it true," Tom pointed out. "We are destroying their world down here."

"Glad the bug is glowing, we couldn't see the truth without it," Curry snipped.

Stacey shook Tom. "Hello, earth to Tom? Look at his face."

Curry snapped his fingers. "Wake up."

"Can he hear us?" Stacey asked.

"Tom, what's happening?" Curry asked. "Are the aliens coming?"

Stacey slapped him hard across the face. Nothing happened. Then she slapped him again.

Tom blocked, stopping Stacey in mid swing. "Don't hit me."

Curry asked. "What were you doing."

"I was listening to the aliens," Tom said. "They don't want us here."

"Ha," Curry laughed. "Really? Tell me what I don't know. I'm more than happy to do just as they say."

"That wasn't all."

"Shoot."

"Don't say shoot," Brew interjected.

"We have to start the engine. Brew, you can figure it out. I have to go to the aliens."

"Are you insane?" Brew asked. "How would I even know where to begin?"

"No, it's what they want."

"We can't let you do that, Tom."

"They killed the scientist, and they need a replacement."

"You're not going to do that," Curry said. "They'll just kill you, too, or you'll become creepy and hate girls with pink hair."

"Tom would never hate me."

"They told me the sub needs to be wired to the power supply to start the engine. It's up to Brew to get everyone out of here. I'm going now."

Curry struck Tom from behind and he fell to the floor unconscious. The symbiote on the back of his head squished, smearing phosphorescent goo across the floor, oozing down Tom's back.

"Good going, Nemo," Stacey said. "The aliens wanted him, and now they are going to be even more pissed, but thank you. I didn't want to be the bad guy."

"When aren't they angry about something?"

Razor Point

"Help me get the wires hooked up." Brew ordered the survivors. "Put that there, and this here, while I get the capacitor hooked up."

"Wha wha huh?" Curry garbled.

"That there, and this here. Got it?"

"The cables are too short."

"Everyone go look for wires and bring them to me," Brew said.

Tom sat up holding his head. The remains of the symbiote fell away and landed in the goo "What happened?"

Stacey looked at Curry. "Now you're gonna get it."

"Not that I have to say it but. . . Sorry, Tom."

"Sorry for what? Where are we?"

"On the sub we found," Curry said. "Don't you remember?"

Tom looked around. "Where's Jackson and Hernandez?"

"Dead."

"Dead? What happened?"

"Dude, you killed Jackson after you put the bug on your head, and Hernandez lost his head."

"We have to get the sub running, fast," Brew said. "The aliens are going to be pissed. They'll smash it like a tin can."

"Long story short," Curry said. "They killed the scientist and want you to replace him."

"No way."

"You put the bug on the back of your head."

Tom felt his head and grimaced, strings of goo pulled away with his hand. "What is this?"

"The bug from the helix, I smashed it."

"Thanks." Curry smiled.

"Thank me," Stacey said.

"All we need to do is connect these four wires together," Brew said. "Tom, hold these by the insulation. Stacey, here."

"Now what?" Stacey asked.

"When I say go, connect the wires to the panels."

The sub rocked. The survivors of the class ran back, holding

224

the wire Brew had asked for. He fiddled with the wires and connected the power cables.

"Okay get ready. Three, two, one. Go."

Tom and Stacey plugged their ends in, completing the circuit. Blue sparks leaped. The power came on. The engine whirled to life, buzzing and popping as arcing ribbons of electricity rode along the walls, burning the air.

A hole ripped in the light, and a creature appeared in the center of the room. Before it attacked, Tom acted, pulling wires from the terminal, punching them into the creature's mouth.

Flashes of light cast dark shadows over the compartment. Arcing wires singed flesh like sizzling meat. The smell of burnt popcorn permeated the air. The creature's arms flailed, then it froze and slumped onto itself, dead. Tom stood like a pillar next to the creature, his eyes closed. His head cleared. "Did I do that?"

"How the hell did you know what to do?" Curry asked.

A strange illumination bathed Tom's face and his eyes opened. He inspected the body. "It seemed natural."

Brew threw his hands in the air. "Everything is fried. That was our only chance."

"Can't we get more wire."

Tom tore at the creature's body, as if possessed. Carapace cracked and sinew popped as the center chest plate came free, spooging out innards.

Brew dropped his arms to his sides. "You don't understand. Everything is fried. "

Tom pushed, digging his arm deep. It disappeared into the chest cavity, angled upward, sinking up to his shoulder. "I know what to do."

Stacey gagged. "That's the sickest thing I have ever seen."

Tom pulled his arm out. Strings of fibers stuck to his arm, and snapped as he pulled away. In his hand, he held a slim covered metallic oval.

"That's. . . ," Curry said.

"Yes, it's their heart. That's why they want the one I have back."

"But it's made of metal."

"They are from Venus and lived in an atmosphere of carbon dioxide and sulfuric acid clouds, perhaps you were expecting a marshmallow? All I know is that I need it."

"Now what are we going to do?

"We are getting out of here. All of us."

Eric Johnson

CHAPTER THIRTY-FOUR
TIME TO SURRENDER


Sparks showered Tom, burning his shirt. He beat out the smoldering patch and moved to Brew. "You have to get it to start again. Don't answer, just do it."

Brew nodded and ordered the class survivors. "Get me more wire."

"Close the hatches," Tom ordered. "We need to figure out what the creatures were doing with the sub."

"This looks like a control console here," Curry said. "But it's designed for alien hands."

"Cut the creature's arms off and stick them into the control slots," Tom said.

"What?" Stacey seemed shocked. "You have more guts than I ever believed possible."

The survivors returned.

"We don't have enough wire to reach." Brew examined the wire. "I don't know how the alien power thingy works. All I did was hook the wires to the terminal. I think all the juice is gone."

"We don't know how to drive it, either," Curry said.

"How much time do we have?" Stacey asked.

"Just do it."

"Tom." Brew grabbed his shoulder. "I'm a skater, not an alien submarine mechanic."

"Then we are dead."

"I can piece the wires together, but don't know if they will hold a current."

"Okay, Tom and Stacey, get into place and hold the wires carefully."

"Too short," Stacey said. "They are never going to reach."

"Pull gently."

"Tom, I have an idea." Stacey stretched her arms out behind her holding the wire, moving closer to Tom.

"What?" he asked. Was this another crazy idea of hers?

"Do what I'm doing," she said, leaning in as close as she could to him. 'If we make it out of here we can go to college together."

"Not on your life."

"But you forgave me."

"That's when I thought we were dead."

Her face was honest. "We need to make the connection."

Tom held the wires behind him. "How?"

"Kiss me." She puckered.

"No way! Are you out of your mind?"

"Don't argue dammit, just do it. I won't puke on you."

Tom pushed his mouth to hers. Sparks flew. Their bodies shook violently as the circuit completed. The engines came to life.

"Who's driving?" Brew shouted.

Curry took the controls. "Don't stop kissing her! We'll lose the engines!"

The ancient submarine creaked and groaned as it shot out of the dock into the ocean and flew to the surface.

"The sub is doing more than moving through the water. We're airborne!" Curry shouted excitedly.

The light of dawn broke over the hills. On the beach were soldiers. The sub crashed to the beach, breaking Tom and Stacey's kiss. Tom opened the hatch. The creatures swarmed past the submarine and heavy gunfire and yellow beams of light erupted across the beach.

Creatures slipped in and out of the light, appearing in the midst of the soldiers' positions and pulling them into the black. The battle raged, but eventually the mermen were driven back and disappeared into the ocean. A squad of soldiers approached the sub with agent Ortega in the lead. They leveled their guns at Tom. "Surrender," Ortega ordered. "There's nowhere to run."

Silently, Tom climbed out of the hatch and jumped down into the surf. He waded out and stood before agent Ortega.

"You've caused a lot of trouble," Ortega sneered.

"Tell me something I don't know," Tom said. "How are you going to cover this up? Are you willing to sacrifice children?"

"In the interest of national security I am ordered to give you a choice. You can come with us where we will relocate you under a new identity. We have wonderful facilities at our Guantanamo retreat, or you can choose to sacrifice yourself for our great nation in the name of peace and stability. But first, you have something we want. Give me the object."

"Those aren't choices," Toms said. "Choose life or death, and the life I'd choose would be a death."

"Do you have the object?"

"You mean this?" Tom held up the oval. "It's one of their hearts. That's why they want it."

"The heart, give it here." Ortega pointed his gun at Tom's head. "Which is it? Life or death?"

Shards of light beamed around Tom, hitting the soldiers and vaporizing them instantly. Tom ducked. Ortega fired. As he did so, another beam melted the gun-holding arm off his body.

Behind him Curry, Brew, Stacey, and Bonnie stood in the sail.

"I found the weapons," Curry cheered. "The really cool ones they use to kill humans."

Ortega staggered back, his eyes wincing. He held his remaining hand up to ward off an attack. "Now listen here. Give it to me."

Tom stepped forward. "Take it."

"That's it?" Ortega asked. "That easy? You're just going to give it up?

Tom pushed the Venusian's heart into Ortega's chest. Spines rose up and thrust through his body armor, fixing itself in place. It glowed, started to spin, burrowing into his chest. Blood poured from Ortega's mouth. His hand went to his chest in an attempt to rip the heart from his body. A loud crunch sounded over the crash of the waves. His eyes flared with shock and wonder, all at the same time.

Tom leaned in. "You don't know me very well, I have a heart. I care."

He turned to see Brew, Curry, Stacey, and Bonnie exit the sub. The creatures returned taking Ortega's body then disappeared, leaving the five them on the beach in the warmth of the rising sun. The class survivors made their way off the beach as the remaining soldiers picked themselves up, regrouped, and retreated.

Brew did a happy dance. "We made it. We made it."

Bonnie hugged Curry.

Curry pushed him away. "Dude, composure please. I'm glad you made it, too. Okay."

Stacey fired a few bursts into the air from the alien weapon and kissed Tom. "These weapons are awesome!"

With one hand, Tom took the alien weapon from her and put his other around her. "This doesn't mean what you think."

"Oh, Tommy, a girl's gotta do."

"She put the ace in Stacey," Curry said. "Nice shooting."

"The ship totally flew," Bonnie said. "We have to go for a ride, see the moon, explore the stars."

"Slow down, Star Trek," Curry said. "Something better, like, be alien invaders, and bomb down on Washington and the world. Take me to your leader and some shit like that."

"I'm down," Brew said. "But we gotta go get my parents first."

"Right, Brew," Tom said. "We need to get my dad, too, and your mom, Curry."

"Hold that thought, skater. My mom's probably worn them out and escaped all on her own."

A hole in the world ripped open before them and out of the blackness stepped a different kind of alien, one that looked a lot like a lizard. He held his hand up, gesturing a greeting. His mouth moved like he was speaking, but made no sound.

Bonnie screamed.

Stacey gasped, "What now?"

Brew raised his fists.

Eric Johnson

Curry lowered his weapon to fire. "I've had enough of this."
Only Tom understood the speech.
"You are not in the right place, Tom. Remember, I promised to get you home?"
"Wait!" Tom stepped forward, holding everyone back. Suddenly, new memories were triggered, things he had long-forgotten, or been made to forget. "Emmett? Is that you? You died on Mars. I remember all that now."
"You understand it?" Curry asked.
Brew cried. "It has human hands!"
"I do understand it," Tom said slowly. "I owe Emmett my life. He transported me home from Mars."
Emmett motioned Tom to come. "You are in the wrong universe."
Confused and shocked, Tom found himself in denial. "Wrong? You got it wrong?"
"Yeah, tell him like it is, Tom," Curry said. "Nobody gets it right around here except us."
Brew stepped in front of Tom stopping him. "All that stuff you told us was true?"
"I told you it was something bigger than me." Tom pushed him aside.
Brew looked at Stacey, "Tom's mind was damaged by Curry smashing the symbiote. He's like, totally lost it this time. Do something."
Tom shushed them and looked at Emmett, "You did get me home. This is it. Where's your brother Winston?"
"Tom, we can't understand him. What's he saying?" Stacey asked.
"We don't have time," Emmett said. "We need to go now."
"I'm not going anywhere. Do you have any idea of what I've been through here? We won, it's over. I got my dad. I have my life. No way."
"None of it's important. None of this should have happened.

I'm sorry, Tom. The machine that I used to send you back to Earth wasn't a teleportation device like we thought. It is a trans-dimensional time machine. This isn't your time or place."

"But it looks right."

"Looks can be deceiving, especially when we desire. I've figured out how to get you home."

The ground shook, sending them to their feet as the ocean slid away from the shore at incredible speed. Brew, Curry, and Stacey stared out to sea. The class survivors followed the receding water in wonder.

"I've never seen anything like it," Brew said, his voice weak and irregular.

Stacey held on to Tom's arm in panic. "Is it real?"

"How'd the tide go out so quickly."

"Don't you ever watch videos?" Curry asked. "The tide is coming back. Tsunami!"

Emmett punched a few buttons on a hand held device. "The Venusians have started their attack to eliminate humans from the planet. We don't have time, you must come now, Tom."

"What about them? I can't leave them, they'll die."

"It is the fate of this Earth. Come."

"This is my home."

"It is only one of many Earths."

"Um, guys, what's that?" Brew bolted to the sub. Curry and Bonnie followed.

A wall as high as the clouds appeared on the horizon, shining golden in the reflected morning sun.

"Brew!" Tom cried.

"We must go now, Tom. You will understand."

Numb, Tom let go of Stacey's hand, moved to Emmett's side, and stepped into the black.

Stacey dove after him into the portal. "Tom!"

The shining wave roared across the beach.

## CHAPTER THIRTY-FIVE

### I CAN

Gravity stretched and squeezed, threatening to pop him like bubble wrap. Lights sparkled and fuzzy amoeba popped and percolated around him, phasing in and out in blinding colors. The sensation of onions rubbing into his eyes subsided. Tom landed, his feet tapping the floor followed by a rush of sea water. The roar of the tsunami was silenced by the portal closing, sealing the passage between worlds.

"Emmett?"

"Stay still, teleportation has effects," Emmett said from somewhere in the dark.

Tom's legs buckled. He lay in the cold pool of sea water. "Send me back! I have to get my dad!"

"That world was destroyed."

"You took away the life that they gave me. I didn't know I was on a different world. Now all of my friends are dead, and I'm left with nothing. If I wasn't supposed to be there, why didn't you come sooner?"

"There is no deus ex machina. There is only me and the machine." Emmett stepped from the shadows, and examined Tom with a device. "I see some of the symbiote survived removal. You are recovering from the teleportation nicely; it could have been worse. That's one thing you can thank the scientist for."

"You knew about him?"

"Don't be naive."

"I only remembered what happened when I used the symbiote."

"Did you think finding you was simple, Tom? By erasing your memory, he hid you. And by chance, your regaining your memory allowed me to find you. His snooping nearly cost a dozen Earths their existence. I'm relieved he is dead. I promised to get you home, we haven't much time. You must prepare to go."

"My Dad is dead. What do I go back to?"

"Dead in that Earth, yes, but only in your mind. The one you left behind is still there."

"The one I knew is dead."

"All versions are essentially the same, only slight variations occur. Imagine that you have been on a long trip, and are returning home. Think of the reunion. Think of the joy you should be feeling. You're going home."

"I can't go back knowing what I know."

"Everyone has secrets."

"The third eye gave you super intelligence. Enough to activate the machine and survive, but don't you see the problem?"

"Intelligence is not about the accumulation of data, it's about deciding what that data means. The good news is I located the point in time where I need to send you. You want to go."

"Do I?"

"Don't be a fool, I'm trying to help you. When you are gone my debt will be nulled, paid in full."

"Then pay your debt by sending me back to the world I know. The one I know."

"There were no guarantees that the machine would work when we used it the first time. It was reckless to use it. I later discovered that it was missing a part. If I had known, I would have never sent you through."

"Send me back now!"

"Fool! Activating the machine opened a gravity maze of different times and spaces. But over the years I was able to figure out a work around. Don't you see the importance? Toying with the balance of the universe is delicate and must be limited."

Emmett stared hard at Tom, but as Tom looked into the reptilian eyes, he knew there was nothing left of the scared teenager that had accompanied him to Mars and been turned into a Lizardman. "How long has it been? How long have you searched?"

"Countless years, but that is unimportant."

"Where's your brother, your twin Winston?"

"Dead, long ago. His natural life ended peacefully."

"What about Anidea? We couldn't have survived any of it without her."

"Lost forever. . ." Emmett stood taller. "Enough! I don't see why you engage in this useless banter. It will change nothing. Prepare to go!"

"Tom," Stacey said, weakly.

"Stacey?"

"A stow away! What are you doing here?" Emmett snapped.

"Where am I?" Stacey asked.

Emmett worked the device in his hand. "You are going to sleep."

"Wait!" Tom said. "Stop!"

A glowing blue field of popping electrical energy surrounded Stacey, freezing her in place.

"What did you do? Free her!"

"She can't be here. She will unbalance this universe like you did to the last one. I can't let that happen."

"She is, and she is alive."

"There is nothing I can do, space time is a harsh mistress."

"Help her."

"Why is she so important, do you love her? You can't afford love, not if it costs you your biggest desire. She must go back."

"Figure out something! Take the data, like you said, and use it."

"It is a waste of time."

"Why isn't our being here causing wherever we are to be destroyed? That means we can stay."

"The machine is encased in a time envelope, we are immune from the effects of time here, but out there she would cause the destruction of the universe. She could never leave, and staying here would drive her insane. Her fate is with the death of her planet. I can't upset the balance."

"Let her stay!"

"One wrong calculation and it is the destruction of billions of lives. The factors are too risky."

"You can keep her frozen until you find a solution."

"Technology eventually fails its purpose, and like any trapped animal she'd try to escape. We can't fight nature. But don't you see, I found you and I know how to get you home. Be happy, Tom."

"I can't let you kill Stacey."

"She's already dead. Her fate is what kills her, not me. There is a small window of opportunity for you to return safely."

"Look, let her stay here. She's already crazy, unfreeze her and see. She'll go along, once you explain."

"I can't do that, there will be unforeseen consequences."

Tom grabbed the device from Emmett and mashed his fingers across the control interface. The stasis field turned off, Stacey screamed and collapsed to the floor.

"Cold, so cold. What did you do to me?"

Tom fell at her side, shielding her, and pointed the device at Emmett. "I can't let you do it."

"Don't be demented. Guards!"

Two dozen Lizardmen entered the room, surrounding Tom.

"After you killed their leader, they treated me like a GOD! You can't imagine the power I have. Now you will go home, as I promised."

Emmett waved his arm and the machine rose up from the floor.

"Let her live! You can't do this, Emmett! "

Emmett placed his hand on the activation pad. "I can. Take the life that is rightfully yours!"

The floor vibrated and a beam of light engulfed Tom.

Coming Soon
Book Three

# The Monster
# A Child Knows Best

Made in the USA
San Bernardino, CA
28 February 2016